MW00533044

SHORT CUTS

BOOKS BY J.L. ABRAMO

Jake Diamond Mysteries
Catching Water in a Net
Clutching at Straws
Counting to Infinity
Circling the Runway
Crossing the Chicken

Chasing Charlie Chan
A Jimmy Pigeon Novel
(Featuring Jake Diamond)

Nick Ventura Mysteries
Brooklyn Justice

Sixty-First Precinct Novels
Gravesend
Coney Island Avenue

Stand Alone Novels
American History

Anthology
Short Cuts

Non-Fiction
Homeland Insecurity

J.L. ABRAMO

SHORT CUTS

*Collected Crime Fiction and
Nonfiction in Smaller Doses*

Collection Copyright © 2023 by J.L. Abramo

"One Hit Wonder" originally appeared in *Fedora III* (Wildside Press, 2004); "Walking the Dog" originally appeared in *Murder Under the Oaks* (Down & Out Books, 2015); "Pocket Queens" originally appeared in *Brooklyn Justice* (Down & Out Books, 2016); "Mysterious Ways" originally appeared in *Unloaded: Crime Writers Writing Without Guns* (Down & Out Books, 2016); "L.A. Freeway" originally appeared in *Mama Tried: Crime Fiction Inspired by Outlaw Country Music* (Down & Out Books, 2016); "Not the Way It Looks" originally appeared in *Coast to Coast: Private Eyes from Sea to Shining Sea* (Down & Out Books, 2017); "Tommy's Birthday" originally appeared in *Greasepaint & 45s* (Down & Out Books, 2019); "One Way or Another" originally appeared in *Mickey Finn: 21st Century Noir: Volume One* (Down & Out Books, 2020). All other stories new to this collection.

All rights reserved. No part of the book may be reproduced in any form or by any electronic or mechanical means, including information storage and retrieval systems, without permission in writing from the publisher, except by a reviewer who may quote brief passages in a review.

Down & Out Books
3959 Van Dyke Road, Suite 265
Lutz, FL 33558
DownAndOutBooks.com

The characters and events featured in the short fiction in this book are fictitious. Any similarity to real persons, living or dead, is coincidental and not intended by the author.

Cover design by J.L. Abramo

ISBN: 1-64396-338-4
ISBN-13: 978-1-64396-338-9

For Friends, Family, and Fans—
and Lance Wright, who I consider all of the above.

CONTENTS

FOREWORD

LIKE TRYING TO CATCH WATER IN A NET
1

SHORT FICTION

ONE HIT WONDER
7

WALKING THE DOG
21

POCKET QUEENS
A Novella
45

MYSTERIOUS WAYS
125

L.A. FREEWAY
133

NOT THE WAY IT LOOKS
143

TOMMY'S BIRTHDAY
159

ONE WAY OR THE OTHER
177

MAJOR CHORDS
195

MENTAL BLOCKS
209

NO MILK TODAY
223

SUITABLE FOR FRAMING
233

VOLUNTEERS
247

MEANS, METHOD AND OPPORTUNITY

THE MYSTERIOUS NATURE OF CRIME FICTION
271

A BRIEF HISTORY OF DETECTIVE FICTION
277

THE PRIVATE EYE AS COLD WARRIOR
Hammer vs. The Hammer And Sickle
281

LOCATION, LOCATION, LOCATION
Dennis Lehane's Journey From
Boston To Brooklyn And Back
283

RESURRECTING JIMMY PIGEON
287

BROOKLYN EASE
You Can Go Home Again
291

SAN FRANCISCO BEAT
299

FOOD FOR THOUGHT
Even Fictional Characters Need To Eat
303

FIFTY ANSWERS
313

CLOSING WITH OPENINGS
321

FOREWORD

LIKE TRYING TO CATCH WATER IN A NET

I am often asked what inspired me to start writing.

My simple answer to the question is *reading*.

Reading books, fiction or nonfiction, has always offered me the opportunity to expand my knowledge and my sensibilities—while doubling as a terrific source of entertainment. I have always found writing to be my preferred tool of expression and creativity—the instrument I wished to master. Poetry, song writing, journalism, and ultimately book-length fiction and short stories.

The summer of 2000 found this South Brooklyn boy working at an office in South Carolina. A fish out of water. In the evenings I would write—working on my first full-length novel. And then one day it was complete. Now what...

It was literally impossible to get a publisher to look at the work unsolicited. So, I was forced to go the prescribed route—attempting to find a Literary Agent who would champion my novel. All of the agencies I researched would only accept *query* letters—would not even take a peek at a chapter or two. If I imagined I could write a good book, I quickly learned I *could not* write a convincing query letter. The responses were short form letters which all said basically the same thing. *Thanks, but no thanks.*

When Van Morrison was asked what he would do if he never

sold a song, he answered without hesitation that he would not stop working at it because, he confessed, *"I can't not write."*

Vincent van Gogh said, *"If you hear a voice within you say 'you cannot paint' then by all means paint, and that voice will be silenced."*

Determined to thwart discouragement, I did the only thing I could think to do. I sat in front of an archaic desktop PC and began to fill in a blank page. I wished to take my mind off rejection. I wanted to write something unlike what I had written before. Without much premeditation it began as a first-person narrative set in the office of a San Francisco private eye, Jake Diamond, and displayed humor that had been absent from my earlier efforts.

I wrote ten pages.

How a new work of fiction begins is as important to the writer as to the reader. For the writer, the opening pages are the seeds that will hopefully grow into a personally satisfying and coherent literary journey. They are the cornerstone. For the reader, the opening pages are the hook that will hopefully inspire the fellow traveler to continue on that journey. When I face the blank first page, I approach it as a quest and try in time to reach some hidden treasure by the end of the excursion—with many detours and sidesteps along the way.

I do not know the final destination when I begin. The characters are created and developed as composites of people I have known, including myself, and by observed human reactions to events. The *plot* develops as a consequence of how these characters react and interact, and is *secondary* to the characters—since it is the people in a story that have always interested me most as a reader and I *get to know* these characters more and more clearly as they move through the story. In a series, as with the Jake Diamond mystery novels, there is the opportunity for the writer, as well as the reader, to learn more about recurring characters in subsequent installments.

Plotting is extremely *challenging*, but when the *theme* of the work finally dawns on me, when I at last understand what it is I am *really* writing about, it provides direction. When I finally discover where the story is headed, I often find it necessary to *backtrack* in order to locate the path I need to be on to get there. But, when I begin, my books and short stories have always been initiated with a scene—one that will hopefully be recalled throughout the tale, by myself and by the reader, as the circumstance that launched the expedition.

A few days after the barrage of rejection letters—and ten pages into the Jake Diamond experiment—I was surfing the internet when I stumbled across the St. Martin's Press/Private Eye Writers of America contest for Best First Private Eye Novel. Interesting coincidence. I decided immediately that I would finish a private eye novel and submit it before the deadline—which was less than a month away. Apparently, for the characters and the dialogue—and certainly not for the convoluted plot—*Catching Water in a Net* was chosen for the award. The prize was publication by St. Martin's Minotaur (following a considerable amount of editing) and an advance against royalties. Holy smoke.

Exactly one year later I received a final hardback copy in the mail. It was a wonder to behold, and a thrill to hold. The novel was released on the first of October in 2001. SMP gave me two more shots before deciding that the Jake Diamond series, though well received by critics and readers alike, was not what they considered a *cash cow*. I continued to write, of course, what other choice did I have—but the work seemed destined to remain out of the public domain. And then, the net held water once again when Down & Out Books reached out to me and gave Jake Diamond and J. L. Abramo a second chance.

Over the course of 18 months beginning in 2011, Down & Out Books reissued *Catching Water in a Net, Clutching at Straws* and *Counting to Infinity* as eBooks and published the stand-alone crime thriller *Gravesend* (which grew out of the first novel no one was interested in looking at a dozen years earlier) in both eBook and Trade Paperback.

Since then, there have been six more novels, a full-length work of nonfiction, and a number of published and unpublished works of short fiction and essays which are collected here for the first time.

We write, we paint, we play music, we sing because we need to. And if we are persistent and honest and somewhat fortunate, perhaps we can catch water in a net and reach an audience.

And we keep writing.

SHORT FICTION

To expostulate what majesty should be, what duty is,
why day is day, night, night and time is time,
were nothing but to waste night, day and time.
Therefore, since brevity is the soul of wit,
and tediousness the limbs and outward flourishes,
I will be brief.

—William Shakespeare, *Hamlet*, Act II Scene II

ONE HIT WONDER

I found myself alone.

The telephone on my desk had beckoned four times.

I was waiting for Darlene Roman to pick up the call. My able assistant was much better at offering salutations, and Darlene had a knack for making it sound as if she were transferring the caller to someone important. On top of that, I might have reminded her, answering calls was one of the things she was being paid to do. But then Darlene might have reminded me that the last time we brought in enough business to earn her a decent paycheck, we were still pounding telegraph keys.

I finally realized that I was alone. I grabbed the telephone receiver, guessing that Darlene had ducked out for a quick drink. A carrot smoothie at the health food bar across Columbus Avenue.

I was trying to decide which of the standard greetings I would use.

"Diamond Investigation, Jake Diamond speaking."

Or, "You have reached the offices of Diamond Investigation, please leave a detailed message. We will return your call as soon as possible, beep."

Before I could utter either, the caller spoke.

"Do it tonight. You know the address; the studio is on the second floor above the market. The last class lets out at ten. By the time all of the students leave and she gets into her street

7

clothing, it could be close to eleven. She always makes a stop at the newsstand, out toward Jersey Street, for a newspaper, and then she goes to her car. The car will be parked behind the school I mentioned. It should be the only vehicle back there, and it will be dark. Make it look like a mugging, and make fucking certain that she's killed. You'll get the other twenty-five grand when the job is done."

I might have told him that he had the wrong number, but the line went dead.

I tried remembering how to get the caller back, how to find out who had dialed our office thinking he had reached his hired assassin of choice. I punched star 80, nothing happened. It was the only number that came to mind, then I realized I was thinking of a Bob Fosse film.

A woman had been marked for death. I had six hours to find her. Somewhere in San Francisco.

"It's in Noe Valley, Jake," Darlene said confidently, examining the wall map of the city, "Jersey is between 24th and 25th and only runs between Douglass and Dolores."

"We're looking for a studio of some kind. Art class?"

"Could be anything," said Darlene, "ceramics, acting, dance, photography."

"Second floor above a market," I said, "north or south of Jersey Street."

"It could be Douglass, Diamond, Castro, Noe, Sanchez, Church or Dolores," Darlene said, rapidly listing street names.

"That'll narrow it down."

"C'mon, Jake. Stop whining. Excuse me for being melodramatic, but a woman's life is at stake."

"The hit-man didn't get the instructions, Darlene."

"We don't know that, Jake. Maybe the man who called realized his error. And the woman needs to be warned, one way or the other. Sooner or later the guy is going to get her killed. He must be determined if he's putting up fifty thousand dollars."

"Why don't we just call the police?"

"Think about it, Jake. By the time the SFPD gets into gear, this woman will be pushing up daisies. And that's if they even take you seriously."

"Pushing up daisies?"

"Give me a little slack, Jake. It's almost five, we have to do something."

"Give Vinnie Strings a call, and Joey Russo. Ask them if they can get over here, as soon as possible; we'll split up the area between the four of us and hit the streets."

"I can't help feeling it, Jake, but this is really exhilarating."

"Just what I needed on a Friday afternoon," I said.

We gathered around Darlene's desk, looking down at the Castro District map she had printed off the Internet. Don't ask me how that's done. Joey Russo was out somewhere doing business. His wife Angela sent their son-in-law, Sonny the Chin, in his place.

We decided we would comb the area between Douglass and Dolores Street, from Alvarado to Clipper. We each selected a quadrant, choosing the intersection of Noe and 24th Street as the starting point.

Darlene, Vinnie, Sonny and I climbed into my Toyota and headed for Noe and 24th. Once there, we would all go out into our sectors on foot and come back together after two hours. If any of us found the studio, it would leave two more hours to decide on a plan of action before class let out at ten.

We avoided considering the possibility that the place wouldn't be found.

I took the southwestern quadrant, nine square blocks. There were small markets everywhere, and newsstands up and down from Jersey Street. I walked into each of them, and other businesses along the way, asking about local studios and public schools. A number of visual and performing arts studios were identified, but none which sat directly above a deli or market. The nearest schools were the James Lick Middle School on the north side of 25th off Castro and the After 6 School opposite, but there were others within the boundaries of our hunt.

Undaunted, I plodded on, grabbing a slice of sausage pizza on Douglass Street for sustenance. I could picture Darlene working on a falafel sandwich as she walked Castro. Vinnie would be searching for a double bacon cheeseburger, and Sonny the Chin would be enjoying a moveable feast that his mother-in-law had brown-bagged for him.

I glanced at my Timex. Nearly half past seven and no luck.

I could only hope the others were having more success, and hope the marinara sauce that had dripped from my slice would one day be purged from the front of my vintage City College of New York sweatshirt.

The last place I entered was a wine shop close to the corner of Castro and Jersey. The owner was from the Bronx and, in spite of the sauce stain, he admired my shirt. He was a fellow City College graduate, who still couldn't get over the 1951 basketball scandal.

He couldn't help with the matter at hand, but he was eager to reminisce and tried his best to sell me a bottle of Cabernet. It was almost eight, so I had to drag myself away. In an attempt to be polite, I handed him one of my business cards.

I spotted Sonny and Darlene when I turned back onto 24th Street. Vinnie was crossing Noe from the east. We crowded together against the strong wind that had come up from the Bay. To passersby, we might have looked as if we were planning to knock off the wine store I had just come out of.

When all of the reports were in, we were huddled at the spot where we had begun with little to show for our efforts.

"What now?" I asked.

"C'mon, Jake, we need a quarterback," said Darlene, "we're running out of time."

"Okay," I said, winging it. "Vinnie, take the Toyota. Drop Darlene off at the Vallejo Street police station. Try to find Lieutenant Lopez, Darlene. Try to convince her that we need help. If she can at least send a few squad cars to cruise the neighborhood, it might scare the guy off. Lopez likes you, maybe she'll bite."

"And if she's not there?" asked Darlene.

"Then look for Sergeant Johnson, but don't mention my name," I said. "Vinnie, you go back to the office and wait there. Maybe, by some miracle, this guy will call again by mistake. I'm going to stick around down here. Call me on my cell phone if either of you has any good news."

"What can I do, Jake," Sonny asked.

"Call your mother-in-law, Sonny, and ask her to say a novena."

Sonny stayed behind with me. We covered the search area again, circling the blocks as we moved out from the center. We were hoping that we might spot student types arriving for some sort of class. We took opposite sides of each street, checking the doorways to every flat that sat above a market or delicatessen, reading the names on door buzzers for anything that might offer a clue.

Darlene rang my cell phone. She had spoken with Lopez and had sweet talked the Lieutenant into sending the troops out. Lopez said she could only spare two cruisers, but she would have them roll through the area until eleven. Darlene wanted to come back and join us in the search. I told her I would rather she go back to the office to check on Vinnie.

It was nearly nine-thirty. Sonny insisted we take a short break for coffee. He suggested that at ten we could go out again, splitting up this time, to look for students letting out.

We sat at the counter of a coffee shop near where we had

started. Sonny finally broke the silence.

"Is this your first contract hit?" he asked.

"Very first," I said, playing along.

"The first is always the toughest," Sonny said.

I gave Sonny a hard look.

"You're joking, right?"

"Yes, Jake, I'm joking. What's on your mind?"

"I'm thinking about the phone call. How I stood there listening dumbstruck. I heard him through without interrupting. Maybe if I had opened my damn mouth, I could have done something."

The counterman came over to refill our cups.

Sonny took a five-dollar bill from his wallet and placed it on the counter.

"Look, Jake. There's a very good chance this guy never realized he called the wrong number, in which case the woman should be safe tonight. If you had cut him short, he would probably have set it up with the real assassin. And you wouldn't have heard enough of the details to get us at least this close to the woman. There's still a chance we may find her, it's almost ten, let's go."

We both rose and moved toward the exit.

"It was strange. After I listened to the guy, I felt as if I had actually accepted the contract," I said.

"In a way you have," Sonny said.

We split up outside the coffee shop. The streets were Friday-night busy. Thirty minutes flew by. I saw a squad car moving slowly up Castro Street; it didn't make me feel much better. I pulled out my cell phone to report in with Darlene. I turned it on and it rang immediately.

"Hell, Jake, I've been calling for more than an hour."

"I must have turned the phone off without thinking, what's up?"

"Some guy from a wine store called, said he had some information about a dance class on Noe Street."

The wine store was less than a block away. I quickly thanked

Darlene and ran back to the shop.

I skipped the formalities.

"Tell me about the dance class," I said.

"A very nice woman stopped in just before nine, for a bottle of Merlot. I'd never seen her before so I tried to make a little conversation. She was in a hurry. She said that she was a dance instructor, working out of a studio on Noe, and had to get to class. I thought she might be the woman you were looking for."

"Where on Noe?" I asked.

"Right around the corner, between Jersey and 25th." I ran out.

I looked up and down the street for any sign. It was much quieter here than on Castro. It was ten thirty-five. Finally I spotted it, a small shoe store in the middle of the block. Above the door was a painted sign, displaying the name of the shop.

The Market.

I had no way of reaching Sonny. I debated whether I should simply walk over and try finding my way up into the studio when a woman came out. She was in her mid-twenties and very attractive. I watched as she moved toward Jersey Street. She stopped into the newsstand and came out with a newspaper under her arm. I followed a safe distance behind as she turned the corner at Jersey, going south.

I looked around to check if anyone else was following. I dug into my jacket pocket and I took hold of the butt of my .38. I had taken it from my desk when we were waiting for Vinnie and Sonny to show up at the office. The woman crossed to the opposite side of Jersey Street and reached into her purse.

Suddenly she was unlocking the door of an automobile parked on the street. The street was comparatively quiet, but it was fairly well lit and there were a good number of pedestrians. I rushed over to the car as she was climbing in. She quickly closed the door, locked it and started the engine. I stood looking at her through the car window. I must have appeared either harmless or pathetic, because she rolled down her window and spoke.

"Can I help you?" she asked.

"Do you teach a dance class over on Noe?"

"That would be Mrs. Landers. She probably came out of the building right after me. I'm one of her students. Is there something wrong?"

"Where does she park her car?" I asked.

"Over on 25th, behind the Middle School."

Then I was running back toward 25th and Castro, my hand deep inside my pocket, still clutching the grip of the thirty-eight.

I caught sight of a woman walking into the driveway alongside the school building. I took off after her. I had unconsciously pulled my hand from my pocket. I held my arm at my side, weapon in hand. I came into the small parking area behind the school. It was unlit. The woman was moving to the solitary BMW parked there.

I heard a sound from the opposite side of the car and I raised my arm.

"Mrs. Landers," I called.

She stopped and turned. She looked at my extended arm and then into my eyes.

"Are you going to shoot me?" she asked.

"No," I said, moving quickly toward the car.

"Jake," a voice called from behind the BMW, "it's Sonny."

I saw Sonny's arms come up over the roof and then he stood.

"I called Darlene and spoke with the wine store guy," Sonny said. "I followed this woman from the studio and came in from the back in case anyone was waiting."

"Would someone please tell me what's going on?" Mrs. Landers asked.

Then we all turned toward the flashing lights and siren of the police cruiser coming up the driveway.

It was nearly midnight. We were sitting outside of Lopez's office at the Vallejo Street Police Station, waiting for the Lieutenant to finish with Sarah Landers.

Lopez had not seemed very happy about having to be there at that hour.

Lopez came out with Landers, asked the woman to take a seat in the hallway and then ushered me and Sonny into her office.

"Sit," she said.

"What do you know, Lieutenant?" I asked.

"Not much," Lopez said, "the woman is a bit eccentric. She's loaded with money; made a bundle dancing on Broadway and in movies. Retired, moved out here, and teaches dance for the love of it, and she can't imagine why anyone would want her killed."

"That kind of thing takes a lot of imagination," Sonny said, "does she have a husband?"

"It was my first thought. She's a widow," said Lopez. "I asked her who she supposed might benefit from her death, she wouldn't even consider it."

"So, what now?" I asked. "Whoever has it in for her is going to try again."

"Not much I can do, Diamond," Lopez said, "I can put a tail on her for a few days, tops. Maybe the guy will call you back, ask you how you fucked it up."

"Cute."

"I have an idea," Sonny said, "but I doubt that either of you will like it."

"Go ahead," said Lopez with little passion.

Sonny was right. We weren't crazy about his idea. For lack of a better one, we decided to give it a shot.

Lopez led me and Sonny out of her office and then she escorted Sarah Landers back in.

The call from Lopez woke me before eight the next morning.

So much for sleeping in late on a Saturday.

Lieutenant Lopez had come down hard on Sarah Landers the

second go around. She learned the woman had one child. A son who stood to inherit everything.

Lopez said she scared the crap out of the woman with talk of obstruction of justice. She warned Landers that if she tried reaching her son, who was now a suspect in a conspiracy to commit murder, she risked imprisonment.

Landers was told not to answer her home telephone.

It was a colossal bluff. Lopez was betting Sarah Landers could not reach a lawyer before nine on a Saturday morning for consultation.

The Lieutenant had a uniformed officer drive Landers to the woman's home, with instructions to remain outside the house.

The BMW remained where it had been parked in the school lot.

Lopez then called the son, reporting that a late model BMW had been discovered abandoned behind a school building. There was no sign of its owner, who had been identified by the vehicle registration as Sarah Landers. The woman could not be reached at her home address. The car would be held at the city auto impound until someone came to claim it.

"Did he sound mildly concerned?' I asked.

"He gave it a good try, he asked if there was anything he could do," said Lopez. "I asked him to phone me as soon as he heard from his mother, and I said we would phone him if we heard anything. Got a pencil?"

"Go ahead," I said.

I jotted down the son's phone number.

"I'm at my office, Diamond. I'll be hunched over my telephone waiting for your call."

"Don't hurt yourself, Lieutenant" I said, and ended the connection.

When the dial tone came back, I punched in the number Lopez had given me.

After three rings a man answered.

"Time to settle up," I said.

"They didn't find her body. What the fuck happened?"

"They will, eventually, I took her for a little ride. Do you have the cash?"

"Yes."

"Meet me in an hour. The Home Plate on Lombard, I'll be at the counter. Don't be fucking late."

"How will I know you?" he asked.

I was very glad to hear that he had to ask.

"I'll wear a fucking carnation," I said, "I'll know you. Don't make me fucking wait."

I hung up and called Lopez.

I sat at the counter of the Home Plate Diner drinking coffee and glancing out the front window waiting for Daniel Landers to arrive.

Before long, a car pulled up and double-parked across the street. I watched as he climbed out from the passenger side, carrying a large brown envelope. A woman behind the wheel rolled down her window to say something to him as he started to cross. I recognized the driver; I had followed her from the dance studio to her car the night before.

Landers walked in and I waved him over. He sat at the stool beside me. He placed the envelope on the countertop without looking at my eyes. I asked if he needed a receipt and he shuddered. He was about to get up when Lopez walked in. It was the first time I had seen her out of a business suit. She looked good.

"Daniel Landers," she said, slapping handcuffs on him in the blink of an eye, "you are under arrest on suspicion of conspiracy in an attempt to commit murder. You have the right to remain silent, I hope you do. You have the right to an attorney; I would not recommend using your mother's attorney. If you cannot afford a lawyer, we'll see what we can do."

"Lopez," I said, as Landers stood frozen in disbelief, "there's a gal in the Pontiac across the street who you may want to talk

17

with."

Lopez took out her two-way radio and called Sergeant Johnson. She told him to pick up the woman in the Pontiac before we came out. I saw Johnson's unmarked Ford pull up beside the other car less than a minute later.

Dan Landers confessed the moment they got him over to Vallejo Street. He claimed that it was her idea, the girl in the Pontiac. He'd met her a few months earlier when he picked his mother up from the studio, one of Sarah Lander's dance students. They began to see a lot of each other and before too long she was filling Dan's head with visions of a rosy and financially secure future for the two of them.

Daniel Landers had no idea who the hired gun was. He had dropped word here and there that he was looking for one and someone contacted him. Landers had deposited the first twenty-five thousand at a drop the previous Sunday night, a trash barrel at the corner of California and Van Ness. The only phone number Landers had was the number for my office, Daniel had apparently written it down incorrectly. Without the contract killer it would be a tough case to prosecute, but the experience would certainly discourage Landers from trying anything like it again and perhaps give his mother reason to reconsider the provisions of her last will and testament.

And that was that. Or so I thought.

Five days later, late Thursday night, I arrived at my apartment from a pinochle game at the Pacific Heights home of a fellow PI. As I pushed the key into the door lock, I felt what could only be the barrel of a handgun pressed up against the back of my head.

"Don't fucking turn around," the voice said.

"Not a chance," I said.

"Word has it that you cost me twenty-five grand, Mr. Diamond, and that really fucking upsets me."

"It wasn't my intention," I said.

"Nevertheless."

"Look at it this way; you *made* twenty-five thousand without having to kill an innocent woman."

"In my business, Diamond," he said, "that is little consolation. If you ever try pulling something like that again, intended or not, you will find yourself at the top of my fucking list. Contract work is getting difficult to come by these days, and I won't have someone pinching any of the few jobs that still trickle my way."

"Don't worry, it was my first and last hit," I said. I felt the gun barrel move away from my head.

I finally found the courage to turn around.

I found myself alone.

WALKING THE DOG

I don't remember hearing the gunshot, but the bullet nearly killed me.

The last thing I could remember hearing before I woke up in a hospital bed twenty days later was a voice calling from behind. I can remember stopping to turn—feeling as if I knew the voice but unable to place it. The moment I came out of the coma, the thought briefly grabbed me and then let go.

There are only two things that scare me more than death.

Most frightening by far is the thought of something truly horrible happening to one of my children.

My son had disappeared for two hours one summer. Charlie was six years old and had strayed from the area where we had been camping. It was a fairly desolate spot, so we weren't afraid he would be abducted. We were terrified he might take a dangerous fall or discover a lake to drown in. Frantically we searched and called out for him, praying darkness wouldn't fall before we could locate him.

Finally, there he was. A good half-mile from our campsite. He was surrounded by fallen tree branches, a kind of makeshift fortress. Sitting there, piling small stones he had gathered to create a squat tower. Totally at ease and fearless—completely glad to see us. I told him what a nice job he had done with the stones, asked him if he was ready to leave, scooped him up in my arms and carried him over to his mother.

It was at least a week before I slept well again.

Next on my list of personal terrors, lurking between concern for the well-being of my children and my own mortality, is the thought of losing my sight or the use of my legs.

Two of my childhood friends had lost their legs, one to diabetes and the other in an automobile accident. One crawled away from life toward an early death while the other passionately embraced life with both arms. I fear my approach would be much more like the former. It is impossible to describe what went through my mind when I found myself in a hospital bed with no feeling at all below my waist.

When I came out of my twenty-day sleep they were all there—my wife, my son, and my daughter.

The moment I opened my eyes Annie, who is thirteen going on thirty, said, "Gee, Dad, you must have been very tired." For an instant I could hear the voice that had called from behind me the night I was shot, and then it was gone. I was happy to see my family. When I discovered I had no feeling below my waist I asked my wife what was going on.

"Don't be afraid, Johnny. The doctors say it will be okay and you shouldn't worry."

Nice try.

I was born on the first day of October, 1973. While my mother was in labor, my dad was in the maternity ward lounge with other expectant fathers watching the baseball game. My mother would often tell us how my father came running into her room bubbling with excitement and cried, "The Mets clinched the East, how are you doing?"

When I came out of the coma, my son Charlie ran and jumped up onto the bed, landing on my knees. I didn't feel a thing.

"Hi, son," I said, "getting excited about the Mets' home opener?"

"That was two weeks ago, Dad."

That was when I asked Maggie what week it was.

Charlie asked me if he was too heavy. I told him he was as light as a feather and to stay right where he was. He laughed and asked me what kind of feather. I was doing whatever it is you do with your mind when you want to move your toes. I began to feel lightheaded and must have passed out.

When I woke again my family was gone and had been replaced by two men in white lab coats and stethoscopes. One held a silver clipboard in his left hand while he twirled a pen like a baton in his right. The other was stroking his chin like a Rodin statue and self-consciously dropped his arm to his side when my eyes popped open.

As I looked up at them, they smiled simultaneously.

I anxiously waited to find out which of these geniuses would be the first to speak.

After a barrage of mumbo jumbo from the Thinker, about where the bullet had entered and exited and how a bone fragment was affecting my ability to feel the entire lower half of my body, he turned it over to medical mastermind number two. Using his clipboard for protection he assured me the condition was almost surely temporary.

Almost surely?

I wondered why doctors insisted on using terms that were absolutely meaningless to their patients. Being a gambler myself, I told him I would prefer simple odds. He said we were looking at a touchy operation but one that was not without a good rate of success and worrying about it would only make my situation more difficult. I wanted to kick him but I couldn't move my leg. As they turned to leave the room they promised they would return soon to complete the touchy operation consent forms and reminded me that all of the resources of the great City of New York were at our disposal.

"The mayor has been here to see you, twice," said Clipboard.

If I had been doing something more in the line of duty than walking my dog in the park on the night I was shot, I suppose the Governor may have popped in also.

I asked them to thank His Honor for me, twice, and to please send my wife and children back into the room.

When my family returned, I asked Maggie to find Sam and beg him to get over to the hospital as quickly as humanly possible.

I met Maggie during my senior year at Queens College. It was the fall of 1995 and on the minds of most Americans was the O.J. Simpson trial. Margaret Kelly sat behind me in a Political Science class called *Law and Social Change* and was constantly voicing her extremely emphatic opinions over my left shoulder. She predicted that, innocent *or* guilty, Simpson would be acquitted. I personally couldn't call that one, but every other student and the professor strongly disagreed.

I bumped into her in the cafeteria the next day and worked up the nerve to approach her as she sat down to her lunch.

"Mind if I ask you one question?" I asked.

"That is a question. Was that the question?"

"Okay, can I ask you another question?" I asked, and then quickly added, "I mean beside this one?"

"Sure, sit."

I sat.

"Do you really believe Simpson will beat the rap?"

Not exactly out of the book on how to pick up girls.

"Yes, I do. And what's more I never say what I don't believe."

"Never?"

"Never, now did you want to ask me out?"

"Yes."

"Then why don't you ask me, before you run out of questions?"

Simpson was found not guilty a few weeks later.

The night of the verdict Maggie and I were sitting in my Bonneville.

"Well, you nailed that one. Are you always that good at predicting the future?"

"Try me."

"Will we both get into Law School?"

"Yes. Though maybe not the same Law School."

"Will we both become lawyers?"

"You will if you really want to."

"Fair enough. Here's one," I said. "If we were married someday, would we be happy together and have lots of kids?"

"Very happy. Two children, but only after I get done with school, and you'll have to help a lot with the kids so I can practice law before I'm an old woman."

"Fair enough."

Margaret Kelly was right about everything. She was accepted into Columbia Law School, completed her studies, passed the New York State bar, had two beautiful children, and was now a prosecutor in the New York City District Attorney's Office. I graduated with a degree in Political Science and Criminology, but I guess I must not have really wanted to be a lawyer, so here I was instead, lying half-paralyzed in a hospital bed waiting to hear from my partner Sam.

Maggie had to take the kids home to feed them and then drop them off with my sister Barbara so she could get back for an evening visit alone. She said she would try to track Sam down as soon as she reached the house.

After they left, I had one thought and one thought only. I wanted a cigarette. Whether smoking was allowed in the hospital room was not an issue. I couldn't care less. The problem was finding a cigarette, particularly a Camel straight.

The chances of finding one in that room were not good. In fact, even if there was a pack two feet from me I would not have been able to reach it in my condition. There was no denying I was going to need some help.

I am not exactly proud of the fact I smoke cigarettes. It is an unhealthy habit and a tough one to kick.

I am, nevertheless, resolved to the fact. I concluded long ago that one thing I am, among many others, is a smoker. I am an Irish-Italian-American, a very good cook, a loving father, a faithful husband, a devoted son to my cantankerous old man, a better than average softball player, a fair harmonica player, a great Pinochle player, an avid reader, a moderate drinker, an opera lover, a lousy car mechanic, a gun control advocate, a movie addict, and a cigarette smoker.

I pushed the button that was pinned to my gown. This would theoretically summon a nurse to my side. The theory was empirically confirmed when two minutes later a nurse, whose name tag identified her as Mary Campanella, walked into the room.

"Can I help you, Mr. Sullivan?" she asked.

"I hope so."

"I'll do my very best."

"Do you mind if I smoke?"

"I don't care if you burst into flames," she said and then added, "sorry, just joking. I've always wanted to say that."

"What are the chances you could get me a Camel cigarette?"

"Slim and none, and slim already left town."

"Let me guess, you've always wanted to say that?"

"No, that one I used every time a patient asks me for a cigarette."

"No exceptions?"

"Well, there is one. If you can give me a really good reason why I should break the rules and bring you a cigarette so you can break the rules, I might give your request some consideration."

"I work with your Uncle Pete."

She walked to the foot of the bed and glanced at the chart hanging there.

"Oh," she said, "you're *that* Mr. Sullivan."

"John."

"Camel you said?"

"Yes."

"Non-filter?"

"Please."

"Give me ten minutes."

"Thank you."

"Don't mention it."

"Don't worry, I won't."

I suppose the cigarette was a little too much for me after almost three weeks cold turkey because the next thing I remembered was opening my eyes to a room lit only by the glow of the television screen on the opposite wall. I don't know how far I made it with the Camel before I fell asleep, but I did notice in the faint green illumination that the ashtray and all other evidence of my transgression had been deftly removed from the scene of the crime. I was reaching for the buzzer on my chest to call for some light when a voice out of the darkness almost got my legs working again.

"How are you feeling, son?"

"Not half bad, Pop," I said. "Why are you sitting in the dark?"

"Didn't want to wake you, want a cigarette?"

"No thanks, I think I just had one. Pete Campanella's niece was good enough to smuggle one in for me."

"Mary?"

"Yeah, she's a real sweetheart."

"She have a boyfriend?"

"She's a little young for you."

"I was thinking about your cousin Jimmy."

"Forget it. She's a nurse, not a psychiatrist. Where's Maggie?"

"She took the kids over to Barbara. I asked her to drop me off here first. Who shot you, son?"

"Don't know. I'm hoping Sam will show up soon with some ideas."

"When I find out, I'm going to kill the bastard."

My father wouldn't hurt a fly unless the fly was involved in an armed felony.

"Thanks, Dad, but maybe we can just rough him up a little."

"Are you going to be able to walk again?"

"That's what they tell me. I certainly hope so."

"Can I do anything for you?"

"Yes, as a matter of fact. Next time you come, bring one of Aunt Tillie's veal parmesan sandwiches on Sabatino's bread and keep Jimmy away from the Campanella girl. And could you change the television station? I think *Jeopardy* is on. And turn on the lights so I can see you."

The lights revealed what was totally hidden from his voice. My tough-as-nails father had clearly been crying. It was almost enough to get me going myself, but I controlled my emotions. I could do that well. After all, I had learned from him. Or maybe I was just saved by the bell, because just then Maggie walked in.

"Hi, Counselor. Thanks for dropping Dad off."

"I'm surprised you two aren't smoking your brains out."

"Did you get hold of Sam?"

"Left a message for him to hurry down here. He's out on the job somewhere."

"I'm missing all the fun."

"Don't worry—there will still be work when you get back. There's never a shortage in your business."

"Hallelujah."

Alex Trebek read the categories for Double Jeopardy.

Maggie and the old man kept the conversation light during their visit. That and the pain medication for the parts of my body that could still feel pain made me sleepy again. I had heard from the hospital grapevine that the operation was tentatively scheduled for the day after next. The theory was that a small bone fragment, which was pressing against my spine, would be carefully removed through a touchy operation and my almost surely temporary lower body paralysis would be history. Terrific theory. And certainly one worth subscribing to. Maggie and Dad said their goodbyes and left me to drift into sleep. I was fighting to stay awake until I heard from Sam, but lost the battle.

In my dream I was reading a book in bed when I heard my father's 1982 Ford Galaxy start up in the driveway. It was October 1986, and Dad was taking my brother to the sixth game of the World Series against the Red Sox at Shea Stadium. The Mets were down three games to two.

Frankie was the logical choice to go with Dad.

Frankie was a diehard Mets fan. I was a Yankee fanatic, but the last time the Bronx Bombers had been in the Series was in 1978, and at five I was too young to go. Regardless of allegiances, I was as jealous as a thirteen-year-old could be that his nine-year-old brat of a brother was going to get to the big game before I did. But in the dream it felt as if something else made me want to jump out of the bed, run to the car, and tell Dad not to take Frankie with him that day. Tell my father to take me instead, and leave Frankie home with Mom. But in the dream I couldn't move my legs, as desperately as I tried, and I lay there helplessly as I listened to the Ford pull away.

When the phone woke me, I was soaked with sweat and I was shaking like a leaf.

Fortunately, the phone was within my reach and I grabbed it after the third ring.

"Spook house," I said.

"Did I wake you?"

"Yes, and I can't thank you enough," I said. "Where are you?"

"I couldn't begin to tell you, partner. It's such a mess that to call it ridiculous would be a gross understatement. I wish you were here."

"I wouldn't mind."

"Margaret tracked me down. How are you feeling?"

"Not bad from the waist up."

"I'm not going to get out of this one soon, but I'll come straight over when I can cut loose. Get some sleep. If you're asleep when I get there, I promise to wake you up."

I wasn't anxious to fall asleep again and pick up my dream where it had left off. I knew all too well how it ended. I wanted another smoke pretty badly, but not enough to bother the nurse again. I turned the television on and flipped through the channels until I came across a martial arts movie already in progress. I watched with the hope that soon I'd be up and kicking again myself.

I was dreaming again. The car was pulling out of the driveway. I was trying to get up from the bed but my legs wouldn't work.

"You will not believe this one." I snapped awake.

The booming voice ricocheted off every wall in the small room and reached my ears with the subtlety of a slap in the face. This is how Sam wakes you. Not like Prince Charming with a whisper and a kiss, but like a hostage negotiator with a bullhorn.

It's one of the character traits that make him so lovable.

"I'm ready to believe anything," I said.

"Picture this, if you will. A guy calls in a pizza delivery order from Di Fara's on Avenue J. Sausage, onion, and green pepper."

"I appreciate the attention to detail."

"It's important. The delivery kid knocks on the door, it's the upstairs of a two-family house on East Fourteenth Street, and the guy opens the door. He keeps the kid waiting on the landing while he goes to get his wallet."

"Cat comes back with a slice on a paper plate, he holds it out to the kid and says, 'Take a bite and tell me if this is sausage, onion, and green pepper'. The kid says he's not really very hungry and he can tell just by looking that it's pepperoni and mushroom. The guy pulls a forty-four Magnum and insists the kid taste it just to be certain."

30

"He forced the kid to eat pizza at gunpoint. Is that a felony?"

"It gets better," said Sam. "The guy forces the poor kid into the apartment and ties him into a chair. Clothesline. Then he calls the pizzeria and he tells the manager it's the third time they've fucked up his order and if they don't get the right pie up to him in twenty minutes he's going to blow the delivery kid's head off. So much for don't shoot the messenger."

"Unbelievable."

"What'd I tell you? The manager calls the owner at home and the old man calls it in to the precinct. So me and Stevie O'Brien— this is who they put me with because you had to go and get plugged—run over to the pizzeria. O'Brien throws on a smock covered with red sauce, and we take a pizza over to Fourteenth Street."

"I can't stand the suspense."

"Wait. We get to the place, O' Brien knocks on the door, I stand out of view of the peephole. The guy says through the door, 'You look a little old for a delivery boy.' Not to mention that O'Brien looks less Italian than I do, his skin is the color of Elmer's Glue-All. Anyway, Stevie starts winging it, rambling about how he owns the joint and he's Irish, the name Di Fara's is a cover but don't tell anyone because it could hurt business and the hostage in there is his sister's son and she'll murder him if anything happens to the kid, and the pizza, which absolutely has sausage, onion, and green pepper and is by the way on the house, is getting cold."

"I'm exhausted just listening to this. Does the guy make the exchange?"

"He opens the door. He's got the forty-four pointed right at O'Brien's head."

"Oh, boy."

"I've got to admit Stevie stayed cool. He takes a step toward the guy and starts to open the pizza box. The guy asks Stevie what the fuck he's doing and O'Brien says he wants to show the guy that the toppings are correct so he can get his nephew the fuck out of there. Meanwhile, I've got my gun out and I'm wondering when this guy is going to take a peek over and spot me. The next thing I hear is screaming. I jump into the doorway and this guy is trying to get hot mozzarella out of his eyes while O'Brien is tackling him to the floor, the weapon drops neatly into the pizza box, Stevie is trying to handcuff the guy, both their hands are slippery with marinara, and I don't know whether to try to help O'Brien or grab a slice."

"You arrest the guy?"

"Oh, yeah. When I left the station, they were still trying to figure out the charge. The gun wasn't registered, but it wasn't loaded either. If we call it a kidnapping, the FBI is going to make us hear about it until the end of time. And all along the guy is yelling about how he's going to sue the city for burning his face with hot tomato sauce. His cheeks look as if they were used to wax a car. So how are you doing?"

"Better than some. Anybody have any ideas about who put the bullet in me?"

"Not a clue, probably someone you locked up once or twice. Maybe we could sit and brainstorm for a while. Can we smoke in here?"

"What are they going to do, arrest us?"

After graduation I had a decision to make. Maggie had been accepted by the Columbia School of Law, but no law school in the city was interested in me. There were a few out-of-town schools that were interested, but the thought of leaving New York City and Margaret Kelly was unacceptable. I enrolled in the Master's program at the John Jay College of Criminal Justice instead. Two years later, newly married and with Maggie still studying, it was time to begin earning a living. The obvious choice, maybe the only choice from the very beginning, was to join the police force.

I met Sam on my first assignment as a homicide detective.

When I arrived he was already at the scene.

"Sullivan," I said, holding out my hand. "John to my friends."

"First homicide call?"

"It is."

"You look Sicilian," he said.

"My mother. My dad was another Irish cop."

"Then we could be distant cousins." He smiled, his white teeth sparkling in his huge black face. "Name's Samson, Sam to my friends."

"Good to meet you, Sam."

"We'll see, John. Gotta minute?"

"Sure."

"Follow me."

He led me into the adjoining room. In the middle of the room was a large bed. In the middle of the bed was a small child. Ten months old maybe. A year at most. A little boy, though you couldn't tell it from his face which looked as if it had been used for soccer practice.

"Welcome to Homicide," Sam said.

That night my father was over for dinner. I asked him what he considered his worst experience in all his years on the job. He reminded me it was the time he came very close to shooting a teenager in the A&P supermarket.

Sam went on and on with a blow-by-blow recapitulation of all the fun I had missed during my three weeks in limbo.

After an hour and a half of non-stop narrative, Sam fell asleep in the middle of a sentence. It was getting on toward eight in the morning. I decided I had best wake him. I expected Maggie to drop in on her way to the office and figured it was time Sam got some real rest.

If I could have reached him from the bed I would have used a gentle shake. Instead I bopped him off the forehead with an empty paper cup.

He opened his eyes and looked at the cup that had landed neatly in his lap.

"Fine shot."

"Go home and get some sleep."

"Good idea," he said, slowly rising. "I'll be back later. Want me to bring you anything?"

"Anything on my assailant would be nice."

"I'm not very optimistic, but I'll do my best," Sam said. "I'm very glad to see you back among the conscious, partner."

Maggie ran in and out just long enough to give me a kiss and a little squeeze between my legs to see if there had been any miracles overnight. Nothing, but I appreciated the gesture.

Soon the Bobbsey Twins materialized with a third person in tow. He was a good-looking kid with all the trappings of a doctor—lab coat, stethoscope and clipboard. He was introduced as Dr. Levine, an intern working with them on my case. Levine looked so young it was all I could do to stop myself from asking if he was looking forward to his bar mitzvah.

The three stooges took turns round robin style going over the operation planned for the next morning. What it would entail, what I could expect, and what the desired outcome would be.

"If all goes well," they let Dr. Levine do the closing argument, "we will eliminate the source of pressure on your spine and you should be able to walk out of the hospital at one hundred percent."

I loved it when they use words like *if* and *should*, straight from the handbook of medical disclaimers.

"Will I be able to tap dance?" I asked Levine.

"I see no reason why not," he answered confidently.

Except for the fact I could never tap dance before.

And, believe me, there had been many times I'd tried.

They turned to leave but I pulled them up short.

"Aren't there some papers I need to sign?"

"Oh, yes," said Moe, or was it Curly, "how silly of us, we almost forgot."

You *did* forget, Einstein, I said to myself. And did he say *silly*? Oh, boy.

I was hoping they would remember to wear their silly little rubber gloves the next morning.

It was still not even nine in the morning, and I had at least twenty-four hours to wonder if I would really be able to walk on my own two legs again. The choices for distraction were *Rachel Ray, Live with Kelly and Michael*, or the paperback Maggie had dropped off. I opted for the book. A murder mystery.

There were visitors coming and going all day. They must have waived the limited visiting-hours policy because I was a hero. Lucky me. When you're a cop and you get shot they always try to make you a hero, no matter what you were doing when you got shot, even if you were walking your dog or holding the weapon in your teeth when it happened.

My father was there most of the morning and the early afternoon. He was taking advantage of my condition, telling me stories I had heard a hundred times since I was four years old. He had a captive audience.

And he had nowhere else to go.

Frank Sullivan was a lonely man, even in a room full of people, particularly since my mother passed away.

It had been proven at many a gin mill and family get-together.

Sam showed up just before noon, looking as if he had slept for a week and needed at least two more. He rescued me briefly by taking Dad down for lunch.

There were others in and out. Other cops, some suit from City Hall bringing best wishes from the mayor, the dynamic duo with more papers to sign, Sam to re-deposit Dad by the bed before he had to *get back out on the street and go do good*, the Campanella kid to check up on my nicotine cravings.

It's amazing how popular you can become just by taking a bullet in the back.

Look at Jesse James.

My sister came to drop my kids off after school and collect Dad.

Charlie had a baseball bat and asked if he could bat my legs to see if I would feel anything. I said, "No, but thanks for asking."

Anne, she insisted her days as "Annie" were officially over, scooped up the mystery novel and went straight to the last chapter.

Maggie showed up after work and took the kids home for dinner, and came back for a few hours in the evening.

Nurse Campanella came in at around nine insisting I'd need my rest for the morning's appointment with the knife. She encouraged my wife to leave without too much coaxing. The Counselor was exhausted.

Maggie kissed me goodnight, asked me not to worry and assured me she would be at my side throughout.

Not long after Maggie left, Nick Ventura walked into the hospital room holding a large flat box with Totonno's written all over it.

Nick and I grew up on the same Brooklyn street. He was a private investigator who tried roping me into his fiascos a little too often.

"Did you bring beer?"

He placed the box on the bedside table and pulled a Sam Adams out of each pocket of his jacket.

"There's a slice missing," I said when he opened the box.

"Bribe to Mary Campanella to let me in after visiting hours."

"If you're here to ask for help on one of your hopeless cases, I'm sort of on sabbatical."

"I just came to see how you were. Carmella sends her regards."

"Have Carmella and the boys got the beauty shop up and running again?"

"Why? Do you want to get your toenails done?"

I had to laugh.

"Did you hear about Sonny Balducci?" Nick asked.

"They find him?"

"A Boy Scout troop stumbled on a shallow grave when they were digging a fire pit at Camp Pouch in Staten Island. When the forensic guys dug him up they found three red snappers sitting on his chest."

"Nice touch."

"What do you think?"

"Good riddance."

We ate pizza, drank beer, smoked Camels, and reminisced about all of the lines drawn and the choices we were forced to make growing up in the Borough of Churches.

"Do you remember my brother Frankie, Nick?"

"Of course I do. He was a sweet kid."

"Yes, he was," I said.

"Everyone is saying you're going to be fine."

"What if everyone is wrong? What if this is it, and I can't dance at my daughter's wedding?"

"Remember junior year when I broke my ankle sliding into third base last game of the season?"

"How could I forget, they could hear you screaming in Yonkers."

"I thought it was the end of the world."

"You were safe at third, the pinch-runner scored, we won the game, and we made it to the Borough Championship."

"It didn't matter to me, I was inconsolable. Two weeks later I was in a cast up to my knee on the day of the championship. My father planned to take me to the ball field. I said I wouldn't go and I locked myself in my room. He warned me if I didn't unlock the door he would bust it down and break my other ankle. I believed him and let him in. He asked me why I wouldn't want to see my team play for the title. I told him I didn't think I could handle it, that it would be hell to be there and not able to be out in the field. My old man never said much worth repeating but what he said that day got me out to the game."

"What was that?"

"When you're going through hell, keep going."

Nurse Campanella came in to chase Nick out and feed me a pill to help me get to sleep.

"Yell if you need anything," Ventura said.

"Could you leave a few of those cigarettes?"

He placed the package of Camels on the pizza box. He stopped at the door.

"John?"

"Yes?"

"How come no one told me little Annie was engaged to be married?"

"Cute," I said, smiling. "I appreciate you dropping by, Nick."

The pill kicked in quickly and I was nodding out before the second commercial break on an old rerun of *NYPD Blue*.

I remember wondering if I would grow up to be like Andy Sipowitz or Larry Flynt. I remember wondering why all the female cops looked like movie stars.

I remember wondering why David Caruso and Jimmy Smits had given up such a great job.

I remember wondering, as I asked a little favor of God, whether the answer was going to be yes or no.

I remember waking up the next morning and being thrown onto a gurney.

I remember being wheeled into the Operating Room with Maggie's hand clutched tightly in mine.

I remember Doogie Levine MD smiling down at me just before I went under.

Then it was 1986 again and I heard my father's Galaxy start up in the driveway below my bedroom window.

I could hear the Ford pulling out of the driveway taking my

father and brother to Shea.

Just as I heard the Galaxy back out onto West 10th Street, my legs suddenly came back to life.

I jumped out of bed, ran down the stairs and rushed out the front door onto the stoop.

I could see the Ford crossing Avenue S.

I could run pretty fast but I knew I'd never catch them before Dad turned onto 86th Street toward the Belt Parkway.

I was almost back into the house when I heard someone call my name from a few doors down. I turned toward the voice to find Bobby Leone yelling for me.

"Johnny."

"Hey, Bobby."

"Get over here."

"What's up?"

"Hurry."

I walked over to where Bobby was pounding on Nicky Ventura's door.

Ventura was up in his window saying he couldn't come down and Bobby was saying if Nicky didn't come down he was going to get the crap beat out of him.

And I was wishing I had stayed inside.

"They stole Tony's bike," Bobby said.

"Who?"

"Three seniors from Lafayette grabbed it on Kings Highway. We're going up there and we're going to get it back."

"High school seniors? Jesus, Bobby, they'll be twice our size."

"Goddammit, Ventura, get the fuck down here," he yelled up at the window.

"I don't know if we want to tangle with high school kids, Bobby," I said.

"What do you mean you don't know? What if it was your fucking bike?"

I didn't have a bike.

"Nicky, I'm getting really pissed," he yelled again.

And he was.

"Where's Tony?" I asked.

"Stop asking a million fucking questions and get a stick or something because when I drag that asshole Nicky down here we're going to Kings Highway."

"I don't want to go, Bobby. It's Tony's bike, so where's Tony? And you're too riled up, you need to calm down."

And then he walked down the steps from Nicky's front door and hit me between the legs with the baseball bat he was holding.

The swing was more Ben Hogan than Mickey Mantle.

And then, in the dream, he said, "You're going to die for this, Frankie."

But Frankie was my brother's name.

I held myself where Bobby had hit me with the bat.

Then I felt myself getting aroused down there.

I opened my eyes and found my wife with her hand down there.

"Look who's back and raring to go," she said.

"I guess the operation went okay," I said.

"Sure feels like it."

"Do you think I should try to get out of this bed?"

"What's the rush?" Maggie said, and she climbed into the bed beside me.

I must have fallen asleep again.

My father walked into my room.

"How was the game, Dad?" I said, "I was looking for you and Frankie on the TV."

"Come downstairs. Your mother and I need to speak with you."

"What is it?"

"Just come down, son."

I followed him down the stairs into the living room. My mother was sitting on the sofa. Her eyes were red. My father sat beside her and wrapped his arm around her shoulder. I rushed over to Dad's vacant TV chair, wanting to grab it before Frankie came in. Come to think of it, where was Frankie?

"Where's Frankie?" I asked.

Dad and Frankie had stopped into the A&P on Stillwell Avenue on their way home from the ballgame. My father always carried his service revolver, even when off duty.

When they came to the checkout, a young neighborhood kid was pointing a gun at the cashier as she filled a paper sack with money from the register. Dad drew his weapon and told the boy to give it up before it was too late, and then it was too late. The kid pointed the gun toward my father and my brother and the gun went off.

"Frankie was killed, John," my father said.

"Was it Bobby Leone?" I asked, shaking.

"No, of course not," he said. "It was a boy from the high school. A squad car picked him up on Kings Highway."

"It's my fault," I said.

I should have gone to that game.

I should have gone with Bobby to Kings Highway.

I should have left Dad's chair empty for Frankie.

I woke up and found Sam sitting beside the hospital bed.

"We got the guy who shot you."

"What was his beef?"

"He thought you were someone else. He was gunning for someone named Frankie Johnson who walks a dog exactly like yours in the same park and who happened to be sleeping with the shooter's wife."

"*You're going to die for this, Frankie.*"

"Huh?"

"That's what I heard, before the gunshot. I thought he was calling *my* name, I thought I knew the voice. I was hearing something else. How'd you find him?"

41

"He killed Johnson this morning. I heard the surgery went okay."

"Yeah, want to see me get up and walk?"

"I was hoping you'd do that little tap dance you do."

"Is Maggie around?"

"Saw her on my way in. She's gone to fetch the kids. She looked somewhat disheveled. You guys didn't decide to do some catching up here in the hospital bed?"

"I'm not sure."

"Don't tell her that."

A week later we had just finished dinner when I asked my father if he would take a walk with me around the block.

What I wanted was a stroll down memory lane.

Maggie said she'd have the coffee and dessert ready when we got back.

Charlie wanted to come along but Annie, in all her teenage wisdom, sensed that I needed to be alone with Dad and she corralled her little brother at the front door, bribing him to stay with the promise of a chocolate éclair.

"Dad," I said, as we moved away from the house.

It was good to be walking.

"Yes, son?"

"The day Frankie died, the day of the World Series game."

"Yes."

"The kid who shot Frankie, he was one of the kids who stole Tony Baretta's bike earlier that day," I said. "Bobby Leone wanted me and Nicky Ventura to go with him to find them."

"And do what, get yourselves shot?"

I guess not.

We were quiet during the rest of the walk, but it was good just to be at his side.

When we returned to the house, the pastries and the espresso were laid out as promised. Annie, I should say Anne, gave me a quick peck on the cheek and said she was meeting her friends at the Kent movie theater on Coney Island Avenue.

"How are you getting there?" I asked.

"Connie's mom."

"Don't let me find out differently."

"Okay, I won't let you find out," she said, and ran out laughing.

I had to laugh also.

Maggie had a legal brief to complete, so she apologized and moved to her study.

My father and my son busied themselves with dessert.

"Dad," Charlie said.

"Yes."

"Remember when I was little and I got lost at the camp place?"

How could I forget?

"Yes, son."

"How come when you found me you called me Frankie?"

"Did I?"

"Yeah. You said, *Thank God, Frankie, I thought I would never see you again.*"

"I guess it was my special way of telling you how glad I was to find you, son."

"Oh, okay," he said.

"He reminds me a lot of Frank, Jr.," said my father, reaching for a pastry.

"Grandpa, the éclair is mine," Charlie said. Then he looked over at me and added, "But I'll share it with you."

I left them to it and took the dog for a walk in the park.

POCKET QUEENS
A NOVELLA

PROLOGUE
THE LINCOLN ASSASSINATION

His head crashed onto the table sending a poker chip floating up into the air end over end like a tiddlywink. I heard Freddy Fingers say "What a fucking game" as the chip settled silently into the growing pool of blood spreading from Lincoln's head onto the sevens near his frozen face. Behind, sounds of shouting, stampeding, bodies tumbling to the ground and I refused to look over my shoulder. Instead, I gazed into the river of red, dark against the green felt, not looking away until the dentist from Philly spoke.

"There are only two things worth dying for. Money is not one of them," he said, "and love is not the other."

I was of a mind to ask which two things he was fucking talking about but, before I could, the knockout in the white dress was at my side posing a question I was almost certain she knew the answer to.

"Are you Nick Ventura, the private investigator?" she asked.

I could only nod.

1

I am sitting at the pot-limit seven-card stud table in the poker room at the Taj Mahal in AC holding pocket queens. I know I shouldn't be here but if I never did anything I shouldn't do I'd be a dull boy. I am here to celebrate and pat myself on the back for scoring two grand in one night for snapping a few nifty photos of the client's husband and his secretary going into a pricey Manhattan hotel and coming out two hours later looking better or worse for it depending on where you're standing.

There are five other players at the poker table, all strangers except Freddy Fingers and I know Fingers all too well and he is fucking stranger than fiction. If I bothered to look around the card room I might spot a familiar face someone I may have played with once upon a time when I sat at the high stakes tables where I could always find a familiar mug if I was so inclined but then the room is not half rocking which leads me to believe there is something going on in Vegas or up at Foxwoods I'm much better off not knowing about.

I'm planted at this table because the betting has been reasonable and I am here to celebrate my windfall not to blow it all in a single game. I'm in Atlantic City because if I can't wander out once in a while to take a look at the ocean I start to forget how tiny I am. The first flop is the third queen and I'm praying I can keep at least one of these mopes in this fucking hand.

I'm stuck there with five other players with no clue about any of them except Fingers who is a totally different story. All I can guess about how these guys play is based on what I have seen in the past few hours and what I know about Freddy and if I sat with Freddy every fucking day of the rest of my life I would have no hint about what to expect from the lunatic. I'm in the fourth seat. The first seat belongs to Sol. The man says he's a dentist from Philadelphia, but the condition of Sol's choppers makes the claim dubious at best. Next is Manny, which is the handle of every cat I ever sat with at a poker table who said he was from Jackson Heights or East L.A. or Sunset Park. The hotdog ahead of me is a dapper dresser called Linc. I can't decide if it's a nickname for Lincoln or short for missing link. Just behind me is a clown who has the nerve to call himself Slim as if being a tall skinny fucker in a Walmart cowboy hat affords him the right. And then there is Freddy Fingers who is less predictable than a dog race.

Sol opens small and I figure him for an unsuited jack-ten, maybe king-ten. Manny calls but the price is cheap so who the fuck knows. Linc raises medium—sitting on an ace or a little pair? I'm holding queens but don't want to scare anyone off, so I call the raise. Slim bails, Fingers calls, Sol calls and Manny folds like an accordion. So when the dealer lays down my third queen there are only four of us still holding.

Sol checks, wouldn't want anyone to surmise he's hoping to fill a straight. Blinkin' Lincoln raises, I'm guessing he does have a pocket pair. Good for him. I stare at the turn card as if the dealer just tossed a garden slug on the table and I call Linc's bump trying like hell to appear hesitant. If there is anyone I want out of this hand it is Fingers but the fucking maniac calls. Sol does the same, Linc checks, I check, Freddy checks and then the dealer flops an ace.

Sol raises bigger this time, if the dip has four to a straight with three cards to go the queens and I may be in a world of hurt. Linc calls, maybe the dude is sitting on an ace in the hole and paired it. I call, Freddy calls, I don't even waste time trying to imagine what the fuck he's thinking about. Sol checks, Linc checks, I check, Fingers checks and the dealer turns the seven of clubs which suits the queen of clubs and ace of clubs that flopped before so now I do begin wondering about Freddy and if the crazy son of a bitch is now holding four to a flush. The seven can't possibly help Sol but Sol can check and stay in so he does. Linc raises, I can only wish he matched a pocket pair of sevens and rides them until they crash against my queens and hope there are no clubs, aces, sevens or picture cards left in the fucking deck and I call. Fingers calls Linc's raise and re-raises and if it were anyone else, I would be positively certain he was holding two clubs in his pocket but it is Fingers so I can't be certain of a fucking thing. Sol crumbles like blue cheese, Linc calls, I call, Freddy checks and the three of us stuck in the horror show watch the dealer flop the seven of hearts which gives me a full house and now I don't care how many clubs Freddy might be hiding because he needs the straight flush to beat me and with the queen, ace and seven of clubs on the board I can be absolutely sure Fingers cannot fucking fill it unless the fucking pest catches another club but I can't chase the feeling that the nightmare to my right just bought his fourth seven and flushed my full house straight down the toilet. When Linc raises huge I think *Oh shit* and I know I have to call because after all I'm holding a full boat and the game has been building from thirty and sixty buck bets to two and four hundred dollar raises and bumps and I think it's about time I raise Linc to find out sooner than too goddamn late if he bought four-of-a-kind but I chicken out and call and without a beat fucking Fingers calls and re-raises like he's got the flush and thinks it's good or he doesn't know what he has or what's good and he just doesn't give a fuck. Linc calls, I can only do the same, Freddy checks and here comes the seventh card down and dirty.

There is nearly three grand in the center of the table, which is a lot or a little depending on the place, date and time. Right here and now it looks awfully good. I wouldn't throw it out of bed. I take my eyes off the card table for the first time in quite a while trying to look as if I have no interest whatsoever in the final down card because I have everything I could possibly hope for already. I notice our little game has attracted a modest audience. I'm instantly drawn to one of the spectators, a leggy green-eyed brunette in a white dress which hugs her body just enough and does a great job setting off her dark skin. She's standing at the dealer's shoulder and I'd swear this apparition was looking straight at me if I wasn't so sure it was good old Linc the dreamgirl was more interested in. I glance to my right and Missing Linc looks at his last card and then up at the lady in white and gives her a smile that has four sevens written all over it and he bets the limit, which is the size of the pot, which is nearly three thousand dollars, which is all I have sitting in front of me. Oh boy. I have no idea how to peek at my seventh card and appear dignified doing it since only a queen can save me. One out and everyone at the table and in this room and in the Taj and in the entire fucking world knows it. I finally manage a peek at my final hole card. Queen of spades. Unbelievable. I call. Freddy folds.

As much as he might have liked, Linc can't raise again because I'm all in. All he can do is show his two sevens which he does without ceremony and with a big old smile for the vision in the white dress and the revelation if not the smile inspires a chorus of *oohs* and *ahs* from the gallery as he pushes his chair away from the table so as not to appear too anxious to rake in the pot. And I don't want to rub it in but I have no choice but to reveal my three pocket queens and the room goes nuts like someone has dropped a bomb on the table which is basically what I just did and before I can turn to Linc with a *good hand, man, tough break*, I hear a small pop and his face is on the table blood spilling out of the back of his head turning his sevens crimson. There is a great deal of screaming and two security guards knocked off their feet as the shooter races out of the poker room. Linc sits to my right stone-cold dead. Freddy Fingers looks at the blood creeping toward the large pile of chips in the middle of the table and he says, "What a fucking game."

And before a single cop shows, the lady in white comes over to me and the dead man and asks, "Are you Nick Ventura, the private investigator?"

I can only nod.

"In that case," she says, "I would like to hire you to find the man who just murdered my husband."

2

An hour later I'm sitting in a police station fielding questions from two detectives who definitely watch too much television. By now I've learned the victim was a hall of fame criminal attorney named Theodore Lincoln who sidelined in divorce cases and made a fortune working Atlantic City because the action here is not conducive to strictly legal activity or successful marriages. No, I never met the victim before tonight. No, I would not be able to identify the shooter, since I was reluctant to look behind when Linc's head hit the table. My mind was drifting. I was thinking about the widow, the smile Linc flashed at her when he turned his hole cards. The man was clearly in love, he had it bad. But when his widow walked over to stand between me and her late husband, she didn't glance at him for a moment, didn't touch him gently or otherwise, simply approached and offered me a job—looking absolutely stunning doing it. I am wondering where she is now, probably wherever they take you when your husband is shot to death at a poker table in AC, but I have no idea where that may be since I don't work Atlantic City. I work Brooklyn, sometimes Queens, occasionally Staten Island if the gig pays me enough to cover the toll on the Verrazano Bridge. Then I recall the poker game and the pile of chips on the table, close to nine grand, and wonder if anyone is keeping Freddy's fingers off my score while I'm being asked about things that I fucking know nothing about.

At the same time, I get this nagging feeling that if a certain stunning green-eyed-disaster-waiting-to-happen in a white dress wanted to tell me all about it I'd be all ears.

"You knew no one at the table?" asked a detective.

"I knew Freddy Fingers, if anyone could really know or care to know the maniac," I said. "You'll probably find him in the Taj Mahal poker room pocketing my money."

"The casino is safe-guarding your winnings, Ventura. No need to worry."

"It's my nature."

"We might have a few more questions."

"I'll be in town through tomorrow evening, bunked down at the Taj. After that, you'll have to pop for a toll call to the Borough of Churches. Have a card," I said, "I'll put my cell number on the back."

I jotted down the number, handed the tall skinny one the business card and inched my way to the exit. He looked at the thing and then at me as I was backing out of the squad room.

"Ventura."

"Yes?"

"Don't stick your nose where it doesn't belong."

"No problem."

Then, as I slip through the door he adds, "Don't forget this is New Jersey."

How could I.

3

When I get back to the casino it is three in the morning and the place is still in an uproar. It takes another hour to locate the eight thousand six hundred forty dollars that was the difference between four queens and four sevens.

I think of Lincoln's sevens and wonder if in this neck of the woods they might replace aces and eights in the vernacular, dead man's hand, and how he looked at her moments before he died.

He died instantly and in love and how bad a way is that to go?

Word is the shooter got away clean, bowled down a pair of guards, dropped the weapon, a muted .38 with a taped grip which would be nothing less than impossible to trace, ducked out of the casino and vanished into thin air.

I'm beat like a drum.

The sun will be up in less than three hours.

So, I find my way to my room and crawl into the rack.

4

At ten in the morning I'm already shaved, showered and dressed in my poker duds, which today is a pair of long shorts, an oxymoron with lots of pockets, and a white dress shirt buttoned up to the neck to hide my bullet wound scar. I think I could eat a horse if it was scrambled with bacon. I'm just about to go looking when there's a rap at my hotel room door. I swing it open and there she stands, different dress same green peepers drawing me in and reminding me how it feels to be lost in the eyes of a beautiful woman. And how dangerous it is to feel that way.

Since gazing into her eyes is like looking down into a bottomless emerald pool feeling a strong urge to dive and I forgot my life jacket up in Coney Island, I looked anywhere else and everywhere else. My baby blues bouncing against the hallway walls like pinballs.

She touches my hand and asks, "Will you help me, Nick?" and I don't even recognize my own name and I forget how to speak.

So, she says, "Can I come in?"

I say, "I don't think it's a very good idea—how about we meet in the hotel coffee shop? Just give me ten minutes, ma'am."

I throw on the rest of my poker outfit, a madras sport jacket and Brooklyn Cyclones ball cap because the thing is I came down to AC to play cards not to fuck around or get fucked around. Ten minutes later I drop into a booth seat opposite the widow Lincoln and a waitress asks if I would like coffee and I say, "Boy, would I."

The widow's name is Katherine she says but please call me Kitty. Okay, Kitty, I say and I offer to buy since I hold a ten dollar comp voucher which should cover the coffee and a few bagels but it's, *no, thanks, I had breakfast before.* I don't ask before what. Feeling extravagant I ordered two bagels for myself—cinnamon raisin hold the butter—and when the waitress waltzed off, Kitty got right down to business.

"I would like to hire you to find the man who murdered my husband," she said, which is pretty much what she said to me when Theodore was face down on the poker table.

I say, "So you said," and then it occurs to me—could be Kitty doesn't need me to learn *who* killed Linc. I'm thinking she needs me to locate the shooter. Then perhaps I'm a bit too hung up on semantics so I take a stab at clarification.

"Hire me to find out who killed your husband?"

"I know who killed my husband, Nick," Kitty said, "I just need your help finding the man."

"I see," I said not seeing at all but loving the sound of my name when she said it and knowing for a fact I would be a lot safer playing poker blindfolded.

"Will you help me?"

"Well, first," I said, as if there was any order to my thinking, "if you know the perp, you should be talking to the personable ACPD detectives who danced me around last night. Second, don't forget this is New Jersey and I'm not licensed to practice here in the Garden State."

"First," Kitty said, "with regard to Theodore's murder the ACPD is AC/DC, they could go either way. Second, the man who shot my husband last night is likely back up in New York City by now, so your Empire State PI license should be perfectly adequate."

"I see."

All I could see were big green eyes and big trouble.

"Well?" she asked.

Well indeed.

There were a number of ways to go. I could sit there staring at four dry bagel halves and hem and haw. I could dive right in libido first. I could procrastinate without hesitation.

I could just say no.

"Look, Mrs. Lincoln," I said, talk about running for cover, "you caught me at a bad time. You're sitting here in that dress. What color is that thing anyway?"

"Jade."

Of course it is.

"Ten-thirty in the morning you're in a jade strapless and all I want to do is look at you sitting there but what I need to do is play poker. I came down here for a reason. Stop me if I you've heard this one before. I need to play every once in a while, like a fix, a little taste to keep me from the perpetual card game that will chew me up and spit out my heart. Tomorrow I'll be back where I am relatively safe behind a desk in a poorly ventilated office above a pizza joint in Coney Island. I recommend you let me purge my dire need to gamble so I can think straight for another month or two. Sleep on it. I'll sleep on it if I sleep at all tonight. Call me if you still want to talk it over—here's my business card."

Kitty Lincoln took the card, her body swaying inside the jade dress. She stood up from the table and said, "Okay, fair enough, good luck with your poker therapy."

"I'll need it," I said. "By the way?"

"Yes?"

"If I help you find this guy," I asked, "what do you hope to accomplish?"

"Accomplish?"

"Let me put it this way. I find the guy what then?"

"I would ask you to do whatever it took to capture his attention so I could ask him a few questions."

"What would you ask him?"

"The man put a bullet in the back of my husband's head right in front of my eyes, I would ask whatever I needed to ask to get the whole picture," she said and walked off, a remarkable sight even going away.

"Mrs. Lincoln," I called.

She stopped at the coffee shop exit and she did a one-eighty, her emerald eyes still within striking distance.

"Yes?"

"Did you love your husband?"

"What's love got to do with it?" she asked and passed through the door to be swallowed up by Atlantic City.

5

My plan for the day had been to do breakfast, play cards, treat myself to something surfy and turfy, and head back up to Brooklyn.

Breakfast had been a total bust. I had been so distracted by the jade strapless I forgot what I was doing sitting there. And Mrs. Lincoln didn't even mention my outfit. After watching her leave the dining room I lost a staring contest with a cup of cold coffee and strolled out onto the boardwalk.

As I may have mentioned, I often found it grounding to look out over the vast Atlantic Ocean and contemplate how small I was. The walkway was jammed with late-August crowds, as was the real estate between where I stood and where the sand gave way to the sea. It only served to make me feel pedestrian, a feeling that was a little more humbling than I was aiming for.

Before searching for a suitable card game, I decided to ditch my room at the Taj to avoid late check-out charges.

I stashed my baggage in the trunk of my 1973 Chevrolet Monte Carlo and made for the casino.

After six hours at the card table, interrupted only by a short break for a fish sandwich that tasted as if it had been shipped in from Omaha and a Mountain Dew that tasted as if it had lost its fizz around 1988, I had skillfully gambled away all but the two thousand dollar grubstake I came down with the day before.

There was no talk of the shooting, which might have surprised me but didn't. The players drawn to these poker tables lived entirely in the moment. Yesterday forgotten, tomorrow no concern. I may have been the only one in the room giving the incident a second thought, but it wasn't the poor bastard with his head lying in a pool of blood I was thinking about.

I politely excused myself from the contest. I could clearly read the disappointment in the faces of the other players who had taken turns relieving me of nearly seven grand. They all looked as if they had lost a rich uncle and were not named in his will.

I escorted myself to the hotel restaurant for what promised to be my first decent meal of the day.

Forty minutes later the waitress removed my two dinner plates. One held the barest remnants of a thick prime rib and half-dozen jumbo shrimp scampi. A bone and six tails. The second plate held an untouched salad. I was eagerly awaiting coffee and key lime pie when Ferdinand Pugno Jr. pulled out a chair opposite mine at the table.

Here is a guy who, if he wasn't such a colossal fuckup, could be sitting poolside at a large Long Island mansion sipping eighteen-year-old single malt scotch and wallowing in all the other perks afforded the son of royalty. Ferdinand Senior was one of those smart Italian-American criminals who got wealthy and got away clean. His namesake was as dumb as a rock.

As a result, instead of enjoying the high life on the Gold Coast, Junior lived in Atlantic City, if you could call it living, funding his eternal poker playing with cash his old man paid him to stay far away from the North Shore.

"So," he said, settling into a chair.

Freddy Fingers was not known for his eloquence.

"Get to the point," I said.

"How much is Kit Kat willing to pay you to find 'The Stick'?" Fingers asked, as the waitress delivered my coffee and dessert.

"Could you translate that into English?"

"How much is Katherine Lincoln willing to cough up to find

Charlie Mungo?" he asked. "That pie looks good."

"Tell me what the fuck you're babbling about, Freddy, and it's all yours."

"Less than a year ago a certain recently deceased lawyer was enchanted by a certain exotic dancer and quickly became her divorce attorney and her new husband in more or less that order."

I picked up a fork and made a move toward the key lime pie.

"Okay, I'm getting to it, hold your horses," Fingers said. "I couldn't help overhearing Katherine's overture to you at the card table last night, and I spotted you and the widow at breakfast this morning. I just thought if you were thinking of signing on you could use a little friendly advice."

"Amiability has never been your strong suit, Freddy, something in this for you?"

"I'm just looking to be liked, Ventura. Everyone treats me like the plague when I buy into a card game."

"You destroy any possibility of sensible wagering for everyone, Freddy. If you learned something about betting a poker hand you would have more pals. And if you would just fucking say what you sat down to say."

"I hardly know where to begin."

"Start with the shooter," I suggested.

Freddy Fingers scanned the dining room and gave the pie another furtive look before elucidating.

"Charlie 'The Stick' Mungo. Trigger man out of Brooklyn. I knew him back in the day, when I was still Dad's number one son. Mungo ran around with a two-time loser named Vincent Corelli. A few years ago, Corelli had to get out of Dodge. He landed here and scored a job dealing blackjack. He soon became infatuated with a very popular showgirl, Katherine Ann Harris, affectionately known as Kit Kat, and before you could say holy matrimony five times fast Kathy Ann slid down her pole and became Kitty Corelli."

I knew of Charlie Mungo by name, but I wouldn't have been able to place him had I been foolish enough to sneak a peek at who popped Lincoln.

I knew Vincent Corelli. We played baseball together in high school and had run into each other occasionally since, as much as I tried to avoid it. I lost track of Vinnie when trouble with both sides of the law chased him out of New York. The fact that he had landed in Atlantic City and taken a bride was news to me.

"Is Corelli still working here?"

"After Kitty dumped him for the mouthpiece, Atlantic City lost its charm for Vinnie. And he was still persona non grata in Brooklyn. Last I heard he was dealing blackjack up in Connecticut. Mohegan Sun."

"Happen to mention any of this to the AC police?"

"I don't speak their language, and Atlantic City cops couldn't find a hockey puck in a bowl of rice. On top of that, this is a Brooklyn thing."

Katherine Ann Harris "Kit Kat" Corelli Lincoln.

Quite a girl.

I slid the pie over to Freddy's side of the table and rose to leave.

"Knock yourself out," I said.

"Don't you want to hear more?"

"I'm good," I said.

I scooped up the guest check and left Freddy sitting there wondering if he had made a new friend.

6

I hopped into the Monte Carlo and took the Atlantic City Expressway to the Garden State Parkway.

Two days at the tables. Nothing lost. Nothing gained. Highlighted by a cinematic sideshow. A bedtime story for the grandchildren, if I ever found a woman who was interested in growing old with me.

I must have been in a hurry to get home because the Jersey State Trooper who pulled me over on the Turnpike claimed I was doing eighty-five. He let me go with a warning. He probably didn't want to look at the Madras sport jacket any longer than he had to. I crossed the Goethals Bridge, cruised across Staten Island and over the Verrazano into the Borough of Churches. As I pulled into a parking spot that miraculously appeared in front of my apartment building, I finally understood what Freddy was trying to tell me in his uncharacteristically friendly way.

It was a warning also.

7

At eleven the next morning, I sat in my office which in turn sat above Totonno's Pizzeria on Neptune Avenue—two blocks from the beach and the ocean that separated me from a thousand places I had only read about.

My great grandfather and Antonio Pero had been childhood friends, since the days at the Little Red Schoolhouse in Greenwich Village when it was the neighborhood grade school for the children of Little Italy before it was a cost prohibitive private school for all but the new upper class. Pero bought the property on Neptune in 1924, a three-story brick apartment building attached to a one-story storefront, and opened a pizzeria with a coal-fired brick oven that would become legendary. It was considered by many aficionados as among the best pies in New York City, never sold by the slice and never traded for anything but cash. When my grandmother died, and my grandfather Giuseppe Ventura refused to be moved into the home of any of his children, Pero's son offered him two small rooms above a beauty salon in the apartment building adjacent to the pizza shop. Antonio's granddaughter, who had been like an aunt to me growing up, now ran the pizzeria and still burned coal. When Giuseppe met his maker, and I needed a place to set up my PI business, 'Aunt' Carmella let me have the rooms for the same monthly rent they had charged the old man. I knew she could get a lot more for the space, and I told her so.

"Think of it like a grandfather clause," Carmella had said, smiling, and we shook hands on the deal.

An ancient window fan was noisily trying without success to battle the elements. The dog day temperature had already soared into the low nineties and the humidity was off the charts. I stripped down to what was referred to as a white ribbed tank top by the youngsters and a wife beater by the old-timers. I had given the widow Lincoln my business card. After Freddy's little history lesson, I was hoping she wouldn't call. I checked the voice mail on the office answering machine. Nothing cooking. I phoned Tom Romano, an old sidekick who had connections, and asked for a favor. He said he would get right on it and we set up a lunch meet for one o'clock at Clemente's in Sheepshead Bay. I went through the mail. All bills, no payments. I leafed through the sports section of the Post, which took up nearly the entire back half of the rag, looking for any news that might offer hope for the Mets. No luck. As it approached noon, I was so hungry I was about to run the two blocks to Nathan's at the boardwalk for a hot dog appetizer when there was a light rap on the office door. I threw on my white button down Van Heusen and tucked it into my black Haggar pleated slacks.

She was dressed for the weather in a little blue number with small white polka dots that could be politely described as a pinafore and more accurately described as too provocative. A blue cloth handbag with wide straps hung from her right shoulder, matching the pattern of the dress dot for dot. There were three tiny beads of sweat on the left side of her neck, just below her perfect jaw line, that had me fighting to hold my tongue. I had hoped she wouldn't call, but forgot to hope she wouldn't drop by.

"Mrs. Lincoln."

"Kitty," she said.

"Right," I said.

60

"Can I take you out for a bite?"

"I've already eaten," I said, untruthfully.

"In that case, can I come in?"

"It's uncomfortably warm in here."

"I can deal with that, unless you're busy."

"Not at all."

She brushed past me, and I closed the office door.

I offered her the client seat and retreated to my own seat on the opposite side of the cluttered table that served as my desk. The matching chairs had been part of my grandparent's ancient oak dining room set, sporting long legs and tall straight backs. I tried but couldn't help appreciating the fact that Kitty was built in much the same fashion.

She placed the bag at her feet. She didn't seem exactly sure what to do about her bare legs with regard to the tall seat and short skirt. She finally crossed them, right over left. She pulled a white lace-trimmed handkerchief from a pocket in her dress and gently dabbed away the drops of perspiration on her neck. She returned the handkerchief to her pocket and placed her hands neatly in her lap. After eventually settling in she looked directly into my eyes, green crashing against blue, and I feared I didn't have a hope.

"So," I said, borrowing a lame conversation opener from Freddy Fingers.

"Have you given my proposition any thought?"

I decided against beating around the bush.

"You said you know the man who killed your husband."

"I said I knew who he was, not that I know him. His name is Charlie Mungo."

"And how did you know who he was?"

"I recognized him from a picture in a newspaper."

I was tempted to ask what newspaper, but she wasn't as enjoyable to look at when she lied.

"Do you have any idea why Mungo would want to kill your husband?"

"That is what I would like to ask the man if you can locate him for me."

"I don't think I can help you, Mrs. Lincoln."

I hated to say it, but I believed it was the truth.

"Listen, Nick. I don't want you to think my interest in seeing you again was strictly business, but I am willing to pay you five thousand dollars if you can successfully point me to Charlie Mungo. Find him, tell *me* where to find him and then, if you wish, we're done."

Five thousand dollars—a handsome figure that bounced around inside my head like a lotto number on a ping pong ball. Before it came to rest her cell phone beckoned from the polka dot bag. She reached in, grabbed the phone, and checked the caller ID.

"I need to take this," she said.

"Sure," I said.

"I didn't expect to hear from you," she said to the caller.

Short pause.

"Where?"

Longer pause.

"I'm on my way."

End of call.

Kitty picked up her bag, replaced the phone, uncrossed her long legs and stood up.

"I have to go," she said, "call me if you have a change of heart."

She quickly turned and walked out of the office.

She had neglected to leave her phone number.

8

On the drive to Sheepshead Bay, I kept asking myself the same question I had asked myself before calling Tom Romano.

If I was hoping Katherine Ann Harris 'Kit Kat' Corelli Lincoln would forget I ever existed, why was I calling Tom?

And now I had said *no* to the lady. Case closed. And as far as the eleventh hour offer of five grand to come on board was concerned, I never had the chance to consider it. After receiving the phone call, Kitty's speedy departure gave me the sneaking suspicion I was suddenly and permanently out of the picture.

If I was smart, I would tell Tom I wouldn't need his help, apologize for the inconvenience, offer to spring for lunch, and enjoy the time catching up with an old friend.

But when something feels very wrong, my intellect goes out the window.

When I walked into Clemente's, I spotted Tom at the bar, sipping what I could confidently guess was a Jack and Coke. He was wearing Bermuda shorts, a cotton Hawaiian print shirt, flip-flops and a straw hat—suggesting he had strolled over from his crib.

"I ordered a couple of Angry Lobster Rolls with fries to go. Should be out any minute," he said in the way of greeting, "I have a very cold twelve pack of PBR on the boat. It might be a little cooler on the water."

"Sounds perfect, I'm buying."

"Too late."

A young woman came from the kitchen and handed Tom two large brown paper bags and I followed Romano out of the restaurant.

Tom's crib was a houseboat that sat parked in a slip on the waters of Sheepshead Bay, a few hundred yards from Clemente's outdoor dining patio.

"How do you sleep on this thing with all the rocking?" I asked when we climbed aboard.

"Like a baby in a tree top."

The deck was equipped with an all-weather green plastic table and matching chairs. Tom dropped the bags onto the table and walked into the cabin. He quickly returned with plates, forks and two cans of Pabst Blue Ribbon.

"I managed to get the information you were looking for," he said as he took a seat opposite me and began plating the sandwiches and fries, "I believe it's reliable."

"Sorry if I wasted your time, Tom, but I'm not sure I'll need it."

"No worries, it took no time at all. Let's eat and drink and you can tell me about your adventure in Atlantic City while you decide."

Twenty minutes later, Tom cleared the table and came back with more cold beer.

"So, both Freddy and the widow fingered Mungo as the shooter."

"With conviction."

"And I suppose I don't have to tell you Charlie Mungo is a very nasty character."

"I got that."

Tom reached into the pocket of his Bermudas, pulled out a folded slip of paper and handed it to me.

"Well, this should tell you where to find him. I won't be offended if you tear it to pieces."

I stuffed the paper into my shirt pocket and didn't pull it out again until I had left Tom's boat and climbed into my car.

I did tear it into pieces—but not before taking a good long look.

9

Four identical brick buildings stood on Avenue J, between East 15th Street and the elevated train station. Each had storefronts on the street level and two floors of apartments above, very much like the building that housed my office.

Tom's note said I would find Charlie Mungo on the top floor above Dave's Supermarket.

I stood on the opposite side of the avenue trying to decide what to say to Mungo if I found him there. Tricky, since I really wasn't sure what I was doing there in the first place.

The decision to throw on a sport coat and transfer my .357

from the glove box of the Monte Carlo to a jacket pocket was not as difficult to make. After all, I was thinking about confronting a cold-blooded killer. The temperature had soared into the high nineties and, as I started across the avenue, I felt blatantly over-dressed.

I climbed the stairs to the top floor, hand in pocket gripping the .357. The door marked 201 was located just off the landing in the front of the building facing the avenue. I moved to the right of the doorway and knocked. The door moved, opening slightly into the apartment. I pulled out the gun and waited, lis-tening for a response or sound of movement.

Nothing.

I finally took a look through the doorway and saw him. I stepped into front room of the apartment.

He was lying on his back and there were two holes in his chest seeping blood.

Vincent Corelli.

I checked for pulse. He was finished.

There was no good reason to stick around.

As I headed down I heard someone rushing up from the ground floor. I ducked through the door that led to the second story apartments and held it open an inch or so, just enough to see who was barreling up the stairs. I didn't know the man. He continued up and I quickly continued down.

On the ground floor landing, at the foot of the exit door, a white object caught my eye. I picked it up and stuffed it into my jacket pocket with the handgun.

It was a white lace-trimmed handkerchief.

The Monte Carlo was parked at the southwest corner of 15th and J, in front of Di Fara's Pizzeria. I sat in the front seat of the car with a Sicilian square on a paper plate and a Cherry Coke. If the man coming up the stairs was headed for Apartment 201, I doubted he would hang around any longer than I had after find-ing Corelli's body. I waited, but before he reappeared a patrol car from the 70th Precinct rolled up in front of Dave's Supermarket.

Two uniforms left the car and walked into the building. One came out minutes later and made a call on the car radio. The other was either holding a *possible suspect* up in the apartment, or the man I had nearly bumped into had found another way out.

I decided it was time to disappear. I knew John Sullivan would be showing up soon and I didn't want to be spotted. Johnny might find it hard to believe I drove all the way out to Midwood just to pay five bucks for a slice of pizza.

I knew John for as long as I could remember. We grew up on the same Brooklyn street, attended the same schools from kindergarten through Lafayette High, dated the same girls occasionally, and shared a common ambition—to wear NYPD blue.

John made it.

Because *where* you are from is one thing, and *who* you are from is another.

Sullivan came from Irish immigrants on his father's side, Sicilian on his mother's. His father was a retired police sergeant. After high school John went on to Queens College, met an Irish-American girl who became his wife and the mother of his children, graduated with honors from John Jay College of Criminal Justice, entered the department and rose quickly through the ranks to Detective Lieutenant.

Homicide.

I was second generation Italian-American. Dad was a gambler and a drinker who was killed by cirrhosis of the liver. I made it out of high school by the skin of my teeth, and couldn't find a girl who could handle me for more than a few months. Although I had magically avoided long term incarceration, my rap sheet forever disqualified me from joining the police force.

I had tried and failed at a number of occupations until I took up the underappreciated trade of private investigation. And my success in that line of work was questionable.

Sooner or later, the discovery of Vincent Corelli's body in Charlie Mungo's apartment would earn Charlie *person of interest* status—and if Mungo was eventually identified as the shooter in Atlantic City, John Sullivan would want to talk with everyone who was in the room when Theodore Lincoln was killed—particularly those who sat at his poker table.

Including me and the unpredictable Freddy Fingers.

Before Sullivan inevitably landed on my doorstep, I felt it would be helpful to know what urged Vincent Corelli to leave his reasonably safe haven on the Connecticut Indian Reservation casinos and risk showing his face in Brooklyn.

And try to discover if Kitty Lincoln had misplaced a handkerchief.

Of course, I could have simply waited for Sullivan to come knocking and told him everything I knew or thought I knew, but suddenly I wanted to know more.

I needed a distraction. A new case wouldn't hurt. I drove back to my office in Coney Island.

10

The only message waiting for me was from Katherine Lincoln.

Nick. I need to see you. Gramercy Park Hotel at 8.
Please.

Short. Sweet.

Not the distraction I was hoping for.

I knew the Gramercy well, though I had never made it past the lobby desk.

With several hours to kill I decided to drop by my place and attempt to make myself look presentable.

I stepped into my apartment and was closing the door when I heard the sound behind me. Too late.

The next thing I remember was the throbbing pain at the back of my head. I wanted to check the damage but found my hands were tied and I was strapped into a chair. When I opened my eyes, I discovered it was one of my kitchen chairs. Sitting opposite me was the man I had almost run into on the stairs of the building on Avenue J. His hand rested on the kitchen table gripping a .44 Magnum.

At least now I knew what hit me.

"Ouch," I said.

"Why did you kill Vinnie Corelli?" he asked.

"I don't know what you're talking about."

He stood up from the table, holding the gun, stepped up and slapped me across the face with his free hand.

"I heard you going down the stairs and spotted you from the window on the third-floor landing as you left the building. I knew who you were. Vinnie had pointed you out to me a few times."

"More than once," I said. "I'm flattered."

He slapped me again.

"Ouch."

"I'm losing my patience."

If what he had been demonstrating to that point was patience, I thought I should adjust my attitude.

"Corelli was dead when I got there," I said.

"Why should I believe you?"

"Because if you believe I killed Corelli, then whoever actually killed him gets a free pass. And you're making me nervous hanging over me with that cannon."

"If you didn't kill Vinnie, what were you doing there?"

"You have me at a disadvantage." I said, almost comical coming from someone tied to a chair. "You know who I am but I'm not sure who you are. But if you happen to be Charlie Mungo, I was there looking for you."

"Why were you looking for me?"

"To ask why you killed Theodore Lincoln."

"I don't know what you're talking about."

"I'd slap you for lying, but my hands are tied and you're holding that Magnum. Looks like a push. Why don't you untie me and then do yourself a big favor."

"Like?"

"Like disappear. If you're not wanted for murder yet, it won't be long."

"Maybe."

There was a short pause in the conversation. I was guessing Charlie didn't know quite what to do. I picked up the ball.

"Who put you up to shooting Lincoln?" I asked.

"Who sent you looking for me?" he asked.

"Untie me, Charlie. I'll make a pot of coffee."

I won't say Charlie and I bonded, but we did have a nice talk over coffee and Entenmann's Cherry Cheese Danish. Being a gracious host, I elected to go first.

"Katherine Lincoln offered to hire me to find you."

"Why?"

"She didn't say."

Okay, I wasn't being totally straightforward.

"Did she tell you I shot her husband?" Mungo asked.

"No."

"Then what makes you think I did?"

"Someone else made you."

"Who?"

"I won't say. But why did you think you could walk up and whack the guy in the middle of a room full of players and not get made?"

"Bystanders are afraid to look at a shooter's face. No one is anxious to be a key eyewitness in a murder investigation, especially the characters in a casino gambling room who prefer remaining low profile. I put my head down, dropped the gun, and got out."

The thing was, he may have been right. I know I didn't care to look, and as far as I knew no one had come forward to identify Mungo. The only two people who seemed certain he was the shooter were keeping it a secret from everyone except me.

Lucky me.

"What happens when Corelli is found dead in your apartment?"

"I'm not an idiot. I can't be connected to that place. It's officially unoccupied. The building is owned by a dummy real estate management company out of Canada. The apartment is essentially a safe house."

"It wasn't too safe for Corelli."

"Vinnie called, asked me to meet him there. I got over there as quick as I could. How did you find the place?"

"Not important. How did you find this place?"

"Directory assistance. Did you tell your client where to find me?"

"Never had the chance. And I think she changed her mind about hiring me."

"So, why come looking for me?"

"Curious."

"Why I killed Lincoln?"

"Yes."

"Corelli offered me twenty thousand dollars to do the deed."

"Where would Corelli find twenty thousand dollars?"

"I didn't ask. I knew Vinnie a long time. If he said he was good for it, I took his word."

"Did he mention why he wanted Lincoln killed?"

"I didn't ask. But Vinnie wasn't very fond of the guy who snatched his woman."

"Love? Jealousy? Revenge?"

"People are funny that way."

"Guess you're out twenty grand."

"Maybe, maybe not. Either way, Vinnie was a friend, and someone is going to answer for killing him."

"So, where are we?" I asked.

"There is no we. Forget it. You forget me, I forget you. Sorry I hit you."

"Forget it," I said.

And he left without further ceremony.

I was ready to forget it until I remembered I had an invitation to the Gramercy Park Hotel— and I hated to miss an opportunity to finally get a look at the inside of the place.

11

I jumped into the shower, rinsed the dried blood out of my hair. The throbbing pain had gone, I thought I would live.

I poured a few inches of Johnny Walker Black over ice and worked on it while I inspected my wardrobe. The August heat hadn't subsided much so I opted for function over form—a lightweight cotton suit and a short-sleeved dress shirt. I managed to get into the shirt and slacks before there was a knock on the door. I checked the time. If I hoped to make it to the Gramercy by eight my caller would have to settle for a very short visit.

I opened the door to John Sullivan.

"Got a minute?"

"Or two," I said. "Come in."

I escorted Sullivan to the kitchen and offered him Charlie Mungo's chair at the table.

"Coffee?"

"I'm off duty. I'll have what you're having."

I poured him a scotch and took a seat.

"What's up?" I asked.

"Do you remember Vinnie Corelli?"

"Sure. Good fielding shortstop, not much of a clutch hitter."

"Bump into him lately?"

"Not since he was chased out of Brooklyn. Looking for him?"

"Found him in an apartment on Avenue J, with two in the chest."

"Dead?"

"Very."

"And?"

"Found this in his pocket."

He reached into his jacket, pulled out a clear plastic evidence bag and placed it on the table. It contained my business card.

"Any idea why he was holding this?"

"None. However, there are a lot of those things floating around. I'm a shameless self-promoter."

"Okay," he said, knocking down the rest of his drink. "Looks like you're getting ready to go out, I won't hold you. Maybe another time."

"Sure. I'll give you a call."

We both rose from the table and I walked him out to the hall.

"Catch you later," he said, and he was gone.

Sullivan was tenacious. Eventually he would have more questions and I always found it easier playing dumb if I actually knew something.

12

I called the Gramercy to let Kitty know I was running late. I was informed that Mrs. Lincoln had checked out. I couldn't blame John Sullivan for causing me to miss the appointment, since she had left the hotel hours earlier—before my chat with Charlie Mungo.

Speaking of Mungo, I had really wanted to know why he was nicknamed 'The Stick' and had forgotten to ask. I had however asked him where he imagined Vincent Corelli would dig up twenty thousand to finance the hit and he didn't seem interested in the particulars.

I was less indifferent.

As far as Kitty was concerned, I could only guess—and I was afraid to guess. I found the invitation to visit her at the Gramercy Park and her early departure difficult to reconcile. If there was anything I felt certain of it was that the short phone call she took in my office changed her game plan. But her plan and her game were still a riddle and I believed the solution was out of reach from this side of the state line.

The decision to go back to Atlantic City so soon was not a happy one. I was very conscientious about keeping my visits few and far between. Proximity to the big poker game was dangerous for me, regardless of my primary mission. And what made the return trip even less appealing was the sad fact that to learn more about the late Vincent Corelli and his ex-wife, and be better prepared for any future interrogation, I would need to enlist the help of an unlikely ally.

Thing is, when you have burning questions, you go where you think the fire hose may be.

13

Shortly past three the following afternoon I checked into the Day's Hotel in Egg Harbor Township off the Garden State Parkway. Fifteen miles from the Atlantic City boardwalk, it was far enough to avoid temptation and keep my return unadvertised. For the time being, I wanted only one person to know I was back in the neighborhood.

If Freddy Fingers was sincere about wanting to make friends, I was ready to introduce him to his new best buddy.

I called to have Freddy paged at the Taj Mahal, expecting to leave a message.

To my surprise, he was on the line a few minutes later. He was either in between poker hands, or still trying to decide which game to sit in on and totally fuck up.

He agreed to meet me. I chose the where, he chose the when. I asked him to keep it under his hat.

"I have just the right lid for the occasion," he said.

I had enough time for a cat-nap, a shower and a quick bite to eat before the meeting with Fingers. I was finishing the last of my order of Southern fried chicken at Sam's Rialto Grill in Pleasantville when my cell rang.

I was curious.

"Mr. Ventura, this is Detective Lawrence of the Atlantic City PD. You may remember me. We spoke the other night after the shooting at the casino. You said we could call you if we had more questions. Do you have time to talk?"

I remembered the two dicks who grilled me at the police station, but had no idea whether Lawrence was the tall one with the really bad complexion or the short fat one.

"What about, Detective?"

"Do you know Vincent Corelli?"

"I know *a* Vincent Corelli. I'm guessing there are more than a few out there."

"Lafayette High School. Class of ninety-one. Varsity baseball. Chess Club."

"Sure."

"When was the last time you saw Mr. Corelli?"

Something in his voice told me it was not a good time to crack wise, but I occasionally lack self-control. And if Lawrence knew Vincent Corelli was dead, then he was fucking with me.

"It's been a while. We were never close, I preferred checkers. From what I've heard he was run out of Brooklyn by the cops, the crooks, or both. That's really all I can tell you, Detective, and I'm running late for an appointment."

"I do have a few more questions, Mr. Ventura. I would hate to have to inconvenience you by bringing you all the way down here from Brooklyn to finish this up."

"No problem. How about I come down to the station tomorrow morning and we can talk. How does ten sound?"

"Ten would be fine."

"Great. See you then."

"Have a safe trip," he said, and ended the call.

I had the uneasy feeling Detective Lawrence somehow knew I was already down from Brooklyn, but I shook it off. I had a rendezvous with Freddy Fingers to think about.

If you want someone to know where you're staying, meet him in the bar at your hotel. If you want someone to think they know where you're staying, invite him to meet you at the bar in a different hotel.

14

I was sitting at the bar in the cocktail lounge of the Howard Johnson's in Pleasantville nursing a scotch when Freddy pulled up a stool beside me.

"Nice tie. What do you call that color?"

"Mauve," I said.

"What brings you back to Purgatory so soon, and why the cloak and dagger?"

"ACPD wants to speak with me about Vincent Corelli."

"Corelli? Why?"

"Don't know. Any theories?"

"None."

"Has Detective Lawrence invited you in for a sit-down?"

"Not yet."

"Do you think they're looking at Charlie Mungo?"

"I suppose someone else in the room may have made him, but I hear a lot of things and that's not one of them. I did hear they couldn't positively ID the shooter from the surveillance camera tapes. His head was down, they have no clear view."

"But you're sure it was Mungo?"

"Absolutely."

"Any chance he made you making him?"

"That's not a pleasant thought."

"When was the last time you saw Corelli down here?"

"Long time, I heard he picked up a gig in Connecticut after the divorce."

"So you said. Any idea where he might dig up twenty grand?"

"None. But if you find out let me know, I'll bring the shovel."

"I need to talk with Katherine Lincoln. Know where I can find her?"

"I can tell you where she lives. Huge house at the end of South Iroquois in Margate, north side. Hard to miss."

"And if Lawrence calls you in?"

"I didn't see the shooter's face, I haven't seen Corelli in half a year, I never spoke with you."

He pulled a pen from his pocket and jotted a number on a cocktail napkin.

"My cell, if you can't track me down at the casino. Can I reach you here?"

"I'll call you. Can I buy you a drink?"

"Thanks, but I need to be somewhere," he said, getting up to leave. "Stay focused with Detective Lawrence. He's smarter than he looks."

With that he headed out the door. I walked over to a window looking out to the parking area. Freddy had been fairly generous with information. I suppose I should have been appreciative, but it bothered me that he was all answers and no questions. Fingers stopped at the driver's window of a red Mustang convertible and exchanged a few words with the occupant before climbing into the Cadillac parked beside it and pulling out of the parking lot.

I walked back to the bar and ordered another scotch. An hour later. Back at my hotel. Another bar. Another scotch. Call it a nightcap because I was ready to call it a night.

A deep, silky voice at my right ear.

"Excuse me."

"Okay," I said.

Tall. Dark hair. Dark eyes. Olive complexion. Unquestionably the fruit of a Mediterranean family tree. Straight off the top of Nick Ventura's favorite types list.

"Are you staying at this hotel?" she asked.

"Excuse me?"

"That must have seemed forward. I'm looking for a place to rest for the night. I noticed this hotel and thought I would check it out. I was fishing for an endorsement."

"It's okay, but if you're looking for Atlantic City you pulled up fifteen miles short."

"I'm headed for a business lunch in Philadelphia tomorrow. I took the Garden State to avoid the Jersey Turnpike. Can I buy you a drink?"

"That sounds forward."

"It was a long drive, I'm thirsty and I don't favor drinking alone."

"In that case," I said, "allow me."

She said her name was Angela. Angela was as easy to talk with as she was to look at. Over the course of nearly two hours, we covered everything from the less than amazing Mets to the New York Giants to the novels of John le Carré to the films of Russell Crowe to the music of Counting Crows—with no mention of the weather or what we did for a living.

"I suppose I should see if I can get a room," she finally said. "Thanks for the drinks and the pleasant conversation."

"Any time."

"I like you," Angela said, before leaving the hotel lounge.

I liked her too. A lot. In spite of the fact that I had spotted her climbing out of the red Mustang convertible that followed me from the Howard Johnson.

15

A wake-up call from the front desk at eight the next morning had me up, showered and dressed for my appointment downtown.

I was thinking about Freddy Fingers. How he had seemed very interested in knowing where I was holed up, but showed little interest in why I was asking about Vincent Corelli's fund-raising abilities or why I needed to see the Widow Lincoln.

I had enough time for coffee and a bite to take the edge off. Before I made it out of the room there was a knock on the door.

Angela.

"Hey."

"Hey."

"I lied to you last night," she said.

"Can we talk about it over coffee?"

"Sure."

I escorted her down to the hotel restaurant.

"Freddy asked me to find out where you were staying, and try to find out what brought you down here," Angela said once the coffee arrived.

"Did he say why?"

"No. And I didn't ask."

"But he did ask you to get friendly."

"Yes. But I was thirsty anyway and wanted a drink and I couldn't resist the mauve tie."

"And it was—what? A personal favor?"

"There's nothing personal between me and Freddy Pugno. It was strictly business."

"He hired you?"

"Yes."

"Private investigator?"

"Yes."

"Have you told Freddy I'm staying here?"

"I'll tell him I lost you."

"Why?"

"Professional courtesy," Angela said, "and, as I may have casually mentioned last night, I like you."

"No reason to give up your fee on my account. You can tell Freddy you followed me here. I can always move over to the Howard Johnson's if I feel compromised."

"You're funny."

"Looks aren't everything," I said. "I need to get downtown for a meeting with a Detective Lawrence of the Atlantic City Police Department. Would you be interested in joining me for dinner this evening?"

"Very," she said. She handed me a business card.

"I'll call," I said, standing and reaching for my wallet.

"I got this," she said.

"Thanks. And thanks for coming clean."

"You're welcome and, Ventura..."

"Yes?"

"I don't know what's up with you and Freddy Pugno or with you and the ACPD—and I don't need to know. Unless you decide I need to know."

"I'll keep that in mind."

"And, watch your step with Detective Lawrence. He's not as dumb as he looks."

16

The Atlantic City Police Department was housed in the Public Safety Building on Atlantic Avenue across from the Tropicana. I was directed to Detective Lawrence's desk and he asked me to take a seat. Turned out he was the tall one with the bad complexion.

"Thanks for coming in."

"Sure."

"We were informed by the NYPD that Vincent Corelli was found murdered in Brooklyn yesterday."

That settled that. Now the question became was he going to bring up the discovery of my business card on Vinnie Corelli's body or take namedropping to the next level and mention Charlie Mungo. I wasn't sure what he wanted me to say, so I said nothing.

"The NYPD reached out because Corelli was carrying a New Jersey state driver's license with an Atlantic City address."

"Are you almost to the point where you ask a question, Detective?"

A little cheeky, but Lawrence had billed it as a Q&A. And if I didn't try to move it along, I would be sitting there all day, hearing about what I already knew.

"Do you know Katherine Lincoln?"

It worked.

"I know who she is, but I don't know her."

"Surveillance camera footage shows her talking to you immediately after the shooting."

"She asked if I saw the shooter's face. I told her what I told you, I didn't. I would guess she eventually asked everyone at the table."

"That would be an inaccurate guess. Are you aware that before she was Mrs. Theodore Lincoln, she was Mrs. Vincent Corelli?"

"No."

"A husband and an ex-husband both murdered in less than forty-eight hours. Don't you find it quite a coincidence?"

"I'm one of those few who believe in coincidence, and I have little interest in the personal lives of total strangers unless I'm paid to be interested."

"I see."

I had no idea what he saw, or what he knew. But it was Atlantic City, so I gambled.

"You specifically asked me to keep my nose out of it, Detective. I had nearly forgotten about it until you called me last evening. I don't know how else I can help you."

"A man was gunned down beside you. I would think it would be difficult to forget."

"When I'm in the mood to think about unpleasant events, I have more horrible memories that take precedent. Is there anything else?"

"Thanks for coming in."

"Sure."

We had come full circle. Lawrence had been fishing, I had avoided the hook. I couldn't decide whether he was smarter than he looked or not as dumb as he looked, but one way or the other I was not anxious to find out. As I walked out of the building, I thought it would be a perfect time to drop the whole thing and get out of his pond. But I'm not always as smart *I* look.

I decided I still wanted to see Katherine Lincoln again before I bowed out.

17

It was a straight shot down Atlantic Avenue from the Public Safety Building to the large house on the beach in Margate City. Four miles. Sixteen minutes. Door to door.

I pressed the doorbell. It played two bars of a classical piece I couldn't place. It took Kitty three minutes to respond. She was wearing a plush white terry cloth robe opened to reveal a two-piece bathing suit. I wasn't sure if the color was fuchsia or magenta, but it didn't really matter. I wasn't sure if she was glad to see me, but she didn't appear very surprised.

"I was out at the pool."

"I see," I said.

She closed the robe and tied it with the matching cloth belt.

"Can we talk?" I asked.

"Sure. Come in."

I stepped inside, shut the door, and followed her back to the kitchen.

"Would you like a drink? Scotch?"

"It's a little early for scotch."

"Coffee?"

"No thanks, I'm good."

"What brings you here?"

I reached into my pocket and pulled out the white lace-trimmed handkerchief.

"This," I said, placing it on the marble-topped kitchen island. "I believe it belongs to you."

She looked at it and then back at me with those big green eyes.

"I must have dropped it in your office. Surely you didn't come all the way down here from Coney Island to return a handkerchief."

"Actually, you must have dropped it on the stairs of an apartment building on Avenue J in Midwood."

"I don't know what you mean."

"Then I was mistaken, I guess it doesn't belong to you," I said, picking up the handkerchief and returning it to my pocket, "sorry to have bothered you."

I turned to leave.

"Wait."

I did an about-face.

"He was already dead when I got there."

"I will have that scotch," I said, and I took a seat at the kitchen table.

Kitty placed two glasses with ice and a bottle of Johnnie Walker Green on the table and sat. I poured.

"I knew Charlie Mungo. Not well, but well enough to recognize him when he shot Theodore. Mungo was a friend of my first husband, Vinnie Corelli."

"You made Mungo and thought Corelli had something to do with it."

"No, I didn't believe that, but I needed to be certain."

"And if Vinnie was involved?"

"I decided early on I wouldn't drop a dime on Vinnie or Mungo. But if it was someone else who sent Mungo, I wanted to know. I actually cared for Theodore, and having to witness his execution offended me."

"What made you think Mungo would talk to you if you found him?"

"He would or he wouldn't. I felt it couldn't hurt to ask."

"You didn't consider it dangerous to confront a killer who you could identify?"

"I'm sure Charlie knew I hadn't named him when I had the chance. And he wouldn't have hurt me, out of respect for Vinnie. In any case, that was my motivation for wanting you to help me find Mungo. Then Vincent called me when I was at your office yesterday and everything quickly changed."

"Go on."

"I hadn't seen or heard from Vinnie since he moved up to Connecticut. He said he needed to see me, that it was very important. He told me where he was, I went there and he was already dead."

"Do you have any idea where Vinnie would get his hands on twenty thousand dollars?"

"Why do you ask?"

"Indulge me."

"He may have had that kind of money. Theodore was a jealous man. I always suspected he paid Vincent off to leave Atlantic City after the divorce."

"I bumped into Charlie Mungo."

"And?"

"He said Vinnie offered him twenty grand to snuff Lincoln."

"And you believed him?"

"I don't see any reason for him to lie."

"Did he say why Vinnie wanted Theodore killed?"

"Mungo guessed it was about Lincoln getting the girl. What do you think?"

"I don't know."

"Any idea who might have wanted Vinnie dead?"

"No."

"Mungo sounded very determined to find out who killed his friend," I said.

"I hope he does. I always liked Vinnie."

"But he could never have put you into a place like this."

"That sounds terrible."

"It sounds pragmatic. They found one of my business cards on Vinnie's body. Any thoughts about that?"

"None."

"I guess you won't be needing my services after all."

"I guess not. But if you speak to Charlie Mungo, I would appreciate it if you explained to him that I had nothing to do with Vinnie's death."

"I hope I never run into Mungo again."

"Another drink?"

"No. I need to get going. But I have one more question."

"Yes?"

"How did you know who I was? When you approached me at the poker table immediately after your husband was shot. How did you know I was a private investigator?"

"That's the irony. About a year ago Vinnie pointed you out to me at the Showboat. He said you played ball together in high school."

Ironic indeed. Particularly since, at this point, I had no clue who was playing ball with who.

"Sorry for your losses," I said. "I'll see myself out."

"I'd like to compensate you for your time."

"No need. You never hired me. I'd prefer to keep it that way."

I pulled the handkerchief from my pocket and placed it on the table before I left.

18

As I slid behind the wheel of the Monte Carlo, I let out a sigh of relief. I was done with Kitty Corelli Lincoln— fantasies and all. I believed I had successfully shaken Detective Lawrence off my back. I had no more reason to bond with Freddy Fingers. And I had a dinner date with the first woman I'd met in a long time who I found attractive in more ways than the obvious.

I pulled out my wallet and found Angela's business card. Her last name was DiMarco. I praised myself for being perfectly correct about her ancestry. I dug out my cell phone and called her. She said she knew a very good seafood restaurant at Mays Landing. She would pick me up at my room at six. I drove to the hotel.

I changed into something casual and was about to go searching for a little bite to eat to hold me until dinner when I heard the knocking. I opened the door.

Charlie Mungo stood at the threshold.

"We need to talk," he said.

"How did you find me?"

"I've been watching Kitty's place. I saw you show up and followed you when you left. We need to talk."

Mungo reached into his jacket pocket and pulled something out. I thought it was a gun. I was about to slam the door shut when I heard the first shot. Mungo's legs went out from under him and he fell forward into the room. I caught him in my arms. Then a second gunshot and we were both knocked to the floor.

When I finally opened my eyes, I found myself in a bed at the Atlanticare Medical Center in Pleasantville. I was hooked up to an IV and felt like I'd been hit by a defensive lineman. Angela was sitting in a chair at my bedside.

"How am I?"

"Better than the other guy. A bullet went through the victim and broke your skin. No internal damage, it popped right out. Another inch or two and you would have lost your ability to be such a smooth talker. Your head took a good hard bounce on the floor, knocked you unconscious. You lost blood. You'll live."

"The shooter?"

"Clean getaway. No witnesses. Detective Lawrence is in a yank to talk to you. My cousin Theresa is a nurse here, she smuggled me in and she managed to hold Lawrence at bay—but he'll be back first thing in the morning."

"I can hardly wait."

"If you wanted to break our dinner engagement you could have simply called."

I discovered it hurt when I laughed.

"When can I get out of here?"

"Don't hold your breath. I collected your things and checked you out of the hotel."

"My car?"

"The hotel manager said it's okay where it is for now. No charge. It's probably as safe there as anywhere while you're stuck in here. Is there anyone you would like me to call?"

"Not really."

"Do you want to talk about what happened?"

"Find me something to eat that's easy to chew and as easy to digest and I'll tell you everything."

"I'm on it," Angela said, and quickly left the room.

I closed my eyes and must have dozed off.

Angela gently shook me awake twenty minutes later. She had raised the bed back and moved the hospital table into the dining position. There was a Styrofoam take-out box, a paper napkin, a plastic fork, and a large paper cup of soda with a straw set in front of me.

"What do we have here?"

"Don't you like surprises?"

I opened the box. Meat loaf and mashed potatoes with gravy.

"How did you know?"

"It was all I could find at the local diner that was soft and warm and not soup. I hope you like Dr. Pepper."

"Diet?"

"No."

"Thank God."

Angela's cell phone belted out a Dire Straits tune. I was liking her more and more.

"I need to take this. I'll be back in a minute. Enjoy your meal. Don't eat too fast."

She left the room. I dug in.

Angela walked back into the room talking.

"The man who was killed at your hotel was identified. Charles Mungo. It made the news at five. Someone saw his mug on the tube, came forward and named him as the perp who gunned down a poker player at the Taj Mahal a few days ago."

"Who named Mungo?"

"My source doesn't know."

"Who's your source? Do you have a cousin at the ACPD also?"

"Glad that bullet didn't kill your sense of humor. Just a

friend at the ACPD. That's all he could say."

"Would you like the rest of this meat loaf?"

"No, but thanks for asking."

"Then please move this table and I'll tell you all I know."

I gave her the no-frills account. Theodore Lincoln, Kitty, Freddy Fingers, Charlie Mungo, Vincent Corelli and the errant business card discovered on Corelli's body.

"So, there's nothing you're really sure of," she said after the synopsis.

"I'm sure of one thing—my name is on a list that is getting shorter by the day."

"Just when you think you're out, they pull you back in."

"Not bad, I said."

"I do Scarface better."

"So, what do you think?"

"I think you need to get some rest and be ready for Detective Lawrence. I'll be back in the morning and I can tell you what I think and you can tell me if you could use my help."

"Thanks."

"I'd do the same for anyone who liked *L.A. Confidential* as much as I did."

19

I found a doctor standing at my bedside early the next morning. He greeted me with a lot of mumbo jumbo about my condition, the prognosis, and told me how lucky I was.

I didn't feel lucky.

"Do you have any questions?"

"When can I get out of here?"

"Not today. We'll take you off the morphine later this morning to see how much it really hurts, and remove the bandages to take a peek at the wound. And I want you to try a walk around the ward."

And adios.

Visiting hours started at eight, and Detective Lawrence was first in line. I wondered if he had camped out overnight like a teen at an Apple store jonesing for the latest iPhone.

I managed to survive another interrogation. No, I didn't know Charlie Mungo. No, I didn't have any idea why he came to my hotel room and he never had the opportunity to explain. Yes, I would be leaving Lawrence's neck of the woods as soon as possible.

"Can you tell me who fingered Charlie Mungo for the Lincoln assassination?" I asked.

"A solid citizen who prefers to remain anonymous."

Fine.

"Is that all, Detective? I think it's time for my sponge bath."

He didn't stick around and neglected to thank me for my cooperation.

Angela popped in at nine, moved the hospital table into place, and set down a plate wrapped in aluminum foil. I uncovered a perfect frittata—eggs, potatoes, garlic, onion, sweet red pepper and grated pecorino Romano. It was a beautiful sight.

"What, no Thomas' English muffin?"

"I couldn't resist, I devoured it on my way over."

"Did you whip this up?"

"All by myself."

"It's a work of art."

"I can have it framed for you."

"It looks too good to eat."

"Well, decide, either eat it while it's still warm or ask it to marry you. How did it go with Lawrence?"

"Same mutual evasion, different day."

"Did you see a doctor?"

"Yes, he booked me for another night."

"Probably the safest place to be until we find out who tried to kill you."

"You think I was the target?"

"I think you and Charlie Mungo were both targets and someone was lucky enough to find you propped in the same shooting
gallery. You said Mungo followed you to your hotel, either
someone followed him or someone was watching you."

"No one knew where I was staying except you and Freddy
Fingers."

"I never got to tell Freddy where you were staying."

"Oh?"

"I left him a message last night, asked him to call me. He
never did."

"Maybe he lost interest."

"Maybe."

"You said we."

"What?"

"You said until *we* find out who tried to kill me."

"Did I?"

"Yes."

"If you want my help, just ask. Think about it. Now, as much
as I would love to spend the day in this hospital, I have to make a
living and I have work to do. I'll come back this evening, I'll
bring dinner."

She walked over to the chest of drawers on the opposite side
of the room, unplugged my cell phone from the wall charger,
and brought it to me.

"It should be fully juiced. You might want to check for messages."

"Thanks."

"You're welcome. Don't lose my grandmother's plate. See
you later," she said, and was quickly gone.

There were four missed calls—three from Tom Romano and
one from John Sullivan.

I called Tom.

"I've been trying to reach you since last evening," he said, "I
have a gig for you, a very good paying gig. How soon can you
get to my boat?"

"As soon as I can get out of this fucking hospital."

"What are you doing in a hospital?"

"Recovering from a gunshot wound."

"What the fuck happened? Did you find Charlie Mungo?"

"He found me, and he took two in the back."

"Jesus. Did you hear Vinnie Corelli took two in the chest?"

"John Sullivan paid me a visit, said they found one of my business cards on Vinnie's body."

"What's that about?"

"No idea."

"Which hospital, I'll come to you."

"A hospital in fucking un-Pleasantville New Jersey. It's a long story. As much as I would love a job that actually pays, it will have to wait. But while I'm trapped down here, I could use your help up there."

"What do you need?"

"Freddy Fingers."

"The exiled son of Ferdinand 'The Fist' Pugno? What about him?"

"Fingers said he knew Mungo, from back in the day when Freddy was still in his old man's good graces. And Fingers seemed to know a lot about Vinnie Corelli. I would be interested in knowing if Freddy had any contact with Mungo or Corelli recently."

"I can ask around."

"Do you know why Pugno Senior banished Freddy?"

"When the old man retired, he handed the reins over to Freddy's brother Carmine. The younger son. Everyone could understand the move. Freddy was never really cut out for it. Carmine was the right choice. But being passed over is still a severe insult in the culture. Freddy wasn't happy, and he wasn't quiet about his discontent. He was complaining a lot, in all the wrong places. He was finally warned to shut up or ship out. Why all the curiosity about Freddy Fingers?"

"Because he approached me, I would never have given him a second thought otherwise, and now he's got me wondering if he's in the middle of this somehow."

"Guys like Freddy are lonely. He may simply be starved for attention."

"I was ready to drop this whole fucking business until someone tried to punch my ticket."

"Perhaps it was just a warning."

"Then I'd like to know who to thank for it."

"I'll see what I can dig up."

"Thanks, Tom."

I was about to return John Sullivan's call when a nurse came in and gave me all the excuse I needed to put it off.

"Your doctor will be in shortly. I'm going to take you off the intravenous pain killer and remove your bandages so he can take a look."

She removed the IV. I experienced a great sense of freedom. I wondered if I would be screaming for another dose in thirty minutes.

"Should I remove the gown?" I asked.

"You can just drop the front. I wouldn't want Angela to get jealous."

"Cousin Theresa?"

"At your service."

I moved the bed clothes up to my waist and pulled the gown off my arms and chest. She carefully removed the bandages.

"How does it look?"

"I've seen a lot worse, and eventually it will match the scar on your other shoulder."

The doctor walked in, took a quick glance, and left.

"Very efficient," I said.

"Let's take a walk," Theresa said.

She hooked me up with a walker and a robe to cover my back and we took a stroll around the ward. My legs were rubbery but I attributed it to the Morphine fix and I was feeling no pain.

Theresa got me back into my bed.

"How do you feel?"

"Tired. And I'm beginning to feel pain in my head and my shoulder."

"I'll be right back."

She returned with two tablets and a paperback book. She dropped the tabs into my hand and poured me a glass of water.

"Morphine?" I asked, knocking them down.

"Tylenol PM. Man up. Angela left this for you, in case you get bored," she said, handing me the paperback. "Ring if you need anything."

And see you later.

I looked at the title. *Italian Americans of Newark, Belleville, and Nutley.* I read until the Tylenol put my lights out.

"Sit up," Theresa said, shaking me awake, "lunch time."

She placed a plate in front of me. BLT on white toast and French fries. I dove in. The toast and bacon were crisp, the fries were crunchy.

"This is unusually good hospital food."

"That's because I brought it back from Essl's Dugout. Eat before it loses its edge."

"I might have to start calling you Mother Theresa."

"I already have two kids, three if you count my husband. Did the book put you to sleep?"

"Not at all. I'm curious about the choice."

"Angela is a Nutley girl. She thought you might be interested in where she comes from, and thought it would help you get a handle on where she's usually coming from. I think she likes you. I hope you're not a heel."

She didn't give me a chance to respond.

"Do you need anything else?"

"Coffee?"

"I'll send some up," she said, and skipped.

I cleaned my plate and reached for my phone. Not my idea of dessert, but it would be smart not to let John Sullivan wait any longer.

Unlike Tom Romano, Sullivan already knew where I was and why.

"I have an unsolved homicide up here, there are two down there that are related, and your name keeps popping up," he said, skipping the small talk.

I decided to tell the truth, just not all of it. Risky since I had no idea what else Sullivan knew.

"I was at the apartment on Avenue J. I found Corelli dead. I still have no idea why he had one of my cards."

"Why didn't you call it in?"

"I saw the patrol car pull up before I had a chance, figured a nine-one-one would be redundant."

"Why didn't you mention it when we spoke?"

"I could say you didn't ask, but I wouldn't want to piss you off."

"I'm already pissed off. What brought you there?"

"I was looking for Charlie Mungo."

"Why?"

"A job."

"For who?"

"I can't say."

"Client confidentiality?"

"Something like that."

"What made you think you would find Mungo there?" John asked, obviously getting impatient.

"Tom Romano did some asking around for me."

"Do you think Mungo killed Corelli?"

"No."

"Why?"

"Mungo surprised me at my apartment later. He spotted me on Avenue J and tracked me down. He thought I killed Vinnie. I convinced him I didn't. He sounded very sincere about wanting to find out who did. He admitted to killing Theodore Lincoln, claimed he was contracted by Corelli, suggested I forget we ever met, and went on his way."

"Did you give this to the ACPD?"

"No, it's hearsay."

"What took you back down to Atlantic City?"

"I wanted to inform my client I was off the case, face to face. Mungo found me at my hotel, said we needed to talk, and then the shooting started."

"How are you?"

"Gee, John, I thought you'd never ask. I should be out of the hospital tomorrow. I told you everything I know."

"No, you didn't. I have an informant who sells rumors on the street like they were I LOVE NY T-shirts and I know you're holding out. We go back a long time, Nick, and I like you, but this is business. Here is my best offer. You have two days to make it up here to see me, time to recover and time to think it over. Then you will honestly tell me everything you know. If you don't show up, I will put out a warrant and have you escorted. Get it?"

"Got it."

"Terrific. I'll see you day after tomorrow," he said, and that was that.

I thought about calling him right back. Give him Katherine Lincoln and Freddy Fingers and let the NYPD and the ACPD sort it all out. But someone had taken a shot at me, and I took it personally. And since I had a two-day grace period, I decided to use it. The thing was John Sullivan knew me well, and I couldn't be sure if he was giving me time to convalesce or time to do some of the work for him. Angela poked her head through the door just before three.

"You're early."

"Theresa says they're cutting you loose around this time tomorrow. She's getting off work now and we're going to move your car over to my place. I need to run. I'll be back around six."

"Angela."

"Yes?"

"There's a three-fifty-seven in the glove box, can you put it in a safe place."

"Done," she said, and was gone.

With three hours to kill, I decided to read a little more about the Brownstone Quarries of Nutley, New Jersey.

Angela returned at half past six with a large bowl of baked Ziti Siciliana. The bowl matched the breakfast plate.

"Whip this up also?"

"I could have, but it was a busy day. I pulled it out of the freezer. My mother never lets me go home from a Sunday dinner visit without taking leftovers. Eat while it's still piping hot from the microwave in the nurses' break room. I need to make arrangements for your release. I expect to see an empty bowl when I get back."

"Or else?"

"Or else I'll tell my mother."

I had no problem complying.

Twenty minutes later Angela was back at bedside and I had told her about my talk with John Sullivan.

"And this guy is your friend?"

"A good friend but not a happy one. John seems convinced I've been less than forthcoming. It would be more like Sullivan to have me extracted by helicopter to Coney Island Hospital, but he's giving me time and I'm not sure why. In any event, I have two days and I need answers. Can you do me a favor?"

"Have I ever said no?"

"No."

"I can't wait until it's my turn to ask a favor. What do you need?"

"Do you have any cousins at the Taj Mahal, like in security?"

"I have friends, what are you after?"

"There's a tape of the Lincoln shooting I would like to look at."

"I'll see what I can do," she said.

"Thanks. Did you ever hear back from Freddy?"

"Sort of. This arrived at my office," she said, reaching into her bag. She handed me an envelope with a Taj Mahal return address, "three hundred in cash, I guess Freddy doesn't need my services any longer and, I almost forgot, there's this."

She handed me a cell phone.

"When I picked up your car the hotel manager said they found it in your room, asked if it was yours. I said yes. Are you comparing phone plans?"

"It's not mine."

"I know it's not yours. It belonged to Vincent Corelli."

"How?"

"Charlie Mungo?"

I remembered Mungo reaching into his pocket before he was shot.

"Wow."

"That's one way of putting it."

"I hate to ask."

"Go for it."

"Can you try to identify all of the calls he made and received in the past week or so?"

"Sure, at least any that weren't deleted. Get any reading done?"

"Yes. You're a Jersey Girl."

"Full-blooded. The doctor has agreed to release you to my care. They'll have the paperwork done by three tomorrow. I'll pick you up," she said, rising to leave.

"Can you stay for a while?"

"You gave me work to do and I can't do it sitting here. I'll see you tomorrow and we'll blow this pop stand."

She collected her grandmother's plates, Corelli's cell phone, and the envelope.

"I don't know how to thank you."

She gave me a quick peck on the lips that put the perfect Ziti

Siciliana to shame.

"I'll think of something," she said, and glided out of the hospital room.

20

I woke up at four in the morning and couldn't get back to sleep. I had nothing to look forward to but eleven hours of impatient waiting. I tried thinking of it as R and R, but there was little rest and less recreation. I tried reading, tried a spin around the ward, and by seven I finally begged Theresa to give me something to knock me out. What she served up was very quick and extremely effective.

By two forty-five I had signed all of the necessary release forms and disclaimers, changed into street clothes, and was being coaxed into a wheel chair by Nurse Theresa.

"Is this necessary?"

"Hospital policy. My cousin is bringing the car up front."

As she pushed me through the exit door, I saw Angela waiting in the red Mustang. Top down.

"Treat her nice," Theresa said.

"Or else?"

"Or else I'll tell her father."

"No threats necessary."

"Good," Theresa said.

She rolled me up to the car and I climbed in.

"Sit back and enjoy the ride," Angela said before I could get a word in, "I'll give you the lowdown when we get to the house."

It was twenty-five miles to Ocean City—through Ventnor, Margate (the home of Kitty the Widow and Lucy the Elephant) and across the JFK Memorial and Ocean Drive bridges. Travelling south, the Atlantic Ocean was always to our left. Beautiful, magnificent and mysterious. It was easy to get lost in its vastness, but I often found myself distracted by the grace and confidence of the driver.

Angela pulled the convertible into the driveway beside my Monte Carlo.

"Here we are," she said, "my bungalow."

It was a small one story, covered in wood siding painted bright white, adorned with green slatted shutters, with a view of the sea. Despite its modest size, its location marked it as a pricey piece of real estate.

"Lovely," I said, not remembering the last time I had used that word.

"My grandfather built it as a vacation home."

"Did your grandfather work the quarries?"

"I see you did your homework. My great grandfather came from Calabria with a wave of immigrants who traded the granite quarries for brownstone quarries. Most of the brownstone in New York City came from Nutley. My grandfather didn't favor that sort of labor. He opened a Salumeria in Avondale."

"Is it still in the family?"

"He passed it on to his son, Vito, Theresa's father. He gave this place to my dad, Dominic. Dom had other ambitions. He's a homicide detective in the Newark Police Department. If you ever get to meet him, you can expect a background check. Let's go in."

She led me back to the kitchen.

"I made up the guest room. You'll find all your things there. Your gun is in the top dresser drawer."

"I could get a hotel."

"You were released to my care, I'm responsible, and I don't think you should be driving. Do you want to argue about it?"

"No."

"Are you hungry? Thirsty?"

"I can wait on food. I wouldn't mind a drink."

"Scotch? Rocks?"

"Sure."

She poured Glenfiddich over ice for me and a tall glass of handmade lemonade for herself.

"I found records of three calls on Vincent Corelli's cell phone, all from this past Wednesday. All of the earlier call records were permanently deleted, which takes two steps and indicates commitment. The first, just before noon, was a call to his ex-wife."

"She took that call at my office in Brooklyn."

"I couldn't identify the second outgoing call, but he made it immediately after he called her."

"Mungo told me Corelli called him. And the third?"

"The third was an incoming call, from *this* number. I found this on the seat of your car," she said, handing it to me.

Freddy Fingers' phone number, scribbled on a Howard Johnson cocktail napkin.

"What time was that call made?"

"Around six Wednesday evening."

"Corelli was already dead. Apparently, Freddy didn't know it yet. But it does tell us Freddy had something to talk with Corelli about."

"Bring your drink," Angela said, "it's show time."

She led me into the living room, turned on the television, and fed a disc into the DVD player.

Surveillance footage of the table where I sat beside Theodore Lincoln when he was shot to death six days before. The camera filmed its subjects from above—taking in the playing area, the players and dealer, and anyone within three feet of the table. It ran for about two minutes, with the gun shooting at midpoint.

"Can you go back to just before the gunshot and freeze it just after."

"What do you see," Angela asked as I stared at the still frame.

"It's what I don't see. Everyone in the game reacted to the gunshot, but no one looked up at the assailant—including Freddy Fingers who immediately turns away and looks ready to jump under the table. What I don't see is how Freddy could have identified Mungo without looking at the shooter. Can you play it again. This time focus on Mrs. Lincoln, stop it again at the gunshot."

Angela replayed it.

"It looks like she spotted him before he reached the table, and she's looking right at him when he fires," Angela said.

"She saw Mungo coming and when he shot her husband she didn't flinch. Do you think she was expecting him."

"It happened so fast," Angela suggested, "she could have failed to react because she was in shock."

"Maybe."

"A fat cat is murdered, a young wife who stands to inherit a bundle of money is always the first person of interest, and yet she is passed over as a suspect by investigators. There must be a reason, and there's nothing here to hang her."

"Devil's advocate?"

"I'm just saying." Angela continued. "Personally, it wouldn't surprise me if she was up to her neck in it. But, with Mungo and Corelli both gone, I don't see how we'll ever know. You might want to forget the whole thing and see to it that everyone who may wish you harm is confident you're out of the game."

"Or I could take another go at Freddy Fingers."

"Sure," Angela said, "why not. Ready for some food?"

"Why not."

My cell phone rang. I checked the caller ID.

"My friend Tom Romano from Brooklyn," I said.

"I'll be in the kitchen slaving over the stove."

"Tom."

"Nick, I'm here at the hospital in Pleasantville. Where are you?"

"Ocean City."

"I have news for you."

"You didn't need to come all the way down here. A phone call would have done the trick."

"I actually came down for Michael Bolton at Harrah's, thought I'd catch you before the show."

It still hurt when I laughed.

"I have an extra ticket," Tom added.

"You're killing me. Hold on a minute."

I walked back to the kitchen still laughing.

"It's my grandmother's apron," Angela said, "control the scathing editorials."

I concluded Tom and Angela were going to get along fine.

"Can I invite a guest to dinner?"

"As many as you like."

I gave Tom directions to the house.

Angela had this thing about not talking business until after the meal, so we didn't.

I insisted on doing the dinner dishes. Angela put up a pot of coffee and entertained us with stories of her summers there as a kid, when the tribe of DiMarco offspring ruled the beach—the last of the working-class families that had originally settled the area. The small house sat on a large piece of property. The closest houses were not near at all, and were all four times as large.

"My grandfather made us all promise we would keep this place in the family. Developers have been chomping at the bit to get hands on this land for decades—tear down the bungalow and put up an eyesore with half a dozen two-million-dollar condominiums. This is one of the rare weekends when there are no visitors down from Newark and Nutley. This coming weekend, for the annual Labor Day family reunion, there will be so many DiMarcos, Caravellas, Martuccis and Falcos here it will look like the Feast of San Gennaro and the Columbus Day parade rolled into one. Why don't you gentlemen retire to the living room, if Tom has to wait any longer to tell you what he came down here to tell you he's going to burst. I'll bring the coffee in."

When we were settled in, Tom began.

"I couldn't tie Vinnie Corelli to Freddy Pugno, but I found someone who saw Corelli having dinner with Pugno Senior at New Corners in Brooklyn two weeks ago."

"How does the old man fit in?"

"I'm not sure, but I did some more digging. Pugno Senior was tried for a felony homicide five years ago. He beat the rap.

New evidence suggests jury tampering, involving his attorney at the time. It's possible the investigators were trying to turn his ex-lawyer, cut a deal."

"And what does that have to do with Vinnie Corelli and Pugno breaking bread in Brooklyn?"

"Maybe Vinnie came to New York to offer the old man some valuable information."

"And how would Corelli know anything about anything?" Angela asked.

"His ex-wife?"

"I'm not following," I said.

"Pugno's lawyer in the murder case was Theodore Lincoln."

"Lincoln's wife claimed she hadn't spoken with Corelli in months," I said.

"She hasn't been exactly reliable," Tom said.

"I need a drink," I said.

"It's a beautiful night, let's sit out on the front porch—I'll bring the scotch," Angela said.

We sat on the porch, faintly moonlit, putting a good dent into the bottle. Angela finally broke the silence.

"Are you going to let it go?"

"It wasn't my idea to get dragged into this mess in the first place."

"That doesn't answer my question."

"Someone took a shot at me."

"I could be mistaken," she said, "maybe Mungo was the sole target and you were just in the wrong place at the wrong time."

"I have that ability down to a science."

"I need to get going," Tom said, "let me know if I can help."

"You're welcome to stay," Angela said, "there's plenty of room."

"I need to get back to New York. I have a very early appointment tomorrow."

"Are you okay to drive?" Angela asked.

"Absolutely."

"Where's your car?" I asked.

"Jesus, I can't remember."

"Tom."

"I'm joking. It's right up the next street."

"Can you stick around until I get back? Ten, fifteen minutes?" I asked.

"Sure, where are you going?"

"Down to the water, it always helps me think."

I stood at the waterline staring out across the ocean, in a trance. I eventually decided I didn't give a fuck about what any of these little people did with each other or to each other as long as they kept me out of it.

Then the shooting began. Rapid, automatic fire, at least twenty rounds.

I ran back toward the house. I saw him get into the car and roar off. There was nothing I could do, but I saw his face clearly in the moonlight—and I knew the face.

I ran to the porch, they were both dead.

I ran to the guest room and grabbed my travel bag, my car keys and the Magnum.

As I drove away from the house, I could hear the police siren.

I don't remember driving the one hundred thirty miles.

Shock, booze, rage.

When I came off the Verrazano Bridge into Brooklyn, it was well after midnight.

21

The house was a large two story at East 23rd Street off Avenue I, near Brooklyn College. The street was deserted. I walked up the front steps and rang the doorbell. Detective John Sullivan opened the door a few minutes later.

"Do you know what time it is?"

"Not exactly," I said, "I need your help."

"It couldn't wait?"

"It can't wait."

"Are you okay?"

"I'm far from okay. Can I come in?"

John let me in. His wife was coming down from the floor above.

"Is everything all right, Johnny?"

"Just an old friend who seems to have lost track of time. Go back to bed, sweetheart."

"Hello, Nick."

"Hello, Margaret. Sorry to wake you."

"Try not to wake the children," she said, and walked back up.

Sullivan led me into the living room.

"What's this about?"

I told him most of it.

"Why?"

"Someone must think Mungo told me something I shouldn't know."

"And you couldn't identify the shooter?"

"Male. Dark car. Raced off before I made it back to the house. He didn't know he missed me."

"And you didn't call it in to the Ocean City police?"

"There was nothing I could tell them."

"What do you need from me?"

"I need to talk to Ferdinand Pugno."

"What makes you think I can get you an audience with Pugno?"

"I'm hoping you can, John, there is no one else I can ask. And it has to be right away, before anyone else knows I'm still alive."

"I don't know what I can do or what I want to do. Why didn't you give me any of this when we spoke before?"

"You were after whoever iced Corelli. I didn't know then and I don't know now. I'm hoping Pugno can give me an idea—give us an idea."

"I'll sleep on it, Nick. You'll stay here tonight and we'll talk about it in the morning."

"I don't want to impose on you and Margaret."

"Too late. You'll stay here."

"Am I under house arrest?"

"Was Tom Romano a very good friend?" John asked.

"Yes. And I believe Angela was going to be a very good friend."

"In that case, I want to make sure you don't run off and let your emotions get the best of you."

"I have no feelings right now, John. I'm numb. I just want to get to the bottom of it before the emotion kicks in."

Sullivan walked me out to the Monte Carlo for my travel bag and showed me to the guest room. I went out like a light.

I dreamed I was at the poker table. I had two queens in my hand and there was a third face up on the felt. I picked up my last down card. It should have been the queen of spades, but instead it was Angela DiMarco. Both eyes closed.

I woke abruptly just as John walked into the room.

"You missed getting the kids off to school. You can use the shower down the hall," he said, laying two towels on a chair, "then come down for breakfast. You have an appointment with Pugno in Queens at eleven. Don't ask how."

Queens.

Perfect.

Il Toscano Ristorante sits off 235th Street and 42nd Avenue, a stone's throw from the Douglaston station of the Long Island Railroad. The restaurant is closed on Mondays, but at eleven a sharp dresser greeted me at the entrance and led me inside. He walked me to a small private room with one table. Ferdinand 'The Fist' Pugno sat alone and invited me to take a seat. My escort left.

"Thank you for seeing me," I said.

"Detective Sullivan was very persuasive," Pugno said, "my time is short."

"You met with Vincent Corelli a few weeks ago. Can you tell me what it was about?"

"Why would that be any of your business?"

"I'm a target for extinction. I would like to know why, and I believe your meeting with Corelli may be pertinent."

"On what do you base that belief?"

"The murder of both Corelli and Theodore Lincoln."

"I heard about Vincent's misfortune. I had not heard of Lincoln's. And I still I don't see how I can help you."

"Please try."

"Vincent Corelli came to me with information he thought might trouble me. I assured him, as I now assure you, that I had nothing to fear from Theodore Lincoln. And I had nothing to do with Vincent's or Lincoln's death. Whether you believe this or not is not my concern."

"Would your son have been worried about Lincoln?"

"Carmine knows what I know."

"And Freddy?"

"I have nothing to do with Freddy. I pay him to stay away. Now, if there is nothing else."

"Just one more question, please, if you will indulge me."

"Let me hear it."

"Do you know where I can find Mario Grillo?"

"You may not want to find him."

"I need to, before he finds me. Is Grillo protected?"

"Mario Grillo has no allegiances. He is available to any who will pay for his services. The man kills indiscriminately. He is under no one's wing. But Freddy."

"Yes?"

"Freddy is a worthless gambler, and I have lost all feelings for him. He has caused our family much grief and embarrassment. He is a great disappointment. If he has earned punishment for a transgression, I would not get in the way of allowing justice to take its course. But for the sake of his mother, I would not tolerate seeing him fatally harmed."

"Understood," I said.

"Try Mom's Bar on Forty-Second Street and Second Avenue in Brooklyn. And forget where you heard it."

"Thank you." I rose to leave.

Pugno's man suddenly materialized and escorted me out to the street.

I had failed to mention Mario Grillo to John Sullivan. Grillo was a stone-cold assassin-for-hire who made Charlie Mungo look like a choirboy. I knew Grillo well enough to easily recognize his moonlit face outside Angela's house the night before.

I climbed into the Monte Carlo and headed back to Brooklyn.

Charlie Mungo had reminded me that the most effective way to get the drop on someone is to surprise your target at his home, and bring the rope. Of course, you need to know where the mark lives and that often takes time and patience.

I got lucky.

I had been staking out Mom's Bar for less than three hours when Mario Grillo appeared and entered the bar. I waited another two hours or so for him to come out and I followed him to his crib. It was a converted warehouse on Kingsland Avenue between Nassau and Driggs Avenues in Greenpoint. He entered the building and the waiting began again. He came out an hour later and took off toward Nassau Avenue, on foot. Good news, he would likely be returning soon. I needed to be ready for him and had little time to lose.

I rapped on his door, hoping no one would be there to greet me. I always carried lock picks, and I was good with them, but Grillo saved me the trouble by leaving his door unlocked. I entered the large open space and waited.

Grillo was back in twenty minutes, and I smacked his head from behind with my gun. He was stunned, but managed to turn toward me. I landed a round house to his jaw with the .357 in my fist and he went down like the Titanic.

I tied him to a chair, gagged him, and looked around the place while I waited for him to come to. I found an FN Five-seveN semi-automatic pistol, with a magazine that could hold twenty 5.7x28mm SS197SR V-Max cartridges.

The weapon Grillo emptied outside the bungalow in Ocean City.

I was sitting in a chair facing Grillo, *his* gun in my hand, when he finally opened his eyes. He looked as if he'd seen Lazarus. I uncovered his mouth.

"Who hired you to kill me?"

"That gun is not loaded."

"I'm aware of that," I said, and I struck him with considerable force on his left knee with the grip of the weapon.

"Fuck you," he screamed through his pain.

"Not likely," I said.

"Are you going to kill me?"

"I want to."

"You won't."

"Why is that?"

"Because you understand that what I did is what I do. It's work. My occupation. It's not personal."

"Tell me who hired you, then we can talk job description."

"The anonymity of my clients is as important as the job itself. I'm a professional."

I was certain I would get nothing out of him. I walked to the kitchen counter. I found a Wüsthof Classic 8" Chef's knife and waved it in front of his face from behind.

"You're mistaken, it is personal," I said, "any last words?"

"Fuck you."

That settled it.

I grabbed Grillo by his hair and slit his throat.

I wiped down the knife and dropped it to the floor.

I wiped down and replaced the FN Five-seveN where I had found it and I left the building.

I made a quick stop at my apartment to throw together suitable travel clothing.

I also collected my best suit, dress shirt and tie and grabbed the shoulder holster for my Smith & Wesson 65-3 .357 Magnum.

I used my cell phone to call John Sullivan.

"Well?" he asked.

"Old man Pugno was no help."

"And it took you all day to find out?"

"I drove back down to Atlantic City." I lied, "I'll keep you posted."

"Don't do anything stupid, Nick."

"Wouldn't think of it."

Mario Grillo had stayed mum to the end.

I headed out to the Jersey Shore to find out if I could find someone who was more inclined to talk.

22

Freddy Fingers was not difficult to find. His address was listed in the Atlantic City phone directory. The house was a two-family on South Kingston between Ventnor and Atlantic Avenues, a minute from the Boardwalk and two miles from the Taj Mahal. Fingers had the first-floor apartment.

It was just before ten in the evening, the last Monday in August, a week before Labor Day and the official end of summer. The first floor was lit up. I walked up the steps to the front porch and rapped on the door.

Fingers looked surprised to see me, but unlike Mario Grillo he didn't seem shocked to see me alive.

"I didn't think you were still in town," he said.

"Are you going to invite me in?"

"Sure, come in. Would you like a drink?"

"Scotch, rocks."

There were two matching armchairs in the front room, separated by a small table. Fingers produced two iced glasses and a bottle of Johnny Walker Black, invited me to take a seat and took the other.

He poured.

I picked up my drink and replaced it with the weapon from my shoulder holster.

"What do you plan to do with that?" he asked.

"I promised your father I wouldn't kill you, but I will beat you with this gun until you wish you were dead if you don't come clean."

"Where would you like me to begin?"

"At the beginning," I said.

"Vincent Corelli approached me a few weeks ago. He said he knew a way I might inspire my father to reconsider his opinion of me, and added I could make some serious cash at the same time. Corelli said I needed to be on call."

"Go on, you're doing fine."

"He called me last Monday, told me to sit in at a card game at the Taj Mahal. I didn't expect to find you in the game. I knew it was about Theodore Lincoln and how he might be planning to hurt my father, but I wasn't expecting to see Lincoln's brains on the table."

"And you never did see the shooter."

"Corelli called me again later that night. I told him about you being there and about Kitty Lincoln approaching you after the shooting. Vinnie named Mungo. I never looked up at the shooter. Corelli asked me to keep an eye on you, learn if you were considering getting involved, and to try discouraging you if you were. I thought I had warned you off until you phoned me at the casino. I tried calling Vinnie to tell him you were back in Atlantic City, but I couldn't reach him. So, I hired a private investigator to tail you from the Howard Johnson after we met there."

"Vinnie was already dead when you tried calling him, and I'm certain Corelli was killed by the same man who killed Charlie

Mungo, a very good friend of mine who was mistaken for me, and Angela DiMarco."

"Please, I swear on my mother's life. I don't know about any of that. All I wanted to do was help my father—get out of this hell hole and back into the family."

Freddy Fingers was clearly terrified.

"If you had asked your old man about it, he would have told you what he told me. Lincoln was not a threat to him."

"My father won't even talk to me. Do you have any idea what that's like?"

"I don't. My father talked so much when he was drinking, I had to shut him up."

I changed the subject.

"The name Mario Grillo ring a bell?"

"I know the name. And Vinnie Corelli asked if I knew how to find Grillo, I told him I didn't."

I believed him.

"You haven't seen me since the day Theodore Lincoln was killed," I said, "do you understand?"

"Yes."

"I can't help feeling you are to some extent responsible for all of this carnage, and it makes me very angry."

I reached across the table, punched Freddy in the head with all I had, and sent him and the chair backwards to the floor.

I finished off my drink and put the weapon back into the shoulder holster.

"If I find out that you are holding out on me or are more than partly responsible for Grillo's killing spree, I will hurt you very, very badly. Meanwhile, I would strongly suggest you stay out of sight. Don't bother getting up," I said, and I left the house.

Someone had contracted Mario Grillo, and had kept him very busy.

It wasn't Vincent Corelli, unless Vinnie put a hit on himself. I couldn't see Corelli dreaming up so imaginative a suicide.

I believed the denials of both Freddy Fingers and his father.

Call it deductive reasoning. Call it the process of elimination. Call it the last resort.

There was only one avenue left to investigate—the road I suspected I would inevitably land on minutes after Theodore Lincoln's head landed on the table. I would need help negotiating that road, and it would have to come from someone with a badge.

Someone who might not hold me accountable for murder.

I ruled out Detective Lawrence of the Atlantic City PD. I didn't really know him, didn't particularly like him, and was not sure I trusted him.

I decided against Detective Sullivan of the NYPD. I knew Sullivan too well, liked him a lot, and I refused to put John in a compromising position.

I was left with one final candidate, and a confrontation which I hated to consider.

But when there is only one choice, even when it is a very difficult choice, it is not a hard one to make.

It would have to wait, until some of the dust had settled and grieving families had time to say their goodbyes.

And the waiting would be the hardest part.

I decided I would wait it out in Newark, to avoid difficult to answer questions in Brooklyn.

So, after leaving Freddy Fingers on the mat in his living room, I once again took a two-hour drive north.

I checked into a Holiday Inn on Route 9 near the airport with a full bottle of scotch and I drank myself to sleep.

The next morning, I woke up famished.

I ordered breakfast and a newspaper from Room Service. Eggs, potatoes, bacon, toast, juice and coffee.

I devoured every scrap and I washed it all down with scotch.

An obituary in the Newark Star Ledger gave me the details on the where and when. The funeral and burial were scheduled for the following day at Mount Olivet Cemetery in Bloomfield.

I kept drinking. Tried reading to pass the time, the book Angela had given me, but I couldn't focus my eyes or my mind.

I kept drinking. Tried watching a shoot 'em up Western on the TV, but I kept drifting in and out of sleep.

I dreamed of Tom Romano, cruising out to sea on his houseboat, never to be seen again.

I dreamed of Theodore Lincoln, his damaged head hitting the poker table, again and again.

I dreamed of Vinnie Corelli and Charlie Mungo, offering to buy me a drink as thanks for cutting Mario Grillo's throat.

I woke up and took another drink.

Drink. Sleep. Drink. Sleep.

Seven in the evening. I needed food again.

I thought about going out for dinner, but realized I could hardly walk—let alone drive.

I called down to Room Service for a grilled Porterhouse steak. Twenty-four ounces, medium rare. Hold the salad. Hold the baked potato. Hold the vegetable.

Bring the beer.

Eat. Drink. Sleep. Drink. Sleep.

When I woke up again it was Wednesday morning.

At one that afternoon I watched as the large gathering at the burial site was breaking up.

Groups of two, three and four walking away to their vehicles.

An embrace between two grieving parents.

The priest led the woman away, leaving the father at the grave.

He stood there for nearly ten minutes, alone, before moving to join his wife.

I intercepted him on his way to the limousine.

I knew he would be tied up most of the day with friends and family. I had written a note on Holiday Inn stationery briefly explaining who I was and why I needed to speak with him.

"I'm sorry," I said, handing him the note.

He read the note, looked at me, looked toward the limousine and back to me again.

"I'll be at the hotel waiting to hear from you," I said.

"I'll come as soon as I can."

He turned and walked away.

As a means of distraction and to kill time, I spent most of the afternoon sightseeing.

The Empty Sky Memorial at Liberty State Park, a ferry ride to Ellis Island continuing on to the Statue of Liberty, a walk down the Hudson Walkway in Jersey City.

At all the stops I watched people.

Those reading the inscribed names of September 11th fatalities. Those hoping to learn something about their ancestors. Those gazing up in awe at the torch-carrying symbol of freedom. Those staring across the Hudson River at the breathtaking Manhattan skyline.

I wondered which of them had deceived another lately, had robbed or cheated or physically harmed another, which of them had been victims, and if justice could or would be served. I returned to the hotel to consider how justice *might* be served.

I sat and waited, in a staring contest with the half empty bottle of scotch, deciding to stay dry for the time being. Hoping I had found an ally.

Going over and over again what I needed to do and how I needed to do it.

He arrived at my room just after nine. I told him everything, from the moment Theodore Lincoln was killed to the moment I left Freddy Pugno on his back in Atlantic City. He listened quietly. Stoically. I told him how I had dealt with Mario Grillo, a confession to first degree murder. He remained silent. His reaction unreadable. I explained what I had in mind for the next day, and told him how he could help.

Finally, he spoke.

"Are you saving that for something?" he asked, indicating the half full bottle of scotch.

I poured the drinks.

We talked it out until we agreed on a worthy plan.

Then he spoke proudly about his daughter until all of the scotch was gone.

24

I woke late Thursday morning. I could not remember being haunted by disturbing dreams. Good sign. I was feeling optimistic. I drove straight down the shore into Atlantic City and to the Resorts Hotel and Casino.

Resorts International purchased the historic site of the Haddon House in 1976 while generously funding the campaign to pass the gaming referendum which became law that year. The Haddon Hall building had been constructed in stages during the 1920's, and was the largest hotel in Atlantic City when completed. Resorts became the first legal gambling casino in the United States outside of Nevada when its doors opened in May 1978. In 2010 renovation of Haddon Hall, now called Ocean Tower, began transforming the hotel and casino to recall the Roaring Twenties.

Boardwalk Empire revisited.

It suited my mood.

I was informed by the desk clerk that I had stumbled across the very last unoccupied room in the building.

"We received a cancellation just a few minutes ago," she said. "I'm sure you wouldn't find another accommodation in town before the end of the holiday weekend."

"Sold," I said.

"I can't get you into your room before two."

"No problem."

"You are very lucky, Mr. Ventura."

"We'll see."

I had a few hours to kill. I decided on lunch, I wasn't sure when I would find another opportunity to eat. Dining accomplished, I took a seat on an empty Boardwalk bench and sent the text message from Vincent Corelli's cell.

CELL PHONE FOR SALE. $250,000. ONE DAY ONLY.

At half past two I went back to the hotel, checked into my room, and did what I had developed quite a knack for lately.

I waited.

A response came within the hour.

BE AT THE HOUSE AT 8. BRING THE PHONE.

I immediately made the call to Angela's father.

"Can you be down to the Resorts Hotel by six?" I asked.

"I'll be there. By the way."

"Yes?"

"I reached out to police ballistics' departments in both Ocean City and Egg Harbor Township. The shooter in Ocean City used 5.7x28mm SS197SR V-Max cartridges, common to the FN Five-seveN. The bullets that killed Charlie Mungo were thirty-two caliber—most commonly used with a Colt positive police special or a handgun out of India called the IOF thirty-two."

"Different weapons."

"Different shooters," DiMarco said. "I'll see you at six."

I called John Sullivan

"Where the fuck are you?"

"I'm still in Atlantic City. I have a question."

"I have a hundred fucking questions," he yelled.

"The two bullets Corelli took in the chest, were they thirty-two caliber?"

"Yes. Lucky guess? Do you know who killed Corelli?"

"I'm working on it. I hope to have something for you later tonight."

"That's it?"

"Yes. Sorry."

"You will be a lot sorrier if I don't hear from you tonight," he said, and ended the conversation.

One of the few useful lessons I picked up from my old man was that the decision to bluff was an educated choice, based on an intuitive understanding of when bluffing was advisable and when to rule it out.

Unfortunately, at the meeting later that evening, folding would not be an option.

25

I rang the doorbell at eight. The door opened almost simultaneously.

She was wearing silk pajamas. Two-piece. Pure white.

Probably cost more than my suit.

White was clearly her color.

"Surprised?" I asked.

"No. I couldn't imagine who else it would be. The text message was very theatrical."

"It got your attention."

"It did. I was curious to see a cell phone worth a quarter million dollars. Are you coming in?"

"Sure," I said.

I followed Kitty Lincoln into the house and back to the kitchen.

"Scotch?"

"No, thank you."

"Make yourself comfortable."

I took a seat at the table and she sat opposite me.

"Why are you still around?" she asked.

If she was asking why I was still alive, I could only call it luck.

"You brought me around, when you approached me at that poker table right after your husband was killed. Remind me why you did."

"I told you, I wanted to find out who was responsible for my husband's death."

"We both know that's not true."

"What's on your mind?"

"Revealing phone calls, voice and text messages between you and Vinnie Corelli."

"I don't believe they exist."

"Because they never existed, or because you can't believe Vinnie was too stupid to delete them all."

"The extent of Vinnie's stupidity could never amaze me, but I'm no idiot. If you have what you say you have, I would love to see or hear it."

Time to bluff and go all in.

"You should have grabbed his phone when you had the chance. When did you and Vinnie decide you could have a future as a rich widow?"

"What are you talking about?"

"I'm guessing it was when you first caught Theodore Lincoln's eye, while you and Vinnie were still hitched."

"What do you want?"

"I want two hundred and fifty thousand dollars for starters."

"And?"

"Some answers."

"Is that it?"

"What else do you have in mind?"

"Doesn't the private investigator always end up in bed with the femme fatale?"

"Business before pleasure. Who killed Vinnie?"

"I don't know. Charlie Mungo?"

"If so, then who killed Mungo?"

"I don't know."

"And with Corelli and Mungo gone, who enlisted someone

to kill me?"

"I don't know."

"For such a clever girl, you don't seem to know much."

"Educate me."

"A showgirl meets a blackjack dealer. Love. Marriage. No real prospects. Along comes a rich attorney with an eye for beauty and a false sense of charm. The perfect mark. Easy prey. Girl and boy find their meal ticket."

"Risky. The wife and her lover are always the prime suspects."

"Both have solid alibis. The shocked wife is in plain sight. The lover is somewhere up in Connecticut. Throw in several red herrings. Freddy Fingers, his father's double-crossing ex-lawyer, a mob hit man, and a Brooklyn PI too curious for his own good."

"And?"

"And as long as Mungo didn't talk, it was clear sailing. Mungo had to be silenced, but Vinnie wouldn't have signed on so Corelli had to go also. Freddy never knew enough to be a serious threat. He conveniently served to muddy the waters. And then there was me, I was the wildcard, a loose end. Mungo may have given me something damning."

"Did he?"

"Vinnie's cell phone."

"It's a very imaginative story, but I don't see how it implicates me. There is no real proof."

"The cell phone is enough to open up a whole new line of investigation. And there is Mario Grillo."

"I don't know who that is."

"Mario Grillo is the man who killed two friends of mine in a failed attempt to murder me."

"That must have enraged you. I'm sure you would like him to pay."

"I dealt with Grillo, after he told me you hired him. Now I would like *you* to pay."

"Are you going to kill me?"

"That's much too melodramatic, and it wouldn't change anything. I gave you my price, two hundred fifty grand for the cell phone and then goodbye and good luck."

"It's a deal, but I would still like to see the phone first."

I took Corelli's cell from my jacket pocket and placed it on the table.

"Would you like that scotch now?" Kitty asked, rising and moving to the liquor cabinet.

"Sure."

She pulled out a couple of glasses. Then she reached into the cabinet again, pulled out a handgun and aimed it at me.

"I've never seen one like that before," I said.

"It's called an IOF thirty-two. I understand it is a favorite of the Singapore Police Force. My husband picked it up on a trip to India. Theodore gave it to me for protection. And so here we are, Mr. Ventura. The frightened woman alone in her home and the terrifying intruder."

"It wouldn't be smart using the same weapon that killed Vinnie Corelli and Charlie Mungo."

"You are absolutely right. Lucky for me the police arrived just in the nick of time," she said, looking past me over my shoulder.

I turned to discover Detective Lawrence of the Atlantic City PD standing behind me gripping a .44 like Dirty Harry.

Talk about being between a rock and a hard case.

"Are you going to shoot me in the back?"

"I would rather you stood up and faced me," Lawrence said.

I did.

"Love or money?" I asked.

"Love of money. Take out your weapon and put it on the table."

I took out the .357 and placed it next to the cell phone.

"I wouldn't trust her," I said.

"I'm really not interested in your opinion," Lawrence said, just before the gunshot that brought him to the floor.

Kitty turned to the shooter and pointed the IOF.

"Don't," he warned, staring straight into her green eyes, and she dropped the gun to the floor.

Lawrence was moaning at my feet. He had taken the bullet just above the knee. I kicked his gun away and wrapped my tie around his thigh to slow the bleeding. Then I turned to Angela DiMarco's father.

"You didn't identify yourself first," I said.

"I forgot. Call an ambulance, and find the local police," Detective DiMarco said, producing a pair of handcuffs, "and you, Mrs. Lincoln, lock your fingers behind your head."

I unbuttoned my shirt and removed the wire while he cuffed Kitty and sat her in a chair. I placed the transmitter beside my gun and Corelli's cell phone.

"I'm guessing from your timely arrival that it did the job."

"Angela used only the best equipment. We got everything we needed, loud and clear. Unfortunately, we missed a little of the conversation you had with the suspect right before she pulled the gun."

All mention of Mario Grillo and his just reward.

We joined the stunned woman at the kitchen table and waited for reinforcements to arrive.

It was going to be a long night.

EPILOGUE
POCKET QUEENS

The Margate City police arrived as the EMTs were preparing to transport Detective Lawrence to the hospital. Lawrence was read his rights and formally arrested, charged with aiding and abetting a felon. The detective was talking a blue streak. Convinced I was somehow involved in the death of Theodore Lincoln, Lawrence had been staking out my hotel in Egg Harbor when he witnessed Katherine Lincoln put two bullets into Charlie Mungo's back. Instead of doing his sworn duty, he approached the widow to suggest a lucrative deal for his silence. Now, before they could get him into the ambulance, Lawrence was offering to make a new deal in exchange for testimony against Mrs. Lincoln.

We probably saved Lawrence's life. The detective had as little chance of surviving Kitty's housecleaning as Mungo and Corelli did. They were doomed from the start, Katherine Ann Harris 'Kit Kat' Corelli Lincoln was entirely prepared to eliminate anyone and everyone who could possibly stand between her and her full inheritance.

DiMarco and I handed Kitty over to the Egg Harbor police, along with the weapon used to kill Charlie Mungo.

I called John Sullivan to inform him that Vinnie Corelli's assassin was in custody.

DiMarco said he would send copies of the conversation in Kitty's kitchen to both Egg Harbor and the NYPD.

Dominic DiMarco drove me back up to the Resorts Hotel.

"I'm very sorry I put your daughter in harm's way."

"It wasn't you who brought her into to it, and Angela always made her own choices. I'm sorry about your friend, and I respect you for not turning your back on them and for doing what needed to be done. We have a family reunion in Ocean City every Labor Day weekend. Angela would have wanted us to keep the tradition. You're welcome to drop in."

"I'll try," I said.

I walked down to the waterside to stare out over the Atlantic, sizing myself up—a small man facing a mighty ocean trying to hold my own and live with my own choices. A huge world filled with little people capable of causing monstrous damage or, for too short a time, shining a faint light in the darkness. Where guilt was often quantified and being innocent could never guarantee victory. And no one was equipped to keep score.

Demons and angels, and those in my business who thought they could jump into the muddy fray and stay clean.

I was too wired to consider sleep so I found myself at a poker table. I was doing well. Not wishing to press my luck, I decided to play one final hand. Two cards were dealt down to each player. I looked at my pocket cards.

A pair of queens.

I folded.

MYSTERIOUS WAYS

I sat at the reception desk of Diamond Investigations at nine on Monday morning. It was unusually early for me to be at the office.

My associate, Darlene Roman, who traditionally occupied the front-room desk much more effectively, had taken off the previous afternoon for a sojourn in Las Vegas.

"What's in Vegas?" I had asked.

"I don't know, nobody is telling."

It was the first day of February, a typical San Francisco midwinter morning—forty-three degrees, humid, mostly cloudy, chance of light rain.

Darlene had taken care of all the first-of-the-month business required to keep the office functioning, lights operational, telephone on line, wolves from the door.

She had left me very little to do other than sit at her desk testing a theory suggesting that if the phone bill was paid the thing might actually ring once in a while.

Or read a book.

At the moment, I was halfway into *Great Expectations* and not feeling particularly optimistic.

Between page turns, I took a quick bite from a buttered hard roll and sipped from a gone-cold paper cup of coffee from the delicatessen below.

There was a rapping at the door.

Two tentative knocks.

I was about to rise, cross the room, and let my visitor into the office—but saw no reason to amend Darlene's customary protocol. I cleared the coffee and roll from the desk instead.

"It's open," I called.

The door swung into the room revealing a man of fifty or so—imposing, six-two, two-twenty, unthreatening. The gray suit was well-tailored but worn. The white shirt was wrinkle-free and the necktie was tight to the collar. The shoes were practical. He took a step across the threshold and stopped short. I nearly said *come in close the door take a seat*—but I stood and walked over to the stranger instead.

"Jake Diamond," I said, extending an arm.

"Henry Campbell," the man replied, accepting the handshake.

I gently guided Campbell clear of the entryway, shut the door, ushered him to the client chair and invited him to sit. I thought about offering a cup of coffee but remembered *no Darlene, none made.*

I moved around to the opposite side of the desk and sat.

Something in the man's demeanor, an absence of any air of superiority, inspired me to go *familiar.*

"So, Mr. Campbell—may I call you Henry?"

"Sure."

"Good. How can I help you, Henry?"

"My daughter, Elizabeth, twenty-six, registered nurse at St. Mary's, shares a flat with two other girls in the Upper Haight."

Campbell stopped there and turned his attention to his hands, which were neatly folded in his lap.

I gave him a few moments.

"Henry?"

Campbell looked up at me—then slowly looked around the room as if trying to recall where he was and why he was there.

"Someone has been using Elizabeth as a punching bag. It's been going on for a while. I noticed small signs weeks ago, but she explained them away—a spill from her bicycle, a low tree branch. When the injuries became more serious, she offered no explanation at all. When she showed up at my house Friday night, she could hardly walk. I'm a widower, she's my only child."

"Have you spoken to the police?"

"She won't tell me who is responsible and insists she will not talk to the police."

"Is it a boyfriend? Someone she's protecting?"

"It may have started that way but I think now she is frightened, afraid to talk. And *I'm* afraid if something isn't done to stop it, she will suffer permanent injury or worse. I need to find out who is hurting my girl."

"And if you do?"

"I haven't thought that far ahead," Campbell said. "Try talking to the man, I suppose."

I shadowed Elizabeth Campbell for two days.

Late Wednesday afternoon I tailed her from St. Mary's to the Barrel Head Brewhouse on Fulton—a hop, skip and jump from the hospital.

I waited ten minutes before following her into the pub.

I spotted them sitting on adjoining stools at the bar and I took an empty seat at the far end.

He was a good-looking man, early thirties, who seemed to have a smile for everyone. At first glance, they may have been seen as a handsome couple. On closer inspection, she physically cowered beside him. At one point, when Elizabeth began to rise from her seat, he roughly grabbed her wrist and sat her down.

A bartender arrived. A nametag on her blue denim vest identified her as *Annie*. I ordered George Dickel—had to settle for Jack Daniels.

"Casanova, at the other end of the bar," I asked when she brought my drink. "Do you know his name?"

She took a quick look as she set the whiskey down.

"Never saw him before," she said, and walked off.

Twenty minutes later he literally dragged Elizabeth Campbell out of the place by her elbow. I thought about following but felt I still had a shot with Annie. I waved her over.

"Another?" she asked.

"I'm good," I said, dropping a twenty on the bar. "Can you help me out?"

"He's not a nice man and he would not be happy with anyone dropping his name."

"What he doesn't know can't hurt you," I said, sliding a hundred dollar bill her way.

"Richard Konnor," Annie said, "with a K. Have a nice evening, somewhere else."

She quickly walked away and I left the pub.

I climbed into my car and pulled out my cell phone.

I was about to call my client, but decided I wanted to know a little more about Richard Konnor before giving his name to Henry Campbell. I still had at least one favor coming from an SFPD Detective Sergeant. I called the Vallejo Street Station to see if Johnson was there.

We sat in front of a computer at the sergeant's desk in the police station.

"I don't suppose you are going to tell me why you are interested in this guy," Johnson said.

I treated it as a rhetorical question. He let it go.

"There had been talk going around that Konnor played rough with the ladies, but no one ever came forward with a complaint. Then a young woman managed to walk herself into the Emergency Room at St. Francis Hospital, badly battered, claiming Richard Konnor beat her and threw her out of his car. He was brought in for questioning and denied everything. A preliminary hearing was scheduled but before the date arrived the woman retracted her statement."

"Scared off?"

"Or bought off. This guy is literally Little Richie Rich. His old man is one of the most successful developers in the Bay Area. Lots of political clout, a ton of money, and very proficient at keeping junior on the street."

"So, this maniac skates?"

"Unless someone without my constraints cancels his skating permit."

Suddenly we spotted Lieutenant Laura Lopez moving across the room to Johnson's desk. The sergeant killed the browser.

"Jake Diamond," she said, "why are you here?"

Lopez was seldom pleased to see me.

"I needed the sergeant's advice."

"About?"

"He's looking for a reliable and honest automobile mechanic," Johnson said.

"Aren't we all," Lopez said.

I thanked Johnson, said my goodbyes, and headed for my car.

I called Henry Campbell.

He said six words before ending the connection.

St. Mary's Hospital Intensive Care Unit.

I found him in the ICU.

He was standing beside the bed, looking down at his daughter. She was encased in a tangle of wires and tubes and bandages.

"Will she be alright?"

"Physically, eventually," Henry Campbell said, "emotionally, hopefully."

"I know how you must feel," I said, having no real idea. "If there is anything I can do."

"You can tell me who did this to my little girl."

"Henry, let the police handle this. They know about the guy—he has a history. There's a Detective Sergeant who will do whatever it takes to drop a net over the animal. If your daughter will come forward, other victims may do the same. He would be put away for a very long time."

"You say he has done this before?"

"Yes."

"He nearly killed her," Campbell said, "this time. What is his name?"

"His name is Richard Konnor. His father is some kind of high-powered developer."

"I would like time alone with her now," he said, finally looking up at me. "What do I owe you?"

"Not a thing," I said.

And I left him standing at his daughter's side.

I'm not sure what brought me back to the Barrel Head—but there I was close to midnight draining my third drink.

Annie the bartender recommended I go with straight Kentucky bourbon as a Dickel substitute this go-around.

"Sorry if I was rude earlier," she said, "and thanks for the C-note. I need brakes for my car. Do you know any reliable, honest auto mechanics?"

"None," I said.

She poured another shot of Booker's, insisting it was on the house.

"He put her in the hospital."

"Who put who in the hospital?"

"Richard Konnor. The girl he dragged out of here. He put her in the hospital."

"I'm sorry to hear that," Annie said.

"He nearly killed her."

"And you're wondering if things might have gone differently if you had followed them out."

"Yes. And why he wasn't locked up in a cage long ago."

"The answer to the first question is *probably not*. The answer to the second question is *there's no good reason*. Have you had anything to eat lately?"

"I don't recall."

Annie picked up the shot she had poured for me and knocked it down herself. She filled a tall glass with water and placed it in front of me.

"I'm done here in ten minutes," she said. "Drink the water, all of it. I'll take you out for breakfast."

Darlene would be back at her post early, so I was in no real hurry to get down to the office on Friday morning.

I sat in the large backyard of my house in the Presidio, drinking strong coffee, smoking a Camel non-filter, gazing at the Golden Gate Bridge partially obscured by clouds.

My cell phone shouted out The Beatles' *Hello, Goodbye*—something Darlene had arranged when she helped set up the voice mail.

It was Sergeant Johnson.

"Do you have time for breakfast?" he asked.

"Sure."

"Pat's Café work for you?"

"Sure, give me an hour."

I found Johnson at a small table near the front window looking out onto Taylor Street.

I sat and he got right to it.

"I thought you might be interested in knowing Richard Konnor was killed late last night."

"Murdered?"

"No. A traffic accident, but whoever hit him didn't stick around—so we're calling it a felony hit and run."

"Was Konnor driving?"

"He was walking, crossing Frederick toward his apartment. According to toxicology he was pretty drunk. He probably forgot to look both ways, and the impact knocked him into next week."

"Witnesses?"

"It was after three in the morning. Two people saw it from a distance. It was a truck. Neither could make out a license plate or any markings. Both described it simply as a very large white truck. Funny."

"Funny?"

"Ironic, then," Johnson said. "Here's a guy who may have killed someone eventually, kept dodging bullets, and he steps in front of a truck."

"Fate works in mysterious ways," I said.

A waitress arrived to pour coffee and take our order.

"You should try the poached eggs with Hollandaise," Johnson said.

"The only way I can eat an egg is if it's scrambled and burned."

When I walked into the office, Darlene was behind her desk. Her trusty canine, Tug McGraw, was curled up at her feet.

"He missed me," she said.

"How was Las Vegas?"

"I was sworn to secrecy. Did Henry get in touch with you?"

"Henry?"

"We were drinking iced tea and he spotted one of your business cards on the kitchen counter. He said he had been looking to hire an investigator, asked if you were any good. I said you were okay and gave him the card."

"And how did *Henry* come to be in your kitchen?"

"Do you remember me telling you my refrigerator died?"

"Vaguely."

"The only solution I could think of was to pop for a new one, so I did. Henry delivered the new box on Saturday."

"Did he drive a truck?"

"A very large white truck."

"How's the new refrigerator?"

"Very cool."

L.A. FREEWAY

I was sitting at the bar in the Power House on Highland Avenue in Hollywood staring at my empty beer bottle.

I had been thinking a lot about getting away from Los Angeles before my chances were less than slim—and before Susanna got tired of waiting.

I must have been thinking out loud because the first thing Jimmy Stills said when he pulled up a stool beside me was, "I found your ticket out."

Jimmy started in about a big score, a valuable coin collection, throwing in catch phrases like *easy pickings* and *falling off a log.*

I didn't know anything about Jimmy's experience with logs—but had seen him fall off a bar stool once or twice.

"What do you know about coins?" I asked.

"I ran into Billy Mullins."

"With your pickup truck I hope."

"Twenty rare gold coins, you could fit them in a Cracker Jack box, worth over a million. Mullins knows how to get at them and he has a buyer lined up. He needs help."

"What for? He and his psychopath brother need a hand finding an empty snack box?"

"Roy is out of the picture, back east on some other gig. Billy just wants to talk with you. He'll be here tonight at ten."

"I'll think about it," I said.

I threw a twenty down for old man Clancy behind the bar

and headed for the door.

Out on the avenue I stood awhile.

Watching the losers and the lost go by.

I needed to hear from Susanna, again, about how desperately she wanted to say goodbye to all this concrete.

Susanna was doing her devil's advocate thing.

"You said you would never work with Mullins again."

"I said I wouldn't be in the same room with Roy Mullins. The man is a head case. Billy is fairly harmless. He's also dumb as a box of rocks, so this may be nothing—but I see no harm in hearing what he has to say."

"And if it's *something*?"

"Then we can decide."

"Together."

"Together. And if it's *really* something, we can pack up all the dishes."

"I guess it won't hurt to hear what he has on his mind," Susanna said, "but I want to know every detail."

I walked into the Power House at ten.

I looked around the room, taking in all the players.

The cast of characters hadn't changed much.

I walked up to the bar.

Clancy was pouring shots for Tommy Conlon and Kevin Doyle.

"Have you seen Jimmy Stills?" I asked.

"He said they needed somewhere private, I said they could use the office. He's with Billy Mullins."

"I know."

"If you're smart, you'll go the other way."

Clancy thought I reminded him of a son he had lost to gambling and alcohol. He tried to look out for me.

"It's my night to be stupid. Pour me a Jameson. Make it a double."

I carried my drink back to the office where Billy surprised me with an impressive presentation.

"The nineteen-thirty-one Saint-Gaudens double eagle. A twenty-dollar face-value coin—weighing a little more than an ounce. The gold value is just over a grand. Market value, mint condition, seventy-five grand. There are twenty of them."

I quickly did the math. One and a half million.

"I have a buyer. Our end is seven hundred fifty thousand," Mullins added.

"Who's going to give us fifty cents on the dollar?"

"The owner. Philip Simon. He scores the insurance settlement and then gets to keep his precious coins. He will be out of town with plenty of witnesses when we hit his place."

"So, why do you need us?"

"Jimmy will stay outside—keep an eye out and the engine running."

"And me?"

"You get us past the security system. It needs to look like a legitimate break-in. Simon can't give us the disarm code, but he gave me everything else you need to know about the system set up. With your talents it will be a walk in the park," Mullins said, handing me the alarm system schematics.

It appeared both Billy and Jimmy had brushed up on their metaphors for the occasion.

I gave the specs a quick look over and had to agree—it would be like taking candy from a baby.

"What's the split?"

"A hundred fifty thousand for Jimmy—you and I split the rest equally. When Simon returns to Los Angeles, we'll all meet him for the exchange."

"How did Simon find you—in the yellow pages?"

"He's a lawyer. He helped me and Roy out of a jam a year ago."

"No offense," I said, although I couldn't care less if I broke his heart. "If I see Roy anywhere near us, I'm gone."

"My brother is in Jersey cooking up some action with Johnny Roselli. He won't be back for at least a month."

"I'll have to think about it."

"Think fast. Simon leaves town on Friday and we go in Saturday night."

My old man was an Indiana farmer and the son of an Indiana farmer and, when he lost the family farm, he moved us down to Texas where he would work on a farm because it was all he knew how to do. And dream.

He mostly dreamed of California. He talked about the sunshine and the palm trees, the convertible sports cars and mansions, and the freeways paved with gold.

He idolized James Dean, the Indiana farm boy who went to Hollywood and became immortal.

I remember my father coming into my room one night when I was eight years old. He woke me. We sat and looked at the pictures in a book. *Los Angeles, the City of Angels.* Dad promised that someday he would take my mother and me to the Pacific Ocean. He died a week later.

After his death I was in and out of trouble, in and out of schools, in and out of reformatories, breaking in and stealing out of people's homes, and finally in and out of Huntsville State Penitentiary where I learned a trade that would help me get past alarm systems in other people's homes.

When my mother passed away, and I was going through her things, I came across the book my father had brought into my room years before.

I decided to live out his dream. The only thing in my life that would be difficult for me to leave behind was Susanna. Luckily, she believed in me and signed on for the move to California.

But luck ran out and it didn't take long to discover the Los

Angeles of my father's dreams was only real in picture books.

I walked into the apartment just before midnight.

It was as unappealing as when I left.

I could hear Skinny Dennis playing his electric bass guitar next door.

Susanna was waiting up for me.

I ran it down for her.

"Three hundred thousand dollars," she said.

"Yes."

"In three days?"

"Yes."

"Do you trust Billy Mullins?"

"About as far as I can throw him—but if push comes to shove, I can throw him pretty far."

"So?"

"So, Columbus took a chance."

If you have a mind to, you can always come up with rationalizations for criminal behavior. A popular excuse is the allusion of a *victimless crime*. I was about to help someone rob himself to rip-off an insurance company. No foul.

I bought it.

The heart of the matter? I came to Los Angeles with nothing and I was determined not to leave with nothing.

At eleven on Saturday night, I was standing out on Vine Street when the late model Infiniti pulled up to the curb with Jimmy behind the wheel and Billy Mullins in back.

"Nice ride," I said, settling in beside Stills.

"Borrowed it off a dealership lot in Van Nuys," Jimmy said.

"How long before someone discovers it's missing?"

"Long enough," Mullins said. "Let's move."

The house was in Manhattan Beach—a hop and a skip from the sand and surf.

It was a modest sized home surrounded by all of the trees and shrubbery necessary for privacy.

It took me less than ten minutes to disable the alarms and another few seconds to get us in through the back door.

The gold pieces were exactly where their owner had said they would be. They sat out in the open on a large desk in the study in a twelve-inch by ten-inch glass-topped mahogany case. Four rows of five coins. Ten displayed Liberty and ten displayed the double eagle on the reverse side.

Billy Mullins placed the box into a plastic grocery bag.

We left the house and walked casually to where Jimmy Stills waited in the car. I was a few steps ahead of Billy and I hopped into the back seat.

Jimmy stopped the Infiniti to let me out on Vine. As I turned to move off, Billy called me back to the passenger side window.

"I'll let you know the where and when for the exchange. Don't forget to bring this," he said, handing me the grocery bag without ceremony.

And Jimmy quickly pulled away.

The bag and its contents weighed less than five pounds.

I carried it into the apartment.

Susanna was asleep on the sofa. I gently laid the bag down on an end table and went to the kitchen to pour a whiskey.

When I came back into the front room, Susanna was sitting up with the display case resting on her lap.

"What do you see?" I asked.

Susanna looked up into my eyes.

"A piece of land back home, room to grow food, raise horses, breathe. A chance to get off of this L.A. Freeway."

"I'll drink to that."

Susanna looked back down at the gold coins.

"They are really beautiful," she said.

. . .

I heard from Jimmy Stills on Monday. The exchange would take place at Philip Simon's office in Glendale. It was a converted warehouse. A number of retail shops and professional businesses.

Doctors. Architects. Lawyers.

The building would be shut down and deserted by nine.

Jimmy would pick me up at eleven.

At ten-thirty, Susanna took a last look at the gold coins.

"I'd love to keep one."

"I could probably buy you one for seventy-five thousand dollars."

She placed the case into the plastic grocery bag and handed it to me.

"Watch your back," she said.

"I thought *you* had my back."

She gave me a hard punch to the chest.

"What was that for?"

"A reminder to dress appropriately," she said, and she left the apartment.

Just before eleven I walked out onto Vine to wait for Stills. He pulled up in his pickup a few minutes later and I climbed in beside him.

As we approached the freeway entrance, Susanna's words echoed in my head.

Get off of this L.A. Freeway.

L.A. Freeway is not found on any map. It is not a single route into or out of Los Angeles. L.A. Freeway is a term sometimes used to describe the maze of interconnected roadways stretching out from the city like the legs of a spider.

Hollywood, Ventura, Santa Ana, Century, Santa Monica, Long Beach.

It's a web—ensnaring the California dreamer like a spider traps a fly.

We exited the leg called the Golden State Freeway at Hyperion Boulevard and crossed the L.A. River into Glendale. As we approached the building, I had one hope.

Get off the L.A. Freeway without being killed or caught.

When we walked into the office they were waiting.

Philip Simon. Billy Mullins standing beside him.

An open attaché case on the desk filled with cash.

I took a few steps toward the desk.

Suddenly Billy had a gun to Simon's temple. He pulled the trigger. The man was dead before he hit the deck.

Then two shots from somewhere behind me and Jimmy Stills went down.

I turned—the plastic grocery bag with its treasure still in my hand.

I recognized Roy Mullins a moment before he shot me.

My last thought before my head crashed to the floor was *Susanna, don't you cry for me.*

When I opened my eyes, I was in my own bed.

Susanna was sitting in a chair watching me.

"What time is it?"

"Morning. You've been in and out all night. How is your head?"

"Feels like it was bounced across a hardwood floor," I said, as I managed to sit up.

"Jimmy is dead. You took three shots to the chest. The vest saved your life."

"The best present you ever gave me. It was Roy Mullins."

"I know. We heard the gunshots and saw Billy and Roy running out just before we ran in."

"We?"

"I brought Clancy along for support. You were out cold.

He's a strong old timer. I could never have carried you out of there alone."

As if on cue, Clancy walked into the room holding a brown paper bag.

"Coffee and donuts," he said.

"Nice."

"The police received an anonymous tip and caught up with the Mullins boys. Billy and Roy tried to shoot it out. They were both killed."

"Thanks for your help."

"No worries. I need to run."

"I thought you didn't open the bar until ten."

"I have to get to Sunday Mass first," Clancy said, and he was gone.

"Well," Susanna said.

"Well?"

"I guess we're here for a while," she said.

"Do me a favor."

"Sure."

"You know the tin box I keep on the mantle?" I asked.

"The one you think you're hiding your cigarettes in?"

"That's the one. Please bring it in here."

"Pretty heavy for a pack of Camel straights," she said when she handed me the tin.

I pulled off the lid and spilled the contents onto my lap.

Ten 1931 Saint-Gaudens double eagle gold coins.

"How much are they worth?"

"At thirty cents on the dollar—twenty to twenty-five grand. Apiece."

"Less than I was hoping for," Susanna said, "but it will work."

Skinny Dennis helped us load the car.

Later, we drank a farewell to the apartment—standing in the

front room with whiskey in paper cups.

"I'm going to gas up the car," Susanna said. "I'll hit the horn three times when I get back."

She gave Dennis a hug.

"We'll be looking out for your hit record," she said.

When she left, I offered Dennis another drink.

"I have to bounce. Band rehearsal. I'm going to miss you guys."

"You and old man Clancy are about all *I'm* going to miss. I hope your dreams come true."

We shook hands and he headed for the door.

"And, Dennis," I said, as he was moving out into the hallway.

"Yes?"

"Say goodbye to the landlord for me."

A few minutes later I heard Susanna's signal.

I stepped out of the apartment and closed the door behind me.

I reached into my pocket, pulled out the key, and left it in the door lock.

NOT THE WAY IT LOOKS

Dominic Ventura was a gambler and a drunk.

Although he never raised a hand to her, he succeeded in making my mother's life miserable.

My old man did raise a hand to me—until I was old enough to warn him against it.

Dominic was a laborer. Some of his days were spent doing backbreaking work. Most of his days were spent not working at all.

I had a troubled youth—I landed in a lot of hot water. Dominic never helped me out of it and he offered no fatherly guidance to keep me from falling into it.

I don't quote my father often—he had little useful to say. But there were a few things he did say before the drinking killed him that were worth storing away.

When someone claims *it's not the way it looks, it's usually exactly the way it is*, was one of them.

Brooklyn.

A stuffy, dusty, cluttered office two floors above a beauty salon on Neptune Avenue in Coney Island.

A light rap on the opaque glass pane.

"It's open."

The door swung into the room.

The visitor stood planted at the threshold.

"Nick Ventura?" he asked.

"How can I help you?"

"I need a very good private investigator."

"Come in," I said, reluctant to ask where he had heard I was very good. "Close the door, have a seat."

He walked slowly to the ancient oak table that served as my desk and offered a handshake.

I accepted.

"Jim Bishop," he said.

"Sit, Mr. Bishop," I said, releasing his hand, "May I call you Jim?"

He settled into the client chair across the table.

"I'm in danger," he began without ceremony. "There is a man out there who I believe will kill me if I say anything about what I saw."

"What did you see?"

"A murder."

"Have you talked to the police," I asked. I always ask.

"The police have no real suspects, and no solid leads. All I know is his face, and he knows mine. If I speak to the police now and he is following the investigation, he will know I came forward. Until he is positively identified and apprehended, I'm in jeopardy. I need to learn who he is before he learns who I am—and I need help."

"What can you tell me?"

"It all happened in a matter of seconds. It was the evening before last. I was walking past the house when I heard what sounded to me like a gunshot. I moved up to the front door and I heard another shot. I tried the door, it was unlocked. I acted impulsively—I'm not a brave man. I opened the door and the shooter turned to me. We made eye contact. We both froze for a moment. He began to raise his weapon and I ran."

"And you would know the man if you saw him again."

"Yes."

"And he would know you."

"Yes. And the intent in his eyes when he turned and saw me standing in the doorway was unmistakable. If looks could kill."

"Can you describe him?"

"I can," Bishop said. "Please, Mr. Ventura. If you can help me find this man—discover who and where he is, and do it without alerting him—then I will bring all I know to the police and pray they capture him before he gets to me."

"I don't know if I can be much help. There is not a lot to go on and, as I've learned the hard way, keeping information from the police, no matter how vague, is a recipe for grief. I need to think about it. If I decide to take the case, my fee is two hundred fifty dollars a day plus expenses. And I will need a retainer."

"Will cash do?" Bishop said, reaching into his jacket pocket.

He placed ten one-hundred-dollar bills on the table.

I do this job of investigation to help people in need, right wrongs, be free to bend rules occasionally, because I failed the NYPD employment background check, and sometimes it pays the utility bills.

There were more than a few debts that needed immediate attention.

"I'll need you to give me everything you can remember about the man—height, approximate weight, what he was wearing, in which hand he held the weapon, every detail of his face, hair color, eye color, distinguishing features. I'll need you to sign a standard client form."

I walked to the file cabinet. I pulled out several sheets of ruled paper, a contract form, and a fresh pen from a box of Sanford uni-ball rollers.

Bishop wrote notes. I tried to keep my eyes off the grand in cash.

He signed the contract.

"How do I reach you?" I asked.

"I'll call you," he said, rising from his seat, "and thank you."

With that he turned and left the office.

I placed the cash, the contract and the pen into the file cabinet and I returned to my chair. I looked at Bishop's notes.

I understood that finding the killer would be like trying to find a needle in a haystack, and that it would help a great deal if I knew which haystack.

I had the victim's name. I knew where he had been killed.

It was a start.

I needed to learn more about the victim, and learn where the police were in their investigation—learn if there were any persons of interest. The closest I had to an ally in the NYPD was Detective John Sullivan of the 70th Precinct.

John had helped me, unhappily, many times. But Sullivan was not fond of giving up information.

If I asked him what time it was, he would ask why.

The killing had taken place in Cobble Hill, covered by the detectives of the 76th Precinct. If I walked into the Seven-six, and asked about an ongoing murder investigation, the detectives would either hold me for questioning or toss me out the door.

I needed the assistance of someone who could ease suspicion—walk in, ask questions, and appear innocent of any hidden agenda.

It would also be useful if I could get Bishop's written description of the perpetrator rendered into picture form.

A sketch, even one lacking in exactness, could still be worth a thousand words.

Luckily, I knew someone who I believed might help on both scores.

Carmella Fazio was like an aunt. The connection between our families went back several generations. Carmella owned the building that housed the beauty shop and my office above. And Carmella was the proprietress of the renowned pizza parlor adjacent to the beauty shop.

Maria Leone was Carmella's niece. She was a graduate student at the John Jay College of Criminal Justice, where she had recently aced a course on sketch artistry. When she was not in class, she helped her aunt manage the restaurant. Occasionally she did a little research or field work for me—for the hands-on experience and a bit of textbook money.

I went down to the pizzeria and found Maria behind the counter.

After seeing Maria that Friday afternoon, asking her to attempt a sketch from Bishop's written description, and proposing a visit to the Seven-six the next day, I did some research on the murder—relying on newspaper accounts which offered little substance.

The victim was Richard Sherman.

Thirty-three years old, single, Caucasian, discovered by the police D.O.A. at his home following a 9-1-1 call Wednesday evening.

The investigation was ongoing.

An obituary posted in the *Daily News* informed me that Sherman was survived by his parents, brother and two sisters. The wake would be held at Cobble Hill Chapels on Court Street on Friday and Saturday, and the funeral service and burial was set for Sunday at Mount Olivet Cemetery in Maspeth, Queens.

I had a thought. Maybe the killer knew the victim. So well, in fact, that he felt obliged to show up at the funeral. I couldn't remember what movie that thought came from—so I put it on the back burner.

Maria needed to be on the upper west side of Manhattan for a class at eleven—so I drove her over to the 76th Precinct early Saturday morning.

Maria would claim she was working on a research paper for

one of her courses and would much appreciate the opportunity to speak with one of their detectives about a current investigation. We were hoping she could subtly steer the conversation toward the case in question.

I sat in my Monte Carlo outside the police station studying Maria's drawing.

It was an excellent rendition given what Maria had to work with. The face was distinct enough to eliminate the vast majority of mankind—but not nearly distinct enough to convict a suspect. I decided I needed to show the drawing to Jim Bishop.

Maria joined me in the car a few minutes after entering the precinct.

"That was quick."

"He's in there."

"Who's in there?"

She pointed to her drawing.

"Are you sure it's him?"

"Or someone who looks exactly like him."

"It would be quite a coincidence."

"Yes."

"I could wait for him to come out."

"You should. I can walk to the subway station from here. And, Nick."

"Yes?"

"If this could be the guy," she said, "be careful."

Maria left the car.

I sat and waited.

A year can seem to pass in a moment.

Sitting alone in a car for sixty minutes without the *New York Post* sports section or an egg, bacon and cheese on hard roll can seem to last forever.

It was the Fourth of July weekend. Manhattan may have been deserted, but Brooklyn was teeming with activity. Brooklynites celebrated their national holidays close to home and mom's cooking.

The suspect finally walked out of the precinct. I followed his car out Union Street. He turned right onto 4th Avenue, heading south. I watched the vehicle enter the Prospect Expressway and followed to a house in Midwood.

I was considering my options when my cell rang.

Jim Bishop.

Checking in.

"Can you meet me at my office?" I asked.

"How about the Del Rio Diner on Kings Highway?"

"Sure. I can be there in twenty minutes."

"Twenty minutes," Bishop said.

The Del Rio was open for business twenty-four hours a day, every day. It featured a menu as thick as a Tolstoy novel. Signed and framed photos on the walls bragged of patrons from Bill Clinton to James Gandolfini to Eli Manning.

I found Bishop at a window booth, hovering over a cup of coffee.

"Is this the man you saw Wednesday night?" I asked, placing Maria's drawing in front of him as I slid into the booth.

"Yes," he said, "do you know who he is?"

"I don't—but I followed him from the 76th Precinct."

"He was at the police station?"

"For more than an hour."

"Do you think he's a suspect?"

"I don't know—and I don't know how to ask without opening myself up to a lot of questions, and my answers could involve you."

"That's still not a good idea. I won't be safe until I know my identification will put him away—and I don't think this drawing will do it. I need to positively identify him. I need to see him. And I need you with me."

I wasn't sure I was ready to go the distance with Bishop, so I hedged.

"I can't take you out there right now," I said, "give me a few hours."

"I'll call you later," Bishop said, dropping a five-dollar bill on the table for the coffee.

And he was gone.

As I left the diner, I had the feeling I was acting recklessly. Granted, I was trying to protect someone in possible danger— but I wondered if it was vanity that had me believing I was a better ally than the men in blue.

On top of that, I knew as little about Bishop as I did about his suspect—and the possibility of putting the two men in close proximity, with me in the middle, made me uneasy.

I had some thinking to do.

With a few hours to kill, I headed to my crib.

I live on a houseboat docked at Sheepshead Bay. It had taken some time to become accustomed to the constant motion of the boat—particularly at bedtime.

Eventually it had become familiar, even soothing.

The Atlantic Ocean, its bays and its inlets, have always been a major part of growing up in South Brooklyn.

We were working class kids who were a stone's throw from the seaside all summer long. We had our own island.

Growing up in Coney Island, alongside the vastness of the ocean and the mysteries that lay beyond it, always helped me appreciate my relative size in relation to the world and the universe.

It could make a kid feel small.

It could make a man battle to become big enough to contend.

I sat on the deck of the houseboat, sipping a single-malt Scotch, and considered the angles. Follow through as the lone ranger, or strongly advise Jim Bishop to head straight to the police.

Maybe it was vanity, the mortal need to feel more significant. Or perhaps it was the thousand dollars sitting in the file cabinet at my office. In any case, I convinced myself it wouldn't hurt to stay in the game a little longer.

When Bishop called, I gave him my verdict.

"We need to go out there," he said.

"Is it absolutely necessary?"

"I need to see him in person, up close. When I'm sure he's the man I saw that night, we can head straight to the precinct, and I'll make a full statement. I can pick you up in front of your office in an hour."

"Take Ocean Parkway to Avenue I, take I to East Twenty-fourth, and turn left."

Bishop pulled over to the curb in front of the house. Brooklyn College was directly ahead of us.

"What now?" I asked.

Bishop began hitting his car horn repeatedly.

A light on the front porch came on.

A man walked out of the house and started moving toward the vehicle.

"Well?" I asked.

"That's him, no question."

A quick movement from Bishop caught my eye, and suddenly there was a gun in his hand. He raised his arm.

I looked from the weapon up to his face.

"It's not the way it looks," he said.

And then the lights went out.

The ammonium carbonate popped my eyes open.

I was on the ground.

A man in a white coat kneeled over me with a jar of smelling salts.

He helped me sit up.

"Sorry it took so long to get to you—we had more critical business to attend to," he said.

The EMT moved away, and a large man in a bad suit suddenly took his place.

"I'm Detective Ray Washington. You took a serious whack to the head, but you'll live," he said, taking care of the preliminaries, "and you have some explaining to do."

"What happened?"

"A man was shot less than thirty feet from where you sit and, I might add, a drawing of the man was found in your jacket pocket. We also found your PI license—your reputation precedes you."

I decided to leave that one alone.

"Is he alive?"

"He was rushed to Downstate Medical Center. The jury is still out."

"Who is he?"

"Paul Banks. He's an NYPD undercover detective."

"Was he on the Richard Sherman murder investigation?"

"Richard Sherman?" he said, helping me to my feet.

"Richard Sherman—murdered a few nights ago."

"That case was tied up this afternoon. We have the perpetrator in custody, with a full confession. The shooter's wife was suing him for divorce. Sherman was her attorney—and her lover. Detective Banks had no connection to the Sherman case."

"Are you serious?"

"I couldn't make this shit up," Washington said, "and you better start making some sense."

"I didn't shoot Banks—but I did lead the shooter straight to him."

"Follow me. I want you to start from the beginning."

We sat in Washington's unmarked motor pool car.

I gave him the story so far.

"So, this client you call Bishop goes to the obituaries, pulls a name out of the hat, and sells you the Brooklyn Bridge? How smart was that?"

I had to admit it was not smart at all.

"I fucked up," I said.

"I'm inclined to believe you."

"Why would you?"

"First, I can't picture you smacking yourself in the head with a handgun. Second, I spoke to Detective John Sullivan about you. He said you were more prone to stupidity than felony."

"Sounds like something Sullivan would say."

"Detective Banks works deep undercover. Donnie Brasco shit. He's a ghost. He makes a personal appearance at a police house once, maybe twice, every three months. I didn't even know where he lived. How the hell did you find him?"

"Just my kind of luck."

"I'm still undecided about your culpability."

"So am I," I said.

"And Bishop—you have no idea how to find him?"

"None. But I could pick him out of any lineup you put in front of me when *you* find him. Am I under arrest?"

"I need to take you in to get a written statement," he said.

And we were off to the 76th Precinct.

Washington took me into an interrogation room with a legal pad and two razor-sharp number two pencils.

I guess he didn't consider me homicidal or suicidal.

"Write it all down."

I wrote and signed a statement that included everything I cared to share with the detective.

He cut me loose with an unambiguous admonition.

"If I find you held out on me," he said, "I will personally feed your investigator's license into a shredding machine."

"Is there any word on Banks?"

"He's going to pull through."

When I left the precinct, I found Detective John Sullivan waiting outside the entrance.

"When are you going to learn, Nick?"

"Learn what?"

"That the police can be your friends—and you don't want them for enemies."

"With all due respect to you and to the Department, I'm not up for a sermon. I was played, John, and I almost got a man killed. I'm not feeling amiable."

"I can't urge you strongly enough to stand down."

"I was paid four days fees in advance. I owe the client a refund, and I would really like to settle up."

"You're making a mistake."

"I'm trying to *correct* a mistake. I need help. I need prints run."

"Go back in and give it to Washington."

"I'm not ready to do that."

"What's stopping me from going in myself and telling Washington you're withholding evidence?"

"I'm hoping you won't. All I want is a day."

"Do you know what you are asking?"

"I do—and I hate having to ask. If you can't help, I understand. I'll find another way. Sorry you had to come all the way down here to preach to me."

"Actually, I came because I thought you might need a ride to your car."

John Sullivan and I went back a long time. Boyhood. To say I made his job as an NYPD detective more difficult than it already was would be an understatement. Knocking heads with each other was a tradition.

John wouldn't commit to helping me—but he did agree to

hear me out.

"If you have an evidence kit handy," I said when we parked on Neptune Avenue, "bring it up with you."

Up in my office, I asked him for a latex glove and a plastic evidence bag.

I lifted the pen from the filing cabinet and placed it in the bag.

"This came unused out of a box, there are only two sets of prints," I said. "One belongs to me and the other belongs to the man we're looking for."

"One condition, Nick. If we get a hit, if we identify and locate this guy, you bring it to Ray Washington."

"Deal."

"I'll call you," Sullivan said, as he moved to leave the office.

"John?"

"Yes?"

"Why didn't he shoot me when he had the chance?"

"Maybe he got to like you. Maybe he didn't want to get blood all over his car seat. Probably, he didn't consider you a threat to him. So..."

"So?"

"So, hope he doesn't remember this pen and change his mind," Sullivan said, waving the evidence bag as he walked through the door.

I had failed to eat a thing all day.

I stopped into the pizzeria.

Carmella hooked me up with a veal parmigiana hero sandwich to go.

"I put a salad and a cloth napkin in the bag," Carmella said when she handed it to me.

"Why a cloth napkin?"

"It's civilized."

I picked up a cold six-pack of St. Pauli Girl on my way to the houseboat.

I took my dinner out to the deck.

I was in the cabin grabbing another beer when I heard John Sullivan call out to me.

"I'll take anything but a Coors Light."

"Drop by to watch the fireworks display?" I asked, handing him a bottle.

"I dropped by to tell you I got a hit on the prints."

"You could have phoned, saved yourself the trip."

"Sure, but then how could I stop you from doing something incredibly stupid?"

"Who is he?"

"Ted Jackson. Paroled from Riker's a week ago. Detective Banks put him away six years ago."

"I really fucked up."

"I won't argue."

"Do you know where to find him?"

"I talked to his parole officer and got an address. Now we give it to Ray Washington."

"I'm very angry, Johnny."

"We made a deal, Nicky. I don't need a debate, and I could really use a beer," Sullivan said, moving to the cabin.

Ted Jackson came out of nowhere.

I was seated with a bottle of beer in my hand.

He lifted his right arm and pointed a gun at my chest.

A sitting duck had a better chance.

I may have closed my eyes for a moment.

Then a bullet smashed into his shoulder, spun him around, and landed him on his face.

Sullivan was on him in a flash and had Jackson's hands cuffed behind his back in seconds.

"This should settle our argument," John said, lifting Jackson to his feet.

I rose from my chair, picked up the cloth napkin Carmella had sent with dinner, and wrapped it around my hand.

"I think the fall broke his jaw."

"What are you talking about? His jaw is fine." John said, as I moved toward them. "Nick, don't do what I think you're thinking of doing."

"It's not the way it looks," I said.

Then I swung for the bleachers and Jackson's broken jaw hit the deck.

TOMMY'S BIRTHDAY

When I was a few months shy of *my* thirteenth birthday, I was invited to Tommy Morea's thirteenth birthday party. Tommy had promised a big surprise. Johnny, Eddie and I tried to predict what was in store. Tommy's father owned and operated a very successful trash removal company, and he could afford to be extravagant.

"Maybe it's a pony," Johnny said.

"Or a ride," said Eddie.

A *ride* was an amusement park type ride that was portable—delivered by truck to the site of the festivities. A Ferris wheel, a pirate ship, a whip. The pirate ship was like a large boat that swung up and down on an axle. At its high point, the passengers were at nearly a ninety-degree angle to the ground twenty feet below. The whip was six two-seated cars on an oval track that violently whipped around its oval ends. We all favored the whip.

"Maybe it's a pony *and* a whip," I said, always the optimist.

When we arrived on bikes to Tommy's house, we looked for signs. There was no truck on the street and no pony manure evident on the lawn. We were disappointed but hopeful.

After a three-legged race, which Eddie and I won handily, and a potato sack race, which left me with two scraped elbows, we were getting impatient.

Finally, Tommy's father announced that the big surprise would be revealed in twenty minutes. I decided I had time to tend to my wounds and went to find a bathroom.

The door was closed and—although since that time I always knock to be certain—I turned the knob, found the door unlocked, and pushed it open.

Talk about surprises.

The man stood in front of the bathroom sink, his back to me. He was big. He had a head of wild orange hair, a puffy purple shirt with big yellow polka dots, and matching pants that were pulled down below his knees partially covering very large red shoes. Before he turned to me, I caught his reflection in the mirror. A white painted face with a thick red outline around the mouth, and a good-sized red ball for a nose. When he did turn my way, I saw Tommy's mother propped on the edge of the sink with her legs in the air.

"Get out," the man said, "and if you tell anyone what you saw I will kill your whole family."

I quickly beat it.

I didn't take the threat seriously but, since I didn't really care what Mrs. Morea did in her spare time and I didn't want to ruin Tommy's big day, I decided to keep it quiet. The sight of the woman with her knees up above her shoulders and the man's creepy voice were unnerving and instilled in me an instant and lifelong dislike of clowns rivaled only by my distaste for raw green peppers or runny eggs, and my disenchantment with any cover of a Dylan song other than Jimi Hendrix's "All Along the Watchtower."

I decided to leave the party before Tommy's dad introduced the clown—who had been doing his wife—to a backyard packed with anxious adolescents.

I told Eddie and Johnny that my injuries were hurting badly and I needed the healing powers of my mother. They both knew better than to question my toughness. I pedaled my Schwinn home, hoping that my father was not at the house to belittle me for being a clumsy good-for-nothing.

For the hundredth time.

My mother applied the age-old remedy, mercurochrome, which

burned like hell and left both elbows painted as orange as the wig on the man in Morea's bathroom.

Even at twelve years old I had heard stories of young people running off with the circus to escape what they perceived as a dead-end existence in a middle-of-nowhere Midwest town.

But when Tommy's mother walked away from her family—a few weeks after Tommy's birthday party—that was a new one on me.

Frances Morea had left a short note.

I'm sorry. I'm not happy here. I need to go.

And she was never heard from again.

Tommy's father was devastated.

He had truly loved his wife, and her actions were as unexpected as snow in August.

He was left lonely, embarrassed, and bewildered.

And Mike Morea was totally unprepared for single parenthood.

The demands of building and running his business had left him little time for learning the nuances of child rearing. After his wife's abrupt departure, he threw himself entirely—body and mind—into his work. Becoming even further detached from his only child.

And clueless as to Tommy's needs.

Tommy was effectively orphaned.

A combination of our general goodwill—and more than a small amount of prompting from our mothers—persuaded Eddie Caravella, Johnny Sullivan and me to welcome Tommy into our tight little circle.

Tommy was not a great fit.

We were all sports fanatics. We religiously followed the Mets and the football Giants.

We all loved, played and knew baseball.

Tommy couldn't tell you the difference between a ground rule double and the infield fly rule, on the playing field he was all thumbs, and at the plate he couldn't hit anything smaller than the broad side of a barn.

On top of that we were tough. Rather than avoiding confrontations with kids from other blocks, we invited and embraced them.

The Three Musketeers of West 10th Street, a title we didn't originate but gladly adopted, were respected from McDonald to Stillwell Avenues.

Tommy Morea was soft.

We drifted apart after high school—different colleges, different interests, time consuming girlfriends.

The last time I had seen Tommy was at Eddie's wedding.

Soon after, Eddie and his new bride left Brooklyn for Las Vegas—where they live with their three children and where Eddie has been very successful selling real estate. Eddie and I get together for a drink once or twice a year when he comes in to visit his parents or I go out there to play poker with the big boys.

John Sullivan is an NYPD detective out of the Seventieth Precinct in Midwood.

John and I see each other if and when he is willing to respond to one of my frequent calls for help. My work can often benefit from having an old friend inside the department—but John rarely has anything to gain from going out on a limb for me.

And Sullivan never lets me forget I owe him big time.

Those long-neglected memories of the party—and the old gang—revisited me moments after Tommy Morea called my office and insisted he had to see me as soon as possible.

A light rapping on my office door interrupted my trip down memory lane.

I called out that the door was open, and rose to meet my visitor.

Tommy Morea stepped into the room.

I met him halfway with my hand extended but, instead of accepting the handshake, he took a quick step closer to me and gave me an awkward hug.

I offered him a seat across from mine at the antique table I used as a desk.

We both sat.

Tommy hadn't changed much. He was a chubby kid at thirteen, a chubby twenty-six-year-old at Eddie's wedding, and a chubby thirty-six-year-old in the chair facing mine.

He was wringing his hands, looking as if he had absolutely no idea about how to begin a conversation.

I, on the other hand, could never be accused of being unable to get the ball rolling.

"So," I said.

"I think my mother was murdered."

Tommy's face told me he believed what he'd said, but it had come from out of left field.

I took a few moments before responding, and then tried to sound as if I didn't consider the suggestion absurd.

"Why would you think that? I was always led to believe your mother left home voluntarily."

"I was only thirteen and, as I'm sure you remember, very awkward and immature for my age. I could never understand why my mother would have simply walked away, or understood why we never heard a single word from her after she left. Until I saw this."

He reached into his pocket, removed a newspaper article, and he handed it across the table.

I took a look.

A woman, Lorraine Gorman, had been found shot to death in her home the previous August.

Harold Gorman claimed he had left the house very early, to mow the front lawn before it became unbearably hot outdoors. His wife still asleep in bed.

After completing only half the job, the lawnmower ran out of gas.

Gorman drove to a service station, filled a gas can, came back to finish the work, and went back into the house.

Curious about why his wife was not yet up and about, he entered the bedroom where he found her body on the floor at the foot of the bed.

After determining his wife was dead, Gorman phoned the police. It appeared a lot like suicide, but without murder cases homicide detectives would be out of a job.

So, as is customary in such instances, the husband was considered a person of interest.

Harold Gorman was suspected in the murder of his wife.

He remained free, on bail, while prosecutors tried to build a case to present to a grand jury for indictment.

Gorman's defense was well thought out, and somewhat persuasive.

The weapon was registered to his wife, and Gorman claimed to have no knowledge of its existence.

There were no fingerprints on the weapon other than those of the victim.

According to Gorman, his wife had been unresponsive and depressed since having been diagnosed with breast cancer—faced with the probability of radical surgery.

The position of the woman's body and the location of the weapon were consistent with what would be expected had she put a gun to her head and pulled the trigger.

No neighbors came forward with reports of knock-down battles or outside love affairs.

The case developed by the prosecution was not as compelling.

They pointed to a life insurance policy held by the victim, which did not preclude death by suicide, as a conceivable motive.

There was the testimony of the victim's sister who swore under oath that Lorraine had been dealing courageously and optimistically with her illness—and insisted that, as a devout Catholic, Lorraine would never have considered taking her own life.

Finally, there was a record of a past complaint against Gorman for domestic abuse. A complaint that was later withdrawn.

It was not enough to convince the grand jury to indict, and charges were dropped.

End of story.

"Am I missing something here?" I asked, after quickly reading the article.

"Does Gorman appear innocent to you?"

"Not very, but neither did Simpson. That's our legal system, Tommy, innocent unless proven guilty. The prosecution couldn't sell their case and that, as they say, was that. But what does all of this have to do with your mother?"

"Look at his picture."

I turned my attention back to the newspaper article and studied the photograph of Harold Gorman.

It rang no bells.

"I recall you left early from my birthday party years ago," Tommy said, "but do you remember that my father had hired a clown?"

Unfortunately, I did.

"Yes."

"I saw him before he left, when my father was paying him. He had removed his costume and makeup," Tommy said. "He was much younger than in the newspaper photograph, but I am sure it is the same man."

I looked at the photograph again, trying to imagine Gorman in an orange wig and a big red nose.

What I saw instead was a pair of puffy purple pants with large yellow polka dots down around his knees.

"You think when your mother left, she ran away with the clown?"

"Yes," Tommy said. "And I believe the clown killed her."

I didn't know what to say, so for a while I said nothing.

Tommy Morea broke the silence.

"Nick."

"Have you considered going to the police?"

"Would you?"

I may have considered taking it to John Sullivan, but not without something a lot more concrete than Tommy's imagination.

"No," I had to admit.

"Can you help me?"

"Help you do what?"

"Find out what happened to my mother."

"I don't know, Tommy. I would like to—but if I *can* is another question. Give me a few days to try to work something out. Leave me a telephone number where I can reach you," I said, pushing a slip of paper and a pencil his way. "How did you find me?"

"Phone directory. Nick Ventura, Private Investigator. Who would have imagined?"

"Not me," I said. "I'll call you."

I devoted the remainder of the afternoon to another case—with the hope I could wrap it up by day's end.

The following morning, ignoring the voice in my head warning me against it, I turned my attention to Harold Gorman.

Harold Gorman was not difficult to find. I located an address and a telephone number.

Roseanna Napoli was the woman of my dreams.

Attractive, smart, funny, and she could cook up a storm.

I called Roseanna and asked if I could borrow Max.

Max was a medium-sized Chow-Shepherd mix with more personality than most of the people I knew.

"Going to try picking up girls at the dog park?" Roseanna asked.

"You know me better than that. I prefer the supermarket or the laundromat."

"In that case, unless you are planning to shop for food or wash your clothing, he is all yours."

. . .

Max and I drove out to Mill Basin, parked, and took a walk through the neighborhood.

Harold Gorman's house was fronted by a well-kept lawn.

On the northside was a paved drive, leading to the attached garage. North of the garage was a narrow side lawn leading to the fenced yard in back. The same pattern repeated all along the street, providing some distance between the homes—as opposed to the houses crammed up against each other in my neck of the woods.

We strolled down the alley that ran behind the houses. Each had a gated wood stockade fence along the alley, and each backyard was separated from its neighbors by the same fencing.

Getting into Gorman's place from the back was definitely the way to go.

All I needed to do was get Harold out of the house for a while.

Back at my office above the pizzeria, Max safely returned, I browsed the internet.

Harold Gorman was, for lack of a better term, a publicity hound.

Major print media and broadcast news had given little attention to the case of Lorraine Gorman, and only at the time of her death and nine months after when the charges against her husband were dropped. But during the time Gorman was considered a suspect, free on bail, he missed no opportunity to talk with reporters from small local news outlets—from *The Brooklyn Eagle* to *The Mill Basin Courier* to Brooklyn 12, a cable TV station covering news particular to the borough.

Since there was no financial compensation for such interviews; money would not have been Gorman's motivation.

I had to conclude that Harold simply liked the attention.

I felt confident Gorman would consider an invitation for an interview with a major publication, with a two-thousand-dollar stipend thrown in for good measure, irresistible.

. . .

Maria Leone was smart, attractive, and charming.

When Maria wasn't helping her Aunt Carmella run the pizzeria below my office, she studied for her graduate degree at the John Jay School of Criminal Justice in Manhattan.

Maria assisted me with cases occasionally. She welcomed the opportunity for hands-on investigative work, and what I could afford to pay her covered the cost of a textbook or two.

She was perfectly suited to play the role of freelance journalist, but she would need credentials.

So, before I approached Maria with the proposal, I phoned Lefty Brenowitz.

Lefty agreed to meet me on the Coney Island Boardwalk.

Lefty was by far the most talented forger I had ever known. And, if that wasn't enough, he was also a cousin from my mother's side of the family.

We sat at a bench near the Aquarium.

"I need an authentic looking Press Card in the name of Maria Franklin."

"I'll need a photograph," Lefty said.

"No problem."

"What else?"

"Back issues of *New York Magazine* and *Esquire* including articles by Maria Franklin."

"Any particular subject?"

"Preferably pieces built around interviews."

"I'll need to substitute her name in the table of contents and in the byline of the piece itself, and substitute a short bio in the list of contributors."

"Can you do it?"

"Of course I can do it, but we're talking multiple pages in two separate magazines. It may take a few days."

"I need it as soon as possible. And, Lefty."

"Yes?"

"Please give my best to your mother. Esther has always been my favorite aunt."

"Get the photograph to me today. I'll have it all done for you tomorrow."

I met Maria at her apartment, picking up a prepaid disposable cell phone on my way over.

I explained, in some detail, what I was hoping she could do for me.

Maria agreed without hesitation, asking only if she could keep the doctored magazines when it was done.

She supplied me with a copy of her passport photo, and then she called Gorman.

I listened in. Maria was very convincing.

She arranged a meeting with Gorman for seven the following evening at the Milk and Honey Café, twenty minutes or so from Gorman's home. She said it would be a short meeting, no more than thirty minutes, just long enough to "get acquainted" and collect some information she would need to work up a feature article proposal to pitch to *The New York Times Magazine*.

"He sounded excited," Maria said, after completing the call.

"I'm not surprised. I'll get the ID and the magazines to you tomorrow afternoon."

"I'll be at the pizzeria until five, and then back here to change from my marinara sauce covered apron into my successful professional woman costume."

I ran the photograph over to Lefty on my way home.

Home was a houseboat docked in the waters of Sheepshead Bay, a stone's throw from Clemente's Maryland Crab House— where I had made dinner reservations for two.

I had promised Roseanna the seafood of her choice as thanks for letting me borrow the pooch.

169

On the boat, I called Tommy Morea. I asked him to give me another day or two.

Tommy seemed to trust that I was doing the best I could.

I poured a double Jameson's, sat out on the deck, and waited for my dinner date to arrive.

The next evening, we sat in the parked car. Roseanna Napoli behind the wheel.

She had insisted on coming along, arguing that she could be both lookout and getaway driver—and when Roseanna had her mind set, there was no talking her down.

We watched Harold Gorman back his car out of the garage and the driveway, pull out onto the street, and drive off.

I looked at my wristwatch.

Six-thirty-five.

Maria said she could keep Gorman at the Milk and Honey Café for at least twenty minutes, and it would take him at least another twenty minutes to get back home.

That would make it at least seven-thirty-five.

I could give myself close to an hour inside.

Roseanna drove around to the north end of the alley, dropped me off, and went to park nearby.

The back gate was latched, but not locked. Getting past the back-door lock was a cinch.

I wasn't exactly sure what I was looking for, but I knew the best place to begin looking.

I found Gorman's bedroom.

I went through all of the dresser drawers, and the drawer in the bedside table.

A wood chest sitting at the foot of the bed.

A few empty suitcases on the floor of the closet.

A heavy metal strongbox also sat on the closet floor.

I knew I wouldn't have enough time to get into the safe.

On the shelf above the hanging wardrobe, I found a shoe

box tucked beneath a blanket.

I took the box out to the living room, set it on the coffee table, sat in the arm chair, and opened the box.

There were a number of photographs.

Wedding photographs, Gorman and a blushing bride. But not the same bride who had died in the house the previous August.

And a long-expired New Jersey driver's license. The name on the license was Anthony Sanders, but the face was Harold Gorman.

I pulled out my cell phone and took photos of the photos, and the driver's license.

I replaced the shoe box.

I went out the back door, relocking it behind me.

I spotted Roseanna's car as I came out of the alley, walked over, and climbed in.

"Did you find anything?" she asked.

"Some things."

I really didn't want to bother John Sullivan.

I had gone to that well far too many times, and understood it was nearly dry.

I had no other option.

There was an officer at the Sixtieth Precinct who often helped me locate a name attached to a license plate, but the driver's license I discovered at Gorman's place was out-of-state, and a decade old.

"What do you need, Nick?" John said, in way of greeting.

"Maybe I'm just calling to say hello."

"What do you need?"

"I'm sending a photo to your cell phone."

Sullivan was silent for a minute, and then back on the line.

"What is it?"

"A driver's license."

"Nick, you must realize you are wasting my time."

"I was hoping you could get me some information on the guy."

"I would ask what your interest is, but I probably don't want to know."

"A favor for an old friend. Tommy Morea."

"Tommy Morea. I haven't seen or heard from Tommy since Eddie's wedding."

"Can you help?"

"You know how much I hate having to deal with New Jersey's finest."

"I do."

"Give me a few hours."

I thought about saying I owe you, John, but that would be like telling him the sky was blue or the Mets had no hope.

I thanked him, and left it at that.

John called two hours later.

Joan Sanders had been found dead, a single bullet to the head, at a heavily wooded area in Northern New Jersey nine years earlier. Just before dawn.

Detectives went to her home to notify family, if any.

Anthony Sanders came to the door in pajamas. Before giving him the news, they asked for his wife. He told them she had left town, a few days earlier, to visit a friend in Chicago.

Then they did break the news, and asked him to come in to identify the body. He said he could be at the morgue in an hour. He never arrived, and no one had seen or heard of him since.

"They took prints from the house," Sullivan said, "but have never been able to find a match. I have to admit, Nick. You've got me a little curious."

"Impatiently curious?"

"Are you asking me to wait?"

"Please."

"You owe me."

. . .

Maria's initial meeting with Gorman had gone well.

She had spread it on thick, and he ate it up.

After speaking with John Sullivan, I reached out to Maria once again.

Maria called Gorman, telling him *The Times* had contracted the story. She arranged a follow-up meeting, for that evening, to go over the particulars.

We chose a coffee shop less than ten minutes from Gorman's home. She would call him a few minutes before the meeting time to apologize for having to reschedule.

It would give me enough time to get into his house again.

I watched Gorman leave for the meeting, entered the house, and waited.

When Harold Gorman returned and walked through the door connecting the garage to the house, I slapped him on the head with a vintage 1940s leather-covered Billy club given to me by my uncle Sal. It had once belonged to a Brooklyn cop, who carried it as he walked his beat in Coney Island, before he retired and later lost it to my uncle in a poker game.

It was a beautiful piece of work, and worked like a charm.

Knocking Gorman out cold.

We had pushed three chairs close together in the living room. We dragged Gorman into the room, tied him into one of the chairs, and gagged him with a dish towel.

Together, we managed to carry the metal safe from the bedroom closet and set it down at his feet.

When he finally opened his eyes, he found me and Tommy Morea sitting.

Watching him.

I held the club in my right hand, tapping it lightly into the palm of my left.

I stood up, and walked to him.

"If you raise your voice," I said. "I will hit you again, this time across the bridge of your nose."

I removed the gag, and returned to my seat.

"Who are you?" he asked.

"I think the more relevant question is who are you—Harold Gorman, Anthony Sanders, or Bozo?"

"I don't know what you are talking about."

"Sure, you do. Your fingerprints will match those of Anthony Sanders who, for nearly a decade, has been wanted for murdering his wife. I'll let the police sort it out. What I need you to do is get me into the safe."

"And if I don't, are you going to kill me?"

"Not right away."

I walked over and reminded him not to raise his voice. I smacked his right kneecap with the club, swinging for the fences. I was sure his cry could be heard clear across the street.

"That was a poor show of self-control," I said, and I hit the knee again.

This time, he did a much better job masking the pain.

"The safe."

Gorman gave me the three-number combination.

Tommy sat watching as I pulled the safe door open. He hadn't said a word.

There was cash, but it didn't interest me.

I pulled out a gun, which I guessed had been used to kill Joan Sanders.

And I pulled out an envelope.

The envelope contained photographs.

Photographs of women. A different woman in each of six separate photos.

Some, I could identify.

Lorraine Gorman. Joan Sanders.

And Tommy's mother, Frances Morea, as I remembered her.

The thought that there had been at least six victims chilled me.

But what terrified me most, was a seventh photograph.

Harold Gorman or Anthony Sanders, or whoever this monster was, in the full costume and makeup of a clown.

I stood up, and handed the photographs to Tommy.

It was one of the most difficult things I have ever done.

Then, I went to look for a drink.

I found a bottle of Scotch in a kitchen cabinet, poured four fingers, and knocked it down.

I poured another, and I made the phone call.

When I came back to the room, Tommy was standing—the photographs on the floor at his feet.

His eyes were fixed on Gorman.

I had seen similar looks in the eyes of witnesses to terrible accidents.

"Can I have some time with him alone?" Tommy asked.

"Sure. I'll wait outside. John Sullivan will be here soon."

I had placed the Billy club on top of the safe.

I thought for a moment about picking it up on my way out, but left it sitting there.

I walked out to the front porch and I lit a cigarette.

Sullivan's car rolled up to the front of the house ten minutes later.

"Well?"

"The suspect is roped and tied inside."

"Did this guy really kill Tommy's mother?"

"I have no doubts. Her and at least five other women. Tommy is in there with him."

"Do you think Tommy could kill the guy?"

"No, not Tommy. I could. Easily."

Tommy walked out of the house and joined us, carrying the leather-covered club.

John and Tommy greeted each other.

"Are you all right?" I asked, when Tommy handed the club to me.

"My mother told him she was going to leave him. She said she wanted to go back to her family. He couldn't talk her out of it. He drugged her, smothered her while she slept, drove her out to Plum Beach and buried her there."

"Did he say where at Plum Beach?" John asked.

"He couldn't remember. It was more than twenty years ago. With the crabs, fox and wild dogs out there, she's long gone."

"I need to take him in, lock him up in a cage, and call for a forensics team," John said, heading for the front door.

For a moment, I wondered if things might have turned out differently if—all those years ago—I had told Tommy or his father what I had seen in the bathroom.

I pushed the thought aside.

"I'm really sorry, Tommy."

"You have nothing to be sorry about, Nick. I'm thankful. I needed to know."

"Let's get out of here, I'll drive you home."

"I should go to see my father."

"No problem, I can take you there."

"Can we stop for something to eat first?"

"Sure. Italian?"

"Italian sounds good," Tommy said. "It's funny."

"What's that?" I asked, unable to imagine anything funny about anything.

"Today is my birthday."

"Well, how do you like that," I said. "I guess dinner is on me."

ONE WAY OR THE OTHER

The old man looked directly into my eyes.

"You know what your problem is?" he asked.

"Which one?"

"You always bet on the wrong horse."

"What can I say? The ponies have minds of their own."

"I'm speaking figuratively. I'm speaking of your decision-making."

"Making a decision necessitates a choice."

"There is always a choice."

"I've used up all my choices."

"If it's about money, maybe I can dig some up. I still have a few friends outside."

"No offense, but you would need a bulldozer to dig up what I need."

"Do you know these people?"

"They found me. Said I was recommended."

"How do you know you can trust them?"

"I don't trust anyone."

"If you're convicted of a felony again, they'll throw away the key."

"It would be free room and board, and keep me out of trouble. Looks like it's working for you."

"Are you trying to hurt my feelings?"

"No, not at all."

"Is there *anything* I can do for you?"

"Yes. Forget we ever had this conversation."

I stood up, turned, and headed for the visitors' hall exit.

"Matthew?" the old man called from behind.

"Yes?"

"Will I see you again?"

"One way or the other, Dad. One way or the other."

We met at Swift's Coffee House on West Colfax.

To iron out a few details.

I had to admit they were a smart-looking couple.

Mid-thirties.

Simon. Clean-shaven. Hair cut short and neat. Button-down shirt. Black slacks. Black laced shoes.

Amanda. Not Mandy. Long brown hair tied back. White blouse. Maroon skirt. Sensible brown flats. No make-up. None needed.

No tattoos. No piercings. Nothing alarming.

"One-hundred-fifty grand. Minimum," Simon said. "Three-way split."

"Doesn't sound like a three-person job."

"I'll be entering alone," he said. "I'll need twenty minutes inside. I need cars and eyes, front *and* back."

"I don't have a car."

"You'll have one."

"So, we get equal shares for sitting in cars?"

"We get equal shares for giving Simon peace of mind," Amanda said.

"When?" I asked.

"One week from today. We meet here at seven-forty-five in the morning. We're in position at eight-fifteen. The mark is out of the place by eight-thirty. He leaves, I go in."

"And you're sure you can get into the safe?"

"It's what I do. Twenty minutes, thirty tops. Look, if you don't

ONE WAY OR THE OTHER

feel right about it, I understand. We were told you were reliable and could use the bread. But we need to know *now* if you're in or out."

"You never mentioned who pointed you in my direction."

"Is it really important?"

"Probably not," I said. "I'm in."

I'd managed to put off the inevitable for months, scraping up minimum interest payments and late penalties—which ate up nearly all of my paycheck from part-time work at a car wash on Lincoln.

The latest correspondence from the bank suggested I would be living out on the street by Labor Day.

My father's small, one-bedroom cottage had been my home since my release.

The home where I had been raised was long gone—as long gone as my mother.

Sold to pay for lawyers who did my father no good.

With what remained, the old man had made a down payment on the cottage and set up an account to cover mortgage payments for a few years.

Then *he* was locked up.

Two years after he was moved to his all-expenses-paid, state-operated residence, the money ran out and payments to the bank stopped.

Before long, the cottage would be off-limits to me as well.

Two days before my next meeting with Simon and Amanda, I left the car wash at two in the afternoon and rode a bus downtown to meet with my parole officer.

A once-every-two-weeks affair.

Leon Harris was not one to waste words.

"Still working?"

"Yes," I said.

"Part-time?"

"It's all they have."

"Is that cutting it?"

"I put in an application with Leprino. I should hear this week."

"Leprino?"

"Cheese-makers. They're looking for a driver to deliver to supermarkets and restaurants. They're the largest producers of mozzarella in the world."

"Good to know."

"If I get the gig, I should manage. It's early mornings, weekdays, and I can still work afternoons and weekends at the car wash."

"And if you don't get the job?"

"The prison counselor gave me lessons in positive thinking."

"You know what happens if you have no place to live."

"Too well."

"Let me know what you hear."

"You'll be the first."

"Good luck," Harris said, and the session was over.

The next day, Leprino offered me twenty hours a week at ten dollars an hour. Monday through Friday, six until ten in the mornings, beginning a week from the following Monday.

I neglected to call Leon Harris with the good news.

On Friday morning, I woke early with a head full of questions.

Who was the mark? What was the mark doing with at least one-hundred-fifty-thousand in cash in a house safe?

Who the fuck was Simon, and how did he know about the cash?

But other questions made those irrelevant.

Could two part-time minimum-wage jobs keep a roof over

my head—in a place where I felt less at home than I had in the joint?

And how soon could I get the fuck out?

I dressed and took a bus ride to find some answers.

When I walked into Swift's at seven-forty, Amanda and Simon were sitting in a booth at the window.

I settled into the bench opposite.

There was an empty mug and a pot of hot coffee waiting for me.

Simon slid a key across the table as I poured.

"It's the blue Camry out front. The house sits on a large lot, northeast corner of Thirty-Eighth Avenue and Cody Street. Park on Cody, just south of the avenue, where you can clearly see the front of the house. When he leaves, Amanda will drive me around to the back where I'll enter. She will stay back there to watch the rear. If you spot anyone coming anywhere near the place, hit your horn three times. When you see us drive out, take off and meet us at this address for the split," Simon said, handing me a small slip of note paper. "Questions?"

"None."

"Good," Simon said, dropping a ten-dollar bill on the table.

He and Amanda headed for the exit.

I followed.

I watched them pull out of the parking lot and slipped on a pair of leather gloves before climbing into the Toyota.

As I drove, I imagined all of the places I might possibly reach with fifty thousand bucks.

I parked at the southeast corner of Cody, across Thirty-Eighth, facing the house.

It was fifteen minutes past eight.

Moments later, the other car pulled alongside.

Amanda at the wheel.

"He left a few minutes ago," Simon said, from the passenger seat.

"You said he leaves at eight-thirty."

"Guess he had an early date. Who fucking cares? Means we get out of here sooner is all. Keep your eyes open and your hand near the horn."

Simon put the window up and they pulled away. Their car disappeared around the rear of the house.

I sat.

Fifteen minutes later, Simon stepped out of the front door of the house.

He waved me over with a few sweeping arm gestures and went back inside.

I started the car.

Every rational instinct told me to beat it.

I was officially known as a two-time loser.

Although the loss column was actually as long as my arm.

But as they say—you can't win if you don't play.

I killed the engine, pulled the key, stepped out of the car, and crossed the avenue.

The front door was wide open.

I stepped across the threshold.

The body was on the floor. Male. Gunshot to the head. DOA.

I went to the back door.

The other car. Simon and Amanda. MIA.

Police car sirens.

I went out the back.

West one block, then south one block, west and south again.

Dropped the car key down a sewer grating.

Ducked into the Wendy's on Wadsworth.

Took a coffee and a bacon and egg sandwich to an empty table and considered my future.

I needed a vehicle.

Pulling out my cell, I wondered how soon the phone would be as dead as the guy on Thirty-Eighth.

I called the only name on my long list.

"Sammy, it's Matt."

"Hooker. What's up?"

"I need a car."

"For how long?"

"Not sure. A few days."

"I have a beater out back. It should fire up. It's registered, but it's not insured."

"Works for me."

"Where are you?"

"Wendy's. Fortieth and Wadsworth."

"I'll pick you up. Twenty minutes."

"I'll be here."

Sammy was righteous.

He had filled the gas tank.

I dropped him off back at his place.

"I appreciate your help, Sammy."

"No problem. Try not to get pulled over. By the way, did Jimmy reach you?"

"Jimmy?"

"Doyle. He asked if I knew how to find you. I gave him your number. Sorry if that was out-of-line."

"Never heard from him. Did he happen to mention what it was about?"

"He didn't say. I didn't ask. I can give you his number."

"I'll take it. Do you know where he lives?"

"I do."

"Give me an address also."

I imagined I would have better luck finding Doyle at home in the evening.

Time to kill, and washing cars wouldn't cut it.

I called in sick. Said I'd be back for my next shift on Thursday.

Simon had given me the location for the split.

Fat chance, but I drove over anyway.

No such address. Fucked over. Any doubt erased.

I headed home.

Back at the cottage, I picked up the cash I had put away for the next useless bank payment and I went shopping for a gun.

I parked on Broadway in front of the pawn shop.

I went in, setting off the loud buzzer.

"Is Don here?" I asked the guy behind the counter who wasn't Don.

"He walked over to the Seven-Eleven."

I left the shop and went looking for Don.

I found him watching a microwave heat up a burrito.

"Those things are not good for you."

"What is?" Don said. "I would say *fancy meeting you here,* but I have a hunch it's not accidental."

"I need a gun."

"What do you have to spend?"

"Three hundred."

"Are you driving?"

"Yes."

"Pull around to the rear of the shop. I'll meet you there in ten minutes. Want a donut?"

"I'm good."

Don came out the alley door of the pawn shop and waved me over.

"Is that Sammy's piece-of-crap Chevy?"

"It is."

"Still running."

"So far."

He ushered me through the door into the back of the shop.

"How is Sammy?" Don asked, as he opened the floor safe and pulled out a .38 Police Special.

"He's Sammy."

"This is the best I can do. I'll take two-fifty."

"Is it clean?"

"You could eat off it."

I gave him the cash and took the weapon.

I rapped on Jimmy Doyle's door just after seven-thirty.

"Matthew Hooker. This is a surprise."

"Can I come in?"

"Sure. Want a beer?"

"Sure."

Jimmy led me into the kitchen, offered me a seat, pulled two cans of PBR from the refrigerator, and joined me at the table.

"So?" he said.

"Sammy said you were asking for me. I'm curious."

"Didn't Jill contact you?"

"Jill?"

"I'll take that as a no."

"Tell me about Jill."

"Something like a friend. Did a few scores together. She came to me with a proposition. I passed. Not my cup of tea."

"What kind of tea was it?"

"The kind that's too hot to handle and takes too long to brew. Paintings."

"You lost me."

"This cat hits on Jill at a bar. Put her in the right outfit, she can be very alluring. He buys her a few drinks, he has a few too many himself. He invites her to his place to *see his paintings*."

"Seriously?"

"Guy has a pair of Monets on the wall. While he's mixing more drinks, Jill snaps a few shots with her phone. She sends me the photos to entice me. But I don't do art heists. Too hard to fence and too long to wait for a payout. And, far as I know, there's no one in Denver who could handle it. They would need to travel. San Francisco. Chicago. Jill asked if I knew anyone who might be game, I thought of you. I called Sammy, I got your number, and passed it on. I have to admit it was tempting. Even at thirty cents on the dollar, those two paintings could bring in more than a half-million."

"How can I contact her?"

"I can give you a phone number."

"How about an address?"

"It's not a good idea to drop in on a stranger uninvited."

"Good ideas are not my strong point."

With some coaxing, Jimmy gave up Jill's address.

Amanda's address.

I figured the chances of finding her or Simon were slim to none, and that slim had probably already left town.

But I had a full tank of gas and nowhere else to go.

I found *Amanda*.

When I turned onto her street, they were wheeling her on a gurney to a waiting ambulance.

A uniformed cop ushered me past the house.

I saw a medic covering her face with a sheet.

I drove a few blocks, called Jimmy Doyle, and left six words in his voice mail.

Jill is dead.

Watch your back.

I drove back to the pawn shop on Broadway.

Don was behind the counter this time.

"Run out of bullets already?"

"I need some more help."

"I was just about to lock up. Meet me at Stoney's on Lincoln. Give me twenty minutes, I'll buy you a drink. Feel free to start without me."

. . .

"What?" Don asked, as he sat beside me at the bar.

"Where would you try to sell two Monets?"

"Like the two Monets that went missing from the dead guy's house in Wheat Ridge? Heard it on the news. Were you in on that?"

"Just until I was out. I was told there's no one here in town who could handle the paintings."

"Only one. Runs an antique shop on South Broadway at Arkansas. Lives above the place."

"Man have a name?"

"They call him Einstein."

"Some kind of genius?"

"I don't know anything about his I.Q., but he's the spitting image of the original."

"Do you have handcuffs in the shop?"

"I have a few pairs in my car."

"What's that about?"

"About thirty bucks a pair."

The antique shop was closed, but lit inside.

There was a door to the south of the storefront.

I knew the setup.

It would open to stairs leading to an apartment above.

The light in the shop died.

When he came out and turned to lock the door, I left the car.

When he moved to the south door, I crossed Broadway.

He unlocked the door, started inside, and I came up behind him.

I pressed the gun against the back of his head.

"Who are you?" he asked.

"Claude Monet. Step inside. Put your hands back."

"Are those really necessary?" he asked, as I cuffed him.

"I don't know, Einstein, you tell me. Move."

I followed him up the stairs and sat him in the living room.

He didn't resist.

Answered every question without hesitation.

He could have won the Nobel Prize for Cooperation.

He already had the paintings. Told Calley he would need a few days for authentication.

Calley would be back on Monday night to pick up the cash.

Five-hundred-sixty thousand dollars.

"Calley?"

"That's what he called himself."

Amanda. Jill. Simon. Calley. Einstein.

What's in a name.

"I'm guessing you don't know where to find Calley."

"Here. Back door of the shop. Monday evening at eight."

"Where do you come up with that kind of cash?"

"A safe-deposit box. A bank downtown."

"And this *authentication*?"

"Done. Not that I had any doubts. Just a formality."

Protocol among thieves.

I was about to ask what he could get for the two Monets.

I decided I really didn't give a fuck.

"Where are the paintings now?" I asked instead.

"The storage room, in back of the shop. Would you like to see them?"

"I believe you."

"They're beautiful."

"I'll take your word for it. Here's the deal. I let you keep the paintings for a quarter million," I said, liking the sound of it. "Less than half price. Or, I call the police right now. They take the paintings and bring you in for accessory to grand larceny, maybe murder."

"And Calley?"

"What about him?"

"If I don't pay him, he'll probably kill me."

"If you *do* pay him, he will *definitely* kill you. I'll take care of Calley."

So, the deal was struck.

Einstein would hand over two-hundred-fifty-thousand in cash at six Monday evening. Then he would make himself scarce. I'd wait in the alley behind the shop.

Wait for Calley. Or Simon.

Or whoever the fuck he thought he was.

I've been a thief for as long as I can remember.

It's been like a hobby since I was a kid.

If I wanted something, I took it.

Whether I really needed it or not.

The first time I was caught at it, I was nineteen.

I had planned diligently.

A small convenience store off the beaten track in Arvada. I visited the place a few times before going in. No outside cameras, one inside behind the cash register. Closed for business at eleven, locked up by the last remaining employee by midnight. A college kid, a year or two older than I was.

I stopped him as he came out, forced him back in at gunpoint, emptied the register, five-hundred-eighty-four dollars and change, tied him up after he handed over the security camera tape.

I slipped out the back door and walked two blocks to my car.

The fucker intentionally gave me the wrong tape.

Since it was my first *known* offense, and the gun was a black plastic number, I got two years followed by two years' probation.

My second arrest and conviction was dumber still.

Went into a liquor store just before closing. This time with a modest disguise—three days' growth, dark-rimmed glasses, long blond wig under a Colorado Rockies cap. That clerk looked like a college student also, only a lot younger than I was by then.

I carried a bottle of Scotch over to the counter.

Twelve-year-old Macallan.

It looked like a good one, if the price was any indication.

"Is this the best you carry?" I asked.

"Personally, I think the fourteen-year-old Balvenie is a lot better."

At that point I pulled out the gun, a real one this time, had him lock the front door and turn the sign over to *Closed*, tied him up in back, and emptied the register. Two-thousand-five-hundred-seventy-six dollars.

I left the change.

Before I walked out, I grabbed a bottle of Balvenie off the shelf.

They lifted my prints off the bottle of Macallan I'd left at the counter.

There had been a time when I tried to lay it on the old man.

The clichés rolled off the tongue:

A chip off the old block. Like father, like son. The apple doesn't fall far from the tree. It's in the genes.

It was bullshit. There was no comparison.

Our motivations were totally different.

My father robbed what he needed, not what he wanted.

All he *wanted* was to keep food on the table and a roof over our heads.

He came back from a war and was greeted like a villain, when he should have been hailed a hero.

Doors were closed. Slammed.

Right or wrong, he had reasons to overlook the law.

I had no excuses.

For me it had always been a game.

Pick a pocket, bet a nag, mug a sap at an ATM, go all-in at a poker table, shoplift a piece of jewelry, buy a fistful of lottery tickets, enjoy the rush.

For the old man there had been necessary gambles.

And he had much more to lose—a wife, a kid, a home, his dignity—and he lost it all.

And I had never helped.

I tried to remember when the old man was scheduled to get out.

I thought about what two-hundred-grand could do to settle the score.

Funny the things you think about while you're waiting for the next thing to go wrong.

I was in Sammy's car behind the antique shop when Don arrived.

Einstein let us in the back door.

He handed me a small gym bag.

Twenty-five neatly bound bundles of one-hundred-dollar bills.

One-hundred C-notes each.

"What now?" Einstein asked.

"Go somewhere and hide."

I gave Don the bag to lock up in the pawn shop for safekeeping—and a ten percent cut.

Once they both left, I sat in the car.

I checked my wristwatch.

It was almost time for Simon says.

As I waited, it became perfectly clear.

There was nothing Simon had to say that I needed to hear.

Nothing I couldn't guess.

He knew the cat with the paintings would be at home and had planned to kill him from the start.

He probably left the weapon there, somewhere, called the cops, and then waved me in to take the fall.

Killed Amanda because he was that much more greedy and evil.

I picked up the baseball bat, another thing Don had handy, and stepped out into the darkness.

When he pulled into the parking area behind the antique shop, I moved.

I cracked his skull as he was climbing out of his car. He hit the ground.

I heaved him into the back seat and threw the Louisville Slugger in after him.

I got behind the wheel, headed over to Santa Fe Drive, and parked at a deserted railroad yard.

The back seat was drenched in blood.

I thought about checking if he was still alive. I tried estimating how long he would last if he *were* still alive.

I decided it didn't matter and I shot him twice in the head.

I left the weapon, trusting Don's assurance that it was untraceable, left the baseball bat, and walked back to the antique shop and Sammy's Chevy.

I drove home to the old man's cottage and slept like a baby.

Tuesday morning.

First thing, head to the pawn shop for some spending cash.

Don handed me a bundle from his safe. Ten grand.

"Plans?" he asked.

"Find a place where I don't need to report to Leon Harris twice a month. Preferably, someplace with sand and surf."

"You won't be able to fly out of here with more than ten-thousand dollars in cash."

"Any suggestions?"

"Bearer bonds."

"I thought they went out of fashion with *Beverly Hills Cop*."

"I know a guy. He'll sell me one-hundred-sixty-thousand in bonds for two-hundred-thousand cash."

"Do it."

"Do you have a passport?"

"No."

"I would get right on that."

"How long will that take?"

"Six, eight weeks."

"I guess it is what it is."

"Yes, it is," Don said.

. . .

I drove out to Sammy's place to return the Chevy.

He drove me up and down Federal Boulevard to shop for wheels of my own. I paid five-thousand cash for an eight-year-old Subaru Outback. Came with five good tires, a new battery, and a temporary cardboard license plate.

We parted at the car lot, and I found a Walgreens where I had my photo taken.

Then off to the post office to apply for a passport.

Don had nailed it—six to eight weeks.

I decided to play the game until the document arrived. Wash cars, haul cheese, make a few token bank payments, visit Leon Harris every two weeks.

I spent the rest of the afternoon in bookstores, gathering travel guides.

South America, Central America, Costa Rica, Dominican Republic.

Maybe I could make use of the Spanish I had picked up inside.

I ended the day with a T-Bone at Elway's and a jazz combo at Dazzle.

On Wednesday, I was determined to celebrate one last day before having to return to a pair of pointless jobs.

I decided gambling and drinking in Blackhawk would fit the bill.

After too many lost blackjack hands and far too many bourbon and Cokes, I knew it was time to leave the casino floor.

I knew that much.

The old man had questioned my decision-making ability.

I had blamed the lack of options.

But that evening, as I walked away from the card table, there were two clear choices.

Drive back to Denver or get a room.

The State Trooper who pulled me over had me at twelve

miles per hour over the speed limit.

He didn't need the standard tests to determine I was DUI, but he ran me through them anyway.

When he discovered I was uninsured, he deposited me in the back of his cruiser.

Handcuffed.

Three offenses.

All parole violations to boot.

Leon Harris was going to be impressed.

I was immediately bounced back in.

Do not pass go. Do not collect two-hundred grand.

I spotted my old man the next day.

I carried my tray across the dining hall and sat at the table facing him.

He was busy playing with the food on his plate.

He raised his head and looked directly into my eyes.

I wasn't surprised that he wasn't surprised to find me there.

After all, I had told him he would see me again one way or the other.

MAJOR CHORDS

"Are you sure you are alright with this?" the man asked.

"I'm certain."

"It's a big move."

"Only six-hundred-seventy-six miles."

"I mean, it's a big change."

"Change is okay."

"What about *your* work?"

"The work I do needs to be done everywhere."

"And your parents?"

"They're moving to Pensacola, and then it's only two-hundred-one miles."

"You know your geography."

"I know *you*. You have wanted this for a very long time."

"What about the boy?"

"What about the boy?"

"His school, his friends, his grandparents?"

"The boy is young. He will adapt to a new school, make new friends, maybe appreciate his grandparents more. You know what they say about absence, and he will love visiting them in Florida."

"You've thought this out."

"Did you expect less?" the woman asked.

"No."

"So there."

Man: Your memories, of places, events, even people, are not about them but about you.
Boy: Okay.
Man: Try to remember that.

"Are you hungry?"
   "Yes."
   "What would you like to eat?"
   "Mom's pancakes."
   "Use your imagination," the man said, handing the boy a piece of bread.

Boy: Are there good people?
Man: Yes, just not enough of them.
Boy: I had a dream.
Man: Yes?
Boy: We met grandfather.
Man: *My* father?
Boy: Yes.
Man: Did he say anything?
Boy: He said he was sorry.
Boy: Did Mom love me?
Man: Of course she did. Why would you ask that?
Boy: Did she love you?
Man: She always said she did.

"Why are you awake?"
   "I'm not really tired," the boy said.
   "Would you like me to read to you?"
   "I know how to read."

"I know you do, but it's not the same."

"Sometimes I forget what she looked like."

The man reached into his coat, pulled out the small mirror, and handed it to the boy.

"Like you," the man said.

Boy: Is it okay to be afraid?

Man: Only if it makes you more careful.

Boy: Why would someone hurt another person?

Man: Maybe to try forgetting how much they hurt themselves.

Boy: Does it work?

Man: Never.

"It was the best of times, it was the worst of times, it was the age of wisdom, it was the age of foolishness..."

"What book is that?"

"*A Tale of Two Cities.*"

"What cities?"

"Paris and London."

"Where?"

"Europe. Paris in France, London in England."

"Are they still there?"

"They must be."

"What makes you say that?" the boy asked.

"Hope," the man answered.

"Where are we going?"

"We are going east."

"How do you know?"

"It's where the sun rises in the morning."
"How far is the sun?"
"As I recall, the sun is ninety-three-million miles away."
"When will we get there?"
"You don't understand," the man said.
"I'm trying," the boy said.

"I need to rest for a while."
"Is it your leg?" the boy asked.
"Yes."
"There's something up ahead."
"What?"
"I'm not sure."
"I don't see anything."
"It's your eyes."
"I need to rest for a while," the man said.

"What is it?" the boy asked.
"A horse trailer."
"Something pulled by a horse?"
"Something pulled by a car or a truck to carry a horse. I wonder where the vehicle is."
"I wonder where the horse is," the boy said.

Boy: When you were my age?
Man: Yes?
Boy: What did you want to be?
Man: A baseball player.
Boy: Were you good?
Man: Good?
Boy: A good baseball player.
Man: I think so.

Boy: You don't know?
Man: Well, yes, I was a very good baseball player.
Boy: I thought so.
Man: What do you want to be?
Boy: Your age.

"There it is."
  "What?"
  "The horse."
  "Are you sure?"
  "Yes," the boy said, "yes."

"Be very quiet."
  The boy didn't make a sound.
  "It's a male. He looks healthy, he must be finding food," the man said.
  "Can we ride him without a saddle?" the boy asked.
  "We have no bridle, no reins."
  "We have rope."
  "He'll probably bolt when we get too near."
  "Maybe he won't," the boy said. "Maybe he's lonely too."

"We need to rest the animal," the man said, "and find water."
  "Maybe if we get down and walk with him, *he'll* find water."
  "You are always surprising me."
  "That's a good thing, isn't it?" the boy asked.
  "Yes, it is."

"Can we swim?"
  "Yes, but it's getting late. We need to keep our clothing dry."
  The man and the boy stripped and waded into the water.

The horse, which they called Horse, drank and watched.

They dried themselves and dressed.

"Can we stay here tonight?" the boy asked.

"Yes. Wash the towels, hang them to dry, and collect some firewood. I'll look for food."

"How about Horse?"

"I don't think he will stray. If it worries you, tie him to a tree."

"No, I mean, how about food for Horse?"

"Of course, I'll look for food for all of us."

"It was a good day," the boy said.

"It was."

"Tomorrow I will do better."

"You are doing fine."

"I found apples, berries and wild asparagus."

"Do we cook the asparagus?"

"We can, if you like. Horse will want it raw. And he will love an apple."

"Do horses eat meat?" the boy asked.

"Not usually."

"So, is Horse a vegetarian?"

"It's called herbivore. He might take cooked meat if it was offered, probably not, and he will not hunt and kill for food."

"Will we?"

"What?"

"Hunt and kill for food."

"If we need to."

"I'll have my asparagus raw," the boy said.

"How long do horses live?"

"Twenty-five years, more or less."

"Is that a long time?" the boy asked.

"It depends."

"On what?"

"On what you compare it to. A fly, for example, lives fifteen to thirty days. A bowhead whale can live two-hundred years."

"How old was Mom?"

When the man opened his eyes, it was morning.

The boy sat near, looking at the man.

"What is it?"

"I was waiting."

"Waiting?"

"To tell you."

"Tell me what?"

"Horse is gone."

"Are you sure?"

"Yes."

"I'm sorry."

"Will we be alright?" the boy asked.

"Yes, we have each other."

"Will Horse be alright?"

"I think so."

"Why did he leave?"

"I don't know."

"Maybe he needed to find another horse."

"Maybe."

"Do you think he'll come back? I do."

"What makes you say that?" the man asked.

"Hope," the boy said.

"Why are we going east?"

"To reach the big river. It is called the Mississippi."

"Why?"

"It comes from two words in a Native American language,

probably Chippewa. Missi meaning *large* and Sippi meaning *flowing water*."

"I mean, *why* are we going to the river?"

"There is a city on the river where we may find a boat to take us south."

"Why south?" asked the boy.

"It will be warmer in the South."

"It's not too cold here."

"It will be," the man said, "soon."

"What is the city called?"

"Saint Louis."

"Why *Saint* Louis?"

"It was named for a French king, who was canonized."

"Canonized?"

"Made a saint, by the church."

"Is it a holy place?"

"I don't know about that."

"Tell me something you do know about it," the boy said.

"The city always had a very good baseball team."

Boy: Do you miss me?
Man: Do I miss you? Why would you ask that?
Boy: No, I asked do you miss *Mom*.

Man: The first time I met her, she caught me in a lie.
Boy: What lie?
Man: I told her I played the guitar.
Boy: And you didn't?
Man: I had never even picked one up.
Boy: Why did you lie?

Man: I don't know. To impress her. I guess.

Boy: How did she know?

Man: She could tell from my fingers. No calluses.

Boy: Calluses?

Man: Pads on the fingertips from pressing the guitar strings.

Boy: What did she say?

Man: She said *that was it*.

Boy: That was it?

Man: She said I would only be allowed one lie for as long as I knew her and that was it.

Boy: And you never lied again?

Man: That was it.

"Would you tell me a story?"

"What kind of story?" the man asked.

"One that starts with *once upon a time* and ends with *happily ever after*."

"A fairy tale?"

"No. A real story."

"Let me think."

"What kind of boat?" the boy asked.

"A riverboat, with a steam engine and paddle wheel."

"Paddle wheel?"

"Long blades that turn like a wheel in the water and move the boat."

"How fast can it go?"

"Fifteen, maybe twenty miles every hour."

"How fast can a horse go?"

"At a gallop, twenty-five or thirty miles an hour."

"So, a horse could get to the south faster than a boat."

"No."

"Why not?"

"Obstacles."

"What are obstacles?"

"Those things that get in our way—always seem to stand between where we are and where we need to be."

"How do we know we're not there?"

"Not where?"

"Where we need to be?"

"It's a feeling. You'll understand when you are older."

"How much older?" the boy asked.

> Boy: Did you hit the dog?
> Man: The dog?
> Boy: The dog that ran in front of the car. Did you hit it?
> Man: No. I turned the wheel. I saw the dog run off.

"Can I see your hand?" the boy asked.

"Sure."

"Can I touch your fingers?"

"Of course."

"Your fingertips are hard and rough, like leather."

"It's from playing the guitar."

"When did you start playing the guitar?"

"When I couldn't play baseball any longer. There was an accident."

"Your leg?"

"Yes."

"Your father said he was sorry."

"Yes."

. . .

Once upon a time there was a young man who was a very good baseball player in high school and in college.

At the beginning of his senior year at the university, he was offered a contract to play for a professional minor league team come spring training.

He visited his parents over the Christmas holidays in the middle of his senior year. He was shoveling snow in the drive when his father returned from last-minute shopping. His father's car hit a patch of ice, skidded, and hit the young man. The young man's leg was fractured in three places.

The young man was in the hospital for nearly six weeks, recovering and doing physical therapy. The doctors told him he would never play ball again.

The man stopped there and was quiet for some time.

"Are you alright?" the boy asked.

"Can we continue later?"

"Okay."

The young man was immediately charmed by his physical therapist. She was bright, and funny, encouraging, and lovely. He wasn't talking much, but she talked enough for both of them. Although she had worked with many athletes, she was much more interested in music than sports. So, the young man lied to her—for the first and last time.

One day, she brought something for him.

"What's this?" he asked.

"It's a guitar."

"I mean *what*?"

"It's a gift. It's something you can do without having to try stealing a base."

"Where do I begin?" he asked.

"Major chords."

Playing the guitar became the young man's passion, replacing the thing he loved but could no longer do. He fell in love with the guitar and fell in love with the woman who had introduced him to the instrument. They were soon married and, before long, they had a child. A beautiful boy.

The young man began playing with other musicians, and his talent was becoming widely recognized and talked about. And one day he was approached with an offer he knew could change his life—the opportunity to play lead guitar in a world-famous band. However, he would have to relocate to New Orleans if he was interested in joining the group.

The man talked to his wife, and she assured him it was the right thing to do. So, it was decided. The man, the woman and the boy packed the car and started the journey from the city of Saint Louis on the Mississippi, to the south where the river ended at New Orleans.

"And they all lived happily ever after," said the boy.

The man went quiet.

"I'm sleepy," said the boy.

"Good night," said the man.

"Did he blame his father," the boy asked, "because he couldn't play baseball anymore?"

"I think so, yes, for a long time."

"His father was sorry."

> Boy: I feel sad.
>
> Man: Would you like to talk about it?
>
> Boy: I don't know how to talk about it.
>
> Man: I've always had trouble talking about feelings. But if you don't find a way to let people know how you feel, you will be very lonely. If you don't find a way to let the sadness go, it stays with you forever.
>
> Boy: How do you tell your feelings if you can't

talk about them?
Man: There are many ways.
Boy: How do *you*?
Man: With the guitar.

"Maybe I could write them down," the boy said.
"What?"
"The feelings. Maybe I could be a writer."

The man felt a nudging at his shoulder and felt the hot breath on his cheek. When he opened his eyes, he saw Horse.
The boy was sitting on the animal's back.
"I have to go," the boy said.
"Are you sure?"
"Yes."
"I'm sorry, son.
"I know, father. It was not your fault."
The man watched them ride away and closed his eyes again.

When the man opened his eyes, he found himself in a hospital bed.
A nurse stood at his side.
"Where am I?"
"University of Tennessee Health Center," she said. "Memphis."
"How long?"
"You were brought in last night. There was an accident."
"The boy?"
"I'm very sorry."
"We were going to New Orleans. Can I be alone for a while?"
"Of course."

. . .

"What happened?"

"You were on Route fifty-five, southbound," the doctor said. "Witnesses say you swerved to avoid hitting a dog, into the path of a truck pulling a horse trailer. Your vehicle plowed into a concrete road divider, your son died instantly. It's a miracle you survived."

"The other vehicle?"

"A man and a boy."

"Are they alright?"

"They are both fine."

"And the horse?"

"I don't know. I can try to find out."

"How long will I be here?"

"It's hard to say. Your leg is fractured in three places. You won't be able to walk for quite a while. Is there anything we can do to help you get through this?"

"You can find me a guitar."

When they had finally arrived home after the terrible incident on the highway, it had been well past midnight.

The boy slept very late the next morning, following a fitful sleep inhabited by confusing images.

He found the man in the kitchen drinking coffee.

"Was anyone hurt?" the boy asked.

"Yes, I'm afraid so."

"Bad?"

"Yes."

"Was it our fault?"

"No, it was an accident."

"I had bad dreams."

"They will pass, son. Now, help me unhitch the trailer and then you can feed your horse while I make breakfast."

"Pancakes?"

"Sure."

MENTAL BLOCKS

"I hope they made loads of money because that had to be the most boring fundraiser I have ever attended, and I've been to quite a few."

"I felt my opening remarks went pretty well."

"Not bad. You might have eighty-sixed the *knock-knock* joke."

"I thought you liked that one."

"Your timing was a little off," Janet said, "and the other speakers. You could market a recording of the mayor's speech as a cure for insomnia. Not to mention the food was awful."

"And such small portions," Ben said.

"Now, that's good. You should have used that one."

Ben Madison pulled the car into the driveway, climbed out, crossed to the passenger side, and opened the door for his wife.

The couple walked hand-in-hand to the front entrance of their home.

"Very quiet," Ben said, as they stepped into the house.

"It's a good sign. Rachel didn't throw a wild party, and April must be asleep."

"Go up and check on the princess," Ben said. "I'll find Rachel, pay her, and see if she needs a ride home."

Ben found the babysitter bound and gagged in the kitchen just as his wife was rushing down the stairs to find out why their three-year-old was not asleep in her room.

A moment after entering the kitchen, Janet screamed.

John Falcone walked into his house and found Cora in the living room. Reading.

"Sorry I'm so late."

John sat heavily on the sofa beside his wife.

"Tired?" Cora asked.

"Very."

"You're off tomorrow. You can sleep late."

"I hope so. I missed the bedtime story."

"Only by thirty minutes. It took nearly an hour to get her away from the blocks."

"Blocks?"

"My mother dropped by. She found a box of wood alphabet blocks at a thrift store. She believes it will get Sara started on spelling."

"From everything I've read or heard, children don't learn to spell before five or six."

"My mother is convinced her first grandchild is a genius, and who could blame her?"

"Maybe I can teach Sara to spell D-A-D."

"Would you like a drink, *Dad?*"

"I could use one."

"So could I. Scotch rocks, please," Cora said.

As Falcone was rising from the sofa to fetch drinks, his cell phone rang.

Sam Harris was waiting on the front porch of the Madison home when Falcone arrived at the scene twenty minutes later.

"Three-year-old girl kidnapped," he said.

Falcone immediately thought of his daughter.

"Parents were out. The intruder gained access through the rear door, off the alley. He took the babysitter, Rachel, tied and gagged her in the kitchen, and walked out with the child."

"One perpetrator?"

"That's all the sitter saw. He was masked, but she felt certain it was a man. She's sixteen years old."

"How did he overcome her?"

"Pointed a gun and warned her to keep silent."

"How did he bind her?"

"Neck ties. Hands and legs, and over her mouth."

"Did he harm her?"

"No. It looked as if he treated her gently."

"That could be the *good* news," Detective Falcone said. "Who are the parents?"

"The child's father is Benjamin Madison."

"The city councilman?"

"Yes. The mother is Janet Gorman-Madison. *Her* father is James Gorman."

"The developer?"

"The developer who built most of the hotels and casinos in Black Hawk and Central City. He's worth millions."

"A good mark for a ransom demand."

"The intruder may have known that the Madisons were away. He may know them."

"Hold on to that thought. Who's in the house?"

"Officers Campos and Jackson. First at the scene. Responding to a nine-one-one call from the father. State police immediately put out an Amber Alert. Additional uniforms are on their way here to canvas the neighborhood."

"Have you been in?"

"Briefly," Harris said.

"And?"

"Found out what the sitter had to say and told the Madisons I preferred to wait for my partner before we spoke. I asked them to write down everything about the child—her birth date, height, weight, hair, eye color, distinguishing marks—and I passed the information on for the alerts."

"Do you think the sitter knows more than she's saying?"

"I don't. She is a very frightened teenager. She needs to get home to *her* parents. If we feel a need to talk to her again, after we speak to the Madisons, we'll know where to find her."

"Okay, when the other uniforms arrive, Campos can take the girl home," Falcone said. "Let's talk with the parents. They've waited long enough. What's the little girl's name?"

"April."

The two Denver police detectives went in to see April's parents.

The only word Falcone could think of to describe Ben and Janet Madison was *petrified*.

The couple sat huddled together on the living room sofa, courageously trying to remain focused during the interview—but they were clearly drifting into dark thoughts no parent would wish to imagine.

Falcone and Harris were racing through the questions. Anxious to leave the Madisons to somehow console each other, because both knew they could offer no assurances.

"How well do you know Rachel?" Harris asked.

"We've known her since she was a child. Her mother is my best friend," Janet said. "She is like a big sister to April."

"Is there anyone you know who might do something like this?"

"Why would you ask that?" Ben said.

"We always ask, Mr. Madison," Harris said.

"No."

"By now television and radio media have been notified," John said, "and everyone with a cell phone has received a text alert. Every law enforcement agency in the state is onboard. Additional police officers will interview all of your neighbors, and we'll follow any leads. Officer Campos drove Rachel home. He and Officer Jackson will remain outside the house all night. If there is anything you need, anything at all, let the officers know and they will see to it. And if anyone contacts you, let them know immediately. We will arrange to have all incoming calls monitored."

"You believe we'll receive a ransom demand?" Madison asked.

"I do," Falcone said.

What Falcone didn't say was *I hope so.* Falcone understood that with child abductions, kidnapping for ransom was the best-case scenario.

Other motives led to far more tragic outcomes.

"Would you mind if we take a look at April's room?" Falcone asked.

"Not at all," Ben said.

When they walked into the child's room, Falcone noted the cloth blocks on the floor at the foot of the bed.

Falcone and Harris walked together down to their vehicles.

Harris held a sheet of paper.

"What do you have there?" Falcone asked.

"The description Janet Madison gave us. Thirty-seven inches tall, thirty-one pounds, blonde hair, blue eyes, birthmark on the right thigh. The child turned three a few months ago."

"When exactly?"

"On the ninth of July."

All of the color left Falcone's face.

"Jesus, John. You look like you just saw a ghost."

"That's the exact same day my daughter Sara was born."

"And?"

"And icy fingers just ran up and down my spine."

It was well after midnight when Falcone arrived home.

Falcone checked the back door and all of the windows before going upstairs.

He slipped into bed as quietly as possible, not wanting to

wake Cora. The moment his head hit the pillow, her bedside lamp came on.

"Bad?" his wife asked.

"Yes."

"Did someone die?"

"No. Something just as horrible. Maybe worse. Can we talk about it in the morning? I'm ready to pass out."

"Sure. Can I show you something before you do?"

"Sure."

Cora reached for her cell phone and brought up a photo.

It showed wood alphabet blocks on the floor of Sara's bedroom.

Centered in the picture were four blocks side by side.

H E L P

"What am I looking at?"

"Just after you left, I went up to check on Sara. She was out of her bed, playing with the blocks. I had to go through the bedtime story routine a second time to get her back to sleep and, when I asked her what the blocks spelled, she said *mommy*. What do you think of that?"

"I'm too tired to think," John said, resisting an impulse to voice what he *was* thinking.

Cora set the phone back on the table and turned off the light.

She kissed her husband on the forehead as he closed his eyes.

Falcone fell asleep immediately, but the bad dreams lasted all night.

He dreamt of a frightened little girl crying out for her mother.

And he dreamt of *his* mother saving his life.

Falcone sat at the kitchen table. Cora poured coffee.

"They were born on the same day?"

"Yes," John said.

"What is the child's name?"

"April. Her father is City Councilman Madison."

"My God, John. They were at University Hospital when we were there. I met her mother, Janet, in the ward. Sara and April were in adjacent cribs in the nursery. Can you imagine how terrified they must feel?"

"I don't want to imagine."

"Please get Sara. I want her here with us."

"Hi, Daddy," Sara said when her father came into the living room.

"Good morning, pumpkin. What are you doing?"

"Playing."

"Let's go have breakfast," he said, reaching down to pick her up.

Wood blocks were scattered across the floor.

In the center were four blocks neatly arranged in line.

K A T T

"What's this?" John asked.

"Blocks, silly."

"What does it spell?

"Cat?"

Falcone called Cora into the room.

"Your mother was right again, her granddaughter is a genius," John said, as the telephone rang.

It was Sam Harris.

"Meet me at the Madison home. They received the call."

Falcone and Harris sat in the living room with Ben Madison, listening to the voice of the man who took April Madison from her bed.

The caller made a ransom demand, gave an assurance that the child would not be harmed if the demand was met, and told the girl's father to expect a follow-up call to make arrangements for an exchange.

"Can the phone call be traced?" Madison asked, as soon as the recording ended.

"We can try," Harris said, "but it was most likely a burner, a throwaway. Can you come up with two hundred thousand dollars?"

"Janet called her father, he's on his way. I need to see how my wife is doing."

Madison left Harris and Falcone alone in the room.

"I believe we're dealing with an amateur. What seasoned criminal uses neckties, probably his own, to restrain a victim?"

"He *did* have a gun," Harris said.

"I would be surprised if it was loaded. He handled the sitter with kid gloves. And the call. It sounded as if it was scripted from an eighties television show. It has me wondering if he's figured out yet how to make the exchange."

"What are you thinking?"

"I'm thinking this is someone without malice toward the child. Someone who needs the money, and made a very poor decision about how to get it."

"Is that good or bad?"

"Good and bad. It means he's not intent on harming the child and will give her up safely for the cash."

"And the bad?"

"When someone doesn't know much about what he's doing, intentions can go terribly wrong."

"The Feds will jump in—*if* we call them," Harris said.

"Let's hold off. Did the uniforms get anything from the neighbors?"

"No one saw or heard a thing."

Falcone's cell phone rang. It was his wife.

"John, can you come home?"

"Is something wrong? Is Sara all right?"

"There's something you *really* need to see. *Please.*"

"I'm on my way."

"Is everything okay?" Harris asked.

"I'm not sure. I need to run home."

"Go."

"I'll be back as soon as I can," Falcone said, and hurried off.

A few minutes later, Ben Madison came back into the room with another man.

"This is Janet's father, James Gorman. Would you and Detective Falcone like coffee?"

"Detective Falcone had to run out for a while," Harris said. "I would love coffee."

They sat at the kitchen table.

Harris sensed Gorman had something to say.

"What's on your mind, sir?"

"You asked my daughter and son-in-law if there was anyone they could think of who might have done this."

"Yes?"

"I may have an idea."

"Tell me, sir."

"Where is Sara?" Falcone asked, when he came rushing into the house.

"She's fine. I put her down for a nap," Cora said. "It was a battle."

"Your call scared me."

"Probably not as much as this scared me," she said, leading him into the living room.

In the center of all the blocks scattered across the floor were five set side by side.

A P R I L

"What is this?"

"I don't know. I came in to take her up for her nap and found it."

"Did she say what it means?" John asked, trying to control his emotions.

"She's only three years old."

"DID YOU ASK HER WHAT IT MEANT?"

"John, you're shouting at me. And you'll wake her up."

"I'm sorry," John said, taking a deep breath, trying to remain composed. "Did you ask her what it spelled, Cora?"

"I did. She said it spelled *girl*. I'm frightened, John."

Falcone took his wife into his arms.

He tried to think of how to assure her there was nothing to be frightened about, but he wasn't truly convinced himself.

"Do you remember the story I told you about my mother saving my life?"

"Yes, and that was creepy also. I'm going up to check on Sara."

Falcone sat on the sofa, staring down at the blocks.

His cell phone rang.

"We may have a lead, from James Gorman," Sam Harris said. "I think we should check it out."

"Can you pick me up? There's something I think you should see."

The three stood in the living room.

Looking down at the blocks on the floor.

"I don't know what to make of this," Sam said.

"We're having the same problem," Cora said. "I need a drink."

"Could you make that two?" Harris asked.

"Three," Falcone said.

Cora left to pour the Scotch.

"I think April Madison is calling out to us through Sara."

"Using the blocks?"

"Yes."

"That's crazy, John."

"When I was a freshman in college, I shared a place with two other students. They were away on a camping trip. I was in the house alone, asleep, and I felt someone shaking me awake and calling my name. I opened my eyes and my mother was standing over me. *Come, John,* she said, and led me out through the smoke. When I reached the street, I was alone—and the house was engulfed in flames."

"And your mother?"

"My mother had passed away more than two years earlier."

Before Harris could come up with something to say, Cora returned with the drinks.

"Tell me about the lead from Gorman," Falcone said.

"Gorman dismissed an electrical sub-contractor because the outfit was using materials that failed to meet legal specifications. It was a half-million-dollar contract. The head of the company pleaded with Gorman to reconsider. He said that losing the income, and the resulting bad publicity, would destroy his business. He promised to correct the problem. Gorman would not back down—and he was threatened."

"Threatened?"

"Gorman was told *he would pay.*"

"Who was the contractor?"

"William Katt."

"Spelled K-A-T-T?"

"Yes."

"DO YOU HAVE THE ADDRESS?"

"Yes. *What is it, John?* Are you alright?"

"I'll explain on the way. Let's go."

"We should wait for a warrant," Harris said.

"We need to go *right now*, Sam."

Falcone rang the doorbell.

Harris stood behind him.

"William Katt?" Falcone asked, when the door opened several minutes later.

"Yes, how can I help you?"

"Tell us where the child is."

"I don't know what you are talking about."

Falcone grabbed William Katt roughly by the shirt collar and shoved the man into the house.

He threw his forearm across Katt's neck and pinned him to the wall.

"WHERE IS THE GIRL?"

The menace in the detective's eyes defeated Katt immediately.

"She's safe, upstairs, bedroom," Katt managed to choke out, struggling to breathe. "I meant no harm."

"MEANT NO HARM?" Falcone screamed, pushing against the man's neck with more force.

"Please," Katt said, gasping for air.

"John," Harris said, pulling Falcone away, "we need to find the child."

Falcone raced up the stairs.

He found April in a bedroom closet, crying.

He lifted the child up into his arms.

Falcone held the child tight to his chest and talked to her softly, trying to soothe her.

"Sara sent us," he said, once she had stopped trembling.

The following day, Falcone walked into the Second Home Thrift Store on South Broadway.

He approached the woman at the counter.

"Good morning," the woman said.

"Good morning. I was hoping you could help me."

"I will certainly try."

"Do you remember selling a set of wood alphabet blocks recently?"

"I do," she said, "to a very nice lady."

"My mother-in-law. She bought them for my daughter."

"She was very glad to find them, they were hardly used."

"Why was that?"

"The woman who brought them in said *her* daughter was throwing the blocks. The child broke an expensive vase, among other things. I suggested she try *cloth blocks*. They serve the purpose and are a lot safer."

"Do you keep a record of who brings donations?"

"Not unless the value is more than one hundred dollars."

"So, you wouldn't remember who donated the blocks?"

"In this case I would, the woman makes contributions often."

"Can you tell me her name?"

"I don't believe I can without permission from the donor."

Falcone showed the woman his identification.

"Just between you and me," he said, "was it Janet Madison?"

"Why, yes. I heard about her daughter. I can't imagine what she and her husband went through. It must have been a living nightmare. Was it you who found the child?"

"We had help," Falcone said.

"If you believe the wood blocks may be harmful, and want to return them—that is no problem."

"No," John said, after a moment's thought. "We'll take our chances."

NO MILK TODAY

"Kill me."

"What?"

"I want you to kill me."

"Are you serious?"

"Yes."

"And how do you suggest I kill you?"

"I don't know. Smother me with a pillow. Throw me off a bridge. Shoot me in the head."

"Why would I do that? Why would you even ask me to do that?"

"I want to die. I don't know who else to ask."

"If you want to die so badly, shoot *yourself* in the head."

"I can't. Suicide is not as easy as murder," Matt said. "Look at the statistics."

A waitress arrived at their table.

"What can I get for you gentlemen?"

"Matt?"

"Yes?"

"What would you order if it was your last meal?" Bobby asked.

"What do you mean?"

"If you were requesting a last meal before going off to the electric chair or firing squad or whatever. What would you want?"

"Warm cherry pie with vanilla ice cream, and a root beer float."

"There you go."

"What?"

"That alone should take care of your death wish. Please bring my friend a warm slice of cherry pie with vanilla ice cream, and a root beer float," Bobby said to the waitress. "I'll take coffee."

"Is that all you're having?" Matt asked, as the waitress walked off.

"That's it. Do you really want to die?"

"Yes."

"Tell me why."

"It's a long list. It could take a while."

"There's nowhere I need to be."

"I lost my job," Matt began, "and can't find anything that pays more than unemployment benefits. My wife filed for divorce and won't let me see the kids. I'm living in a flea bag transient hotel and paying eighteen hundred a month on a house I can't get in to. I'm about to lose my car. I'm paying three hundred a week vig on a gambling debt I'll never cover. Should I go on?"

"I get the picture. And you want *me* to kill you because you can't do it yourself?"

"Yes."

"I have a better idea."

"Will there be anything else?"

"No thanks, Tina," Bobby said, reading the nametag on her turquoise blouse and thinking the color didn't suit her, "just the check."

Tina scribbled a total, placed the guest check on the table, and moved off to another booth.

"Take down a card game?" Matt said.

"Yes. Six players. Each needs to walk in with no less than forty thousand in cash to sit at the table."

"That's two hundred thousand dollars cash."

"Two hundred forty," Bobby said, "minimum."

"When?"

"The last Friday of every month, at midnight."

"Are you talking about Vito Cirelli's Friday game?"

"That's the one."

"Every would-be takedown artist in Brooklyn has known about the game for a long time. And as tempting as a quarter million cash may sound, why do you think no one ever touches it?"

"Because Vito Cirelli would let anyone who tried simply walk out with the money—and then hunt him down, find him, and kill him."

"Exactly," Matt said. "It would be suicide."

"There you go."

It was two in the morning, now Sunday, when they left the all-night diner.

Bobby was behind the wheel.

"Where are we headed?" Matt asked.

"To the shithole you're calling home, to pick up your things. Then to my place, where you can bunk for the time being. You can have the couch. In the morning I'll make breakfast, whatever you like, and we can talk about Cirelli's card game. Do we need to pick up root beer and ice cream?"

"Why are you doing this?"

"An old friend calls at eleven on a Saturday night. Begs you to meet him at the Del Rio Diner. It's important. He pleads with you to kill him because he doesn't know who else to ask. What would you do?"

They slept late Sunday morning.

"What would you like in your omelet? Mushrooms? Cheddar? Bacon? Cherry Pie?"

"Hold the pie," Matt said.

"Help yourself to coffee, pour me a cup, throw some bread

in the toaster, I need to break a few eggs."

Thirty minutes later, Bobby Doyle dropped the breakfast dishes into the sink, grabbed the coffee pot, refilled their cups, sat at the kitchen table across from Matt Mancini, and lit a cigarette.

"Cirelli started the game two years ago, with a ten-thousand-dollar cash entry fee. During the second meeting, two clowns came in and walked out with sixty grand. Less than two weeks later they were both found dead, beaten to a pulp, their bodies dumped in the middle of Grand Army Plaza. A warning."

"Pulp?"

"Looked like they came out of a trash compactor."

"And no one has tried it again since," Matt said.

"And the players have so much confidence in Cirelli's security that Vito has been able to continually up the buy-in price."

"Is that all he has for security? Reputation?"

"We'll get to that."

"Does Cirelli play?"

"Sometimes—but he doesn't need to. Cirelli takes five per cent of every dollar that comes into the game, and another five per cent of the winnings from all players who are walking out with more than they came in with. He can pick his nose and watch Disney movies all night, and still earn twenty grand."

"Smart arrangement."

"If I didn't dislike the creep so much, I would say it was brilliant."

"Do you have something personal going with Vito Cirelli?" Matt asked.

"We'll get to that."

Matt returned the foldout bed to sofa mode, and the two men reconvened in the living room.

"The contest takes place in the rear dining room of Cirelli's restaurant on Eighteenth Avenue in Bensonhurst. The players need to have forty thousand in cash delivered to the place by six on the night of the game in exchange for a receipt that will get them in for the game. The kitchen stops serving at nine. All of the customers and help are cleared out by eleven."

Doyle lit a cigarette before continuing.

"The players can arrive at the rear door of the restaurant between eleven fifteen and eleven forty-five. Show up one minute late, and you don't get in."

"And the forty grand deposit?"

"Non-refundable. Forfeit. Half goes directly into Vito Cirelli's pocket, the rest goes into the kitty in increments during the course of the game. Are you with me so far?"

"Yes."

"The players are greeted at the rear door by a *sentry*, Sal Basilio, hired hand. He collects the receipts. He conducts a thorough pat down, and grants entrance. Vito, the gracious host, supplies drinks. The game begins at midnight, sharp. Time runs out at six in the morning, and then they all leave to either celebrate or lament."

"Where do we come in?"

"We come in with the ricotta and the mozzarella."

"Now you lost me," Matt said.

"Let's go for a walk."

Matt and Bobby sat on a bench on the Shore Road Promenade looking out at the Narrows and the Verrazano Bridge.

"This waterway connects the Atlantic to New York City Harbor, with Fort Hamilton on this side and Fort Wadsworth on the Staten Island side. The first line of defense against British ships during the Revolutionary War. The troops stationed here were the first in the line of fire, equipped with cannon balls and determination."

Doyle lit a cigarette.

"Those things will kill you," Matt said.

227

"Want a few?"

"No. But thanks for asking."

"When my father was in his early teens, he and a couple of his friends caddied at the golf course in Dyker Park. Afterwards, they would sneak into the mess hall at Fort Hamilton and an ancient black man in the kitchen would hook them up with fried chicken and chocolate milk. My old man insisted it was the best chicken and chocolate milk he ever had in his life."

"Speaking of milk?" Matt said.

"Right," Bobby said. "The front door of Cirelli's restaurant is secured with a keypad lock. At five on Saturday mornings, the restaurant receives a dairy delivery—milk, cheese, eggs. The delivery driver has the access code. The stop before Cirelli's is the C-Town Supermarket on Sixty-Sixth Street and Eighteenth Avenue. We wait until the driver has finished making his drop at C-Town, and then we take him."

"Take him?"

"We grab him. We convince him to give up the keypad code, and secure him in the back of the truck. Then you drive the truck over to Cirelli's, I follow in my car."

"Hijack a dairy truck."

"That's the idea. We throw ricotta and provolone onto the two-wheeler, go in through the front door, drop the cheese at the kitchen, go into the dining room, and we collect the cash. Then we walk back out through the front door, jump into my car, and bounce."

"Simple as that."

"It's not rocket surgery."

"And where is Sal Basilio while this is going on?"

"Sal leaves at midnight, and he is not back until six in the morning to let the guests out the rear door. We'll be long gone."

"Free and clear."

"I don't know about that."

"The next game is this coming Friday at midnight," Matt said.

"Right. So we need to find a couple of guns."

. . .

Early Friday evening, Bobby and Matt sat at Doyle's kitchen table.

They had polished off the Sicilian pizza from L&B, washed down with Miller High Life from long neck bottles.

"The simple things," Doyle said. "It doesn't get much better than this."

"Why?"

"Why?"

"Why take the risk?" Matt asked.

"I've been wanting to take a trip around the world, ending in Ireland, for a few years. Your end of the take could go a long way to easing some of your troubles. It may not win your wife back, but you could find a divorce lawyer bright enough to keep you from losing your kids. Pay off your gambling debt, find a decent place to live, make a car payment, and maybe have enough left over to hire an employment specialist."

"And?"

"And I want to hurt Cirelli. If we pull this off he will be a quarter million in the hole and his Friday night goldmine will be history."

"So," Matt asked. "What is it between you and Cirelli?"

"Vito Cirelli killed my father."

"Your father died in an automobile accident."

"It was anything but an accident. Do you remember my father's business?"

"He moved freight. I remember him taking us for a ride on one of the trucks when we were kids."

"Cirelli was squeezing dad for a percentage of the business. What they called *protection*, back in the day. My father wouldn't pay. Cirelli had him run off the road on the Belt Parkway."

"How do you know that?"

"I got a call a few weeks ago. A patient at Coney Island Hospital needed to see me. His name was Johnny Bardo. Cancer was eating him alive, he must have weighed eighty pounds. They were giving him less than two weeks. Bardo said he needed to get it off his chest. He told me Vito Cirelli paid him to force my dad's car into the concrete barrier at the approach to the Verrazano."

"That was twenty years ago."

"Twenty-two. I was nine years old. It was my parents' anniversary that day. There were a dozen long-stemmed red roses on the seat beside his body," Bobby said. "I asked Bardo to talk to the police. He said he needed to think about it. He died the next day."

"Cirelli will stop at nothing to track us down and kill us."

"It will become his life's mission. He'll give it everything he's got."

"And?" Matt asked.

"If he gets real close, I'll kill you myself if you prefer."

At four on Saturday morning, Bobby and Matt sat in Doyle's car near the delivery entrance of the C-Town Supermarket. It was well before sunrise, and the street was dark and deserted.

"I don't know if I can use this thing," Matt said, looking down at the .38 resting on his lap.

"It's just for show. It's loaded with blanks, but it will make an awful lot of noise. If anyone seems uncooperative, aim high and pull the trigger. Never fails to regain order in the classroom."

"Where did you find the masks?"

"Party City on Atlantic Avenue. Would you rather be Batman or the Joker?"

"Batman."

"Try it on."

Matt slipped the mask over his head.

"You complete me," Bobby said. "Here's the delivery truck."

They waited until the delivery driver had completed the drop at C-Town, and *took him* as he was pushing the truck ramp back up into its track.

The Joker was holding a weapon, and the driver gave up command of his ship without an argument. They closed him in the rear of the vehicle.

"Turn off the refrigeration," Bobby said, as Matt climbed up into the cab. "It's cold back there. I'll be right behind you."

Minutes later, Bobby parked his car. He crossed the avenue and joined Matt at the rear of the delivery truck, now sitting in front of Cirelli's restaurant.

Doyle carried a blue gym bag sporting a New York Giants logo.

Bobby jumped up into the truck and handed down the two-wheeler and a couple of cases of dairy product. The driver sat there doing his best to ignore the two men.

"You'll be fine," Doyle said to the driver.

Bobby jumped down, closed and latched the rear door.

Matt rolled the hand truck up to the front of the restaurant.

Bobby punched in the keypad code and they were in.

"We didn't load any milk," Matt said.

"No milk today."

They left the hand truck in the hall just outside the kitchen.

"Did we really need to bring this in at all?" Matt asked.

"Probably not, but I thought it was a nice touch. Are you ready?"

"Yes."

They adjusted their masks and pulled their weapons.

When they walked back to the dining room they found seven men sitting at the card table, including Vito Cirelli. The table was covered with cash.

One hundred dollar bills, loose or in wrapped bundles.

Doyle's voice was slightly muffled through the rubber mask.

"Cirelli, slowly move your chair away from the table and stay seated with your fingers locked behind your neck," Bobby said. "Everyone else, get down on the floor, face down, legs wide apart, arms fully extended above your heads. Don't make me wait."

Everyone but Cirelli hit the deck.

Bobby handed Matt the gym bag.

Matt put his gun into the gym bag, moved around the table, and filled the bag with cash.

He stood holding the bag, not quite sure what to do next.

Bobby moved to Matt and handed him a ring of keys.

"Go," he said. "Bring the car up front. I'll be out in a minute."

Matt walked out with the gym bag.

Doyle looked around the room. The men on the floor were not moving. When Bobby's eyes finally met Cirelli's, Vito was smiling.

"You're a dead man," Cirelli said.

"Eventually."

"How much time do you think it will take for me to hunt you down and kill you?"

"More time than you have," Doyle said.

Bobby raised his weapon, pointed it at Cirelli's chest, and pulled the trigger six times.

SUITABLE FOR FRAMING

There was no denying he had learned a thing or two from dear old dad.

His father had been a con man until the day he died.

Good at what he did—better at not getting caught.

It could have been a successful, if dubious, calling had it not been for the drinking and the violence. His old man hurt people—and he seemed to enjoy it as much as he did the booze.

He inherited his father's con-artistry, love of the game, and uncanny ability to avoid arrest and imprisonment.

He also inherited the compulsion to punish.

After years of drifting and conning and doing damage, he took a good long look in the mirror and saw a man destined for a jail cell or an unmarked grave.

There was a rumor going around.

He had been hearing it his entire life.

Everyone has choices.

That may be true at the start but, over time, possibilities continually diminish.

The choices made early limit the choices allowed later.

Until you are forced to admit there's only one choice left.

And then, finally, you find yourself right back where you started.

He returned to Denver, and he began again from square one.

And hoped he could control his impulses.

He was thinking about how well he was doing when his cell phone rang.

"Slow down, Laura, I can't follow you."

"There are two men walking up the driveway. I can see them from the pantry window. There's absolutely no reason for them to be here. I'm on my cell phone."

"Are you alone?"

"Yes. Jimmy left a few hours ago. I recognize one of the men, Charlie Sanders. Works for Jimmy. It wouldn't alarm me so much if I didn't believe Jimmy would like me better dead."

"Why would your husband want you dead?"

"Jimmy is an animal. He hits me, then keeps me locked up in this prison until the bruises heal. I told him I was planning to leave him. He glared at me as if he wanted to strangle me on the spot, and he swore I would never see a penny."

"Why did you marry him?"

"Because *you* never offered. They're at the back door."

"Call nine-one-one."

"I'm calling you."

"There needs to be a record of a distress call. Get upstairs, hide, and call it in. I'm on my way."

Detective John Holden answered before the second ring of his cell phone.

It was his partner, Sam Gentry.

"What?"

"Emergency call, home invasion, Cheesman Park at Tenth Avenue. A patrol car is on the way. I'm ten minutes out."

"I'll meet you there."

. . .

The large home sat on nearly an acre of property up against the park.

It was completely enclosed by walls, with the exception of two wrought iron security gates. One at the main entrance at the front of the mansion, and the other on the south side. The south gate gave access to a driveway wide enough for one automobile and led to a parking area which could accommodate four vehicles. There were uniformed officers at both gates.

Holden entered from the south gate, walked up the drive, and found another uniform at the rear door.

"Woman, Caucasian, mid-thirties, DOA," the officer said. "Detective Gentry is inside."

Holden walked through the mudroom into the large kitchen and called out for his partner.

"In here, John."

Coming out of the kitchen, Holden saw Gentry standing in the dining room at the foot of the stairway leading up to the second story. When he reached Gentry, he saw the body lying across the bottom stairs.

"Laura Pappas, she lived here with her husband. It appears she was alone in the house. Shot in the back, twice. Looks as if she was starting up the stairs."

"Where's the husband?"

"We're trying to locate him," Gentry said. "Do you know who her husband is?"

"Should I?"

"Jimmy Pappas owns the two most successful bars downtown on Market Street, near the ballpark. Pappas is one of the richest businessmen in the city. This place alone is valued at four million."

"Organized crime connections?"

"From what I know, he's a self-made man. He started with a few greasy spoon diners in Capitol Hill. The guy has a lot of political clout."

Officer Lewis came in from the kitchen.

"Detectives."

"Yes?" Holden said.

"They located the husband. He's on his way."

"Thank you," Holden said. "Let us know as soon as he arrives."

"Attractive lady," Gentry said, after Lewis left the room. "I need some air. I'll wait outside for the medical examiner and the crime scene unit, and make sure the uniforms are keeping civilians at bay."

Holden put on a pair of latex gloves and stepped up to take a closer look at the body.

Something caught his eye. A reflection of light.

He pulled a cell phone from under the victim and checked the most recent incoming and outgoing calls.

He moved past the body and climbed the stairs.

Ten minutes later, Holden was heading to the back door when he ran into Gentry leading the medical examiner into the kitchen from the mudroom. The two-man forensics team followed at their heels.

"Has Jimmy Pappas arrived?" Holden asked.

"He just pulled up. We don't want him in here yet. I'll be right out," Gentry said, and he led the other men to the victim.

Holden moved out to the front entrance, where two uniforms were doing their best to keep Jimmy Pappas from charging through the security gate and up the stairs to the front door.

"Sir, please remain where you are," Holden called as he approached.

"Who the fuck are you?"

"Detective Holden, sir."

"This is *my* fucking home, and it's *my* wife in there."

"I understand, sir. But there's nothing you can do for her now. I'm very sorry. Your home is now a murder scene and we can't have any civilians in the house until the medical examiner is done and the body is removed. You can see the victim when you come down for the identification. That would be sometime tomorrow morning."

"I don't appreciate your tone, Holden. Do you know who I am?"

"It's Detective Holden, Mr. Pappas, and I appreciate your co-operation, sir. While we allow the technicians and medical examiner to do their jobs, I need to ask you a few routine questions."

Detective Gentry joined them at the gate.

"Is that your vehicle, sir?" Gentry asked Pappas, spotting the Lincoln Town Car in the middle of the street in front of the house.

"Yes."

"What is your driver's name?"

"Stanley."

Gentry walked down to the limousine and spoke to the driver through the car window.

"You need to move the vehicle, Stanley," Gentry said, "and then I have a few questions."

Gentry and Holden sat at a picnic table near the rear door and compared notes.

The two-man ambulance team stood with a wheeled gurney at the door, waiting for the body to be released.

"The driver picked Pappas up here a few hours ago," Holden said. "They went directly to one of his clubs. Pappas was at the club when the emergency call came in, and he was there until receiving the call about the break-in."

"Witnesses?"

"He said there were at least fifty people who could put him at the club."

"The driver said the same. Stanley sat in the back office until Pappas had him drive back here."

"In the office alone?" Holden asked.

"Said he was playing cards with another guy who works for Pappas."

"Get a name?"

"Charlie Sanders. Does this feel like a robbery to you?"

"You see it differently?"

"I don't know," Gentry said. "This place is like a fortress. How did the shooter get in? And there was nothing upset in the place."

"The shooter could have scaled a wall. The back door may have been unlocked. Maybe he intended a robbery and when he discovered someone at home he decided to bail."

"But why *shoot* the woman?"

Before Holden could voice an opinion, the medical examiner walked out and told the ambulance team they could take the victim.

"We found this under her body," he said.

He handed Gentry a plastic evidence bag holding a cell phone.

"I'll get on the autopsy first thing in the morning," the M.E. said. "Please, don't let anyone bother me before ten."

Jimmy Pappas sat in the back seat behind his driver and watched the ambulance pull away.

Detective Holden tapped on the door of the Lincoln.

"You can go in now if you need to," he said, when Pappas put down the window. "The forensic team will be here for a while longer, please try to stay out of their way. Two uniformed officers will also be remaining. If you would come down to the coroner's office at ten tomorrow morning, sir, we need you to positively identify the deceased."

If Pappas had anything to say, Holden didn't wait to hear it.

"Want to grab an early breakfast, Sam?" Holden asked as they walked toward their cars.

"I'm beat."

"I'll see you in the morning."

"You will," Gentry agreed.

Holden decided on a few drinks instead.

He drove to the Skylark Lounge on Broadway, planted himself on a stool at the bar, and drank scotch until last call.

. . .

Stanley Wilson was sometimes known as *Stan the Man*. The nickname seemed inappropriate to him this morning. The words *Stan Back in the Can* briefly ran through his mind, which was still clouded by sleep.

Wilson straddled the windowsill with one foot planted on the bedroom floor and a leg dangling twelve feet above the sidewalk below.

A noise that could only have been the sound of a door being kicked in had got him moving off the bed. Then seven words—spoken from behind with a chilling calmness as he started through the bedroom window—halted him in mid-escape.

Stop, or I will kill you, Stanley.

It sounded convincing.

Wilson wore only a plaid pajama bottom.

Its stretched out elastic waistband revealed the words *Semper Fi*, neatly tattooed just above his left buttock.

Wilson soon regretted he had stopped, had not risked calling what could have been a bluff.

He turned to see a chrome-plated Smith and Wesson .38 pointed at his chest. Good for six shots—but he was sure one would do the job.

He looked up from the weapon to the gunman's face.

Wilson recognized the face immediately.

He was now certain it had been a mistake to turn back from the street below to heed the warning at his back.

The voice spoke again.

Please step back inside, Stanley.

Wilson hesitated. Half inside, half outside, half asleep.

The first light of dawn peeked through the window above Wilson and reflected off the weapon. For a split second, he considered going the other way—but there was a chilling calmness in the man's voice.

Wilson recognized a determination he could not ignore.

Wilson accepted he was caught.

But, hey, he was alive. He would deal with it.

He stepped back into the room.

He somehow felt less threatened once he had squared his feet to confront his assailant.

"Okay, chief, take it easy. You win."

"Walk slowly to the foot of the bed, Stanley, face the headboard and put your arms behind your back."

"Whatever you say."

Wilson moved slowly to the bed, faced the wall, put his hands behind him and waited.

"You need to answer for the murder of Laura Pappas."

"I don't know what you're talking about. I was at the club when she was killed."

"You were with Charlie Sanders when she was killed, and he was in that house. Who did the shooting? You or Sanders?"

"I'm done talking."

"Are those your last words?"

"My last words are *fuck you*."

"Got it."

From a few feet away, the gunman put a bullet into the back of Wilson's head.

Wilson landed face down on the bed, his pajama pants slipping down just far enough to reveal the entire tattoo. *Semper Fi My Ass.*

Over the ringing of church bells, repeated five times, the shooter heard a riot of sounds.

Doors opening, footsteps, a chorus of voiced alarms from neighboring apartments.

He stood at the door, reached out, and put two bullets into the hallway ceiling.

The shots echoed through the building like cannon blasts. He heard frantic movement and doors slamming.

When he stepped out into the hall, it was deserted.

He pocketed the weapon and took the stairs down to the

ground floor, unrushed.

The door at the rear of the building opened to an alley.

He walked calmly to his car and drove off.

The phone woke John Holden early Sunday morning.

"What?"

"How soon can you get down here to the morgue?" Gentry asked.

"What time is it?"

"Eight."

"I thought we were meeting there at ten."

"There's a new wrinkle."

"What?"

"Are you going to grill me or get down here?"

"Give me an hour," Holden said.

"Follow me," Gentry said, when his partner arrived.

He led Holden to a sheet-covered body on a stainless-steel table.

"Washington and Martinez caught a homicide earlier this morning."

"And?"

Gentry pulled back the sheet.

"Fuck," Holden said. "Is that who I think it is?"

"Stanley Wilson, he's looked better. One in the back of the head."

"Witnesses?"

"Neighbors heard a shot, around five, then two more gunshots chased everyone back into their apartments. No one could ID the shooter."

"What do you make of it?"

"Your guess is as good as mine," Gentry said.

. . .

Jimmy Pappas arrived just after ten with a second man in tow.

"Thanks for coming down," Detective Gentry said. "Where's your driver, Stanley Wilson?"

"He was supposed to pick me up at my club. He never showed. I couldn't reach him. I had Charlie drive me down," Pappas said, indicating his companion.

"Too bad," Gentry said. "We had a few more questions for Wilson. If you follow me, Mr. Pappas, we can view the body."

Gentry and Pappas started off, the other man began to follow.

"You'll have to wait here, Charlie," Holden said. "It's Charlie Sanders, right?"

"Right."

"When we spoke to Wilson last night, he said he was with you from the time he brought your boss to the club until the time they left again to drive to the Pappas home."

"Right. Stan and I hung out in the office, playing cards."

"Any idea why he didn't show up this morning?" Holden asked.

"None."

Gentry and Pappas returned.

"Can we reach you at home if we need to, Mr. Pappas?" Holden asked.

"I'll be staying at my loft downtown until the house is cleaned up. The address and phone number are listed. I would rather not hear from you until you know who killed my wife."

Pappas headed straight for the building exit. Sanders hurried after him.

"He confirmed it was his wife," Gentry said.

"Charlie confirmed the card game with Wilson," Holden said.

"The crime scene unit came up with nothing."

"Did they get anything from her cell phone?"

"The last call was the nine-one-one. Other than that, nothing unusual. They found three thirty-eight-millimeter shell casings at the Wilson homicide, and some trace evidence."

"What?"

"Hair. They're sure it's not his, and that it was deposited *after* he was shot. But so what?"

"I need some sleep," Holden said.

"Go ahead, it's Sunday."

Holden turned to leave.

"John."

"Yes?"

"Is this going to turn into one of the ones that got away?"

"I hope not, Sam."

Charlie Sanders walked into the front room of his small detached house near Sloan's Lake and closed the door.

The blow hit him from behind.

When he regained consciousness, he found himself bound tightly to a chair in the center of the room. The man pointing a chrome-plated .38 at his chest sat in a chair facing him.

"Laura Pappas called me. She saw you coming. I couldn't get there in time."

"You have nothing that puts me in that house when she was killed."

"I have Stanley Wilson's word for it, but he wouldn't tell me who did the shooting. I was hoping you would."

"I'm not telling you anything."

"Was it you or Wilson who shot a defenseless woman in the back?"

"Why would it matter?"

"I would like to know."

"Do you think I fucking care what you would like?"

"No, I guess I don't," the gunman said.

And he pulled the trigger twice.

Jimmy Pappas must have felt untouchable, because he opened the door without checking who was on the other side.

He was knocked down to the floor with a blow from the grip of a Glock nine-millimeter semi-automatic.

"Are you insane?"

"I'm angry. Get up."

The intruder guided Pappas to the kitchen and pushed him onto one of the chairs. Then he sat, keeping the gun pointed across the table at Pappas.

Jimmy Pappas noticed that the man wore a latex glove on his free hand.

"I knew Laura my entire life. We grew up on the same street, not very far from where she was killed, went to school together, kindergarten through East High. Her father was a worthless bum. Her mother had no use for her. I was her protector, her big brother, all she had for family."

"Listen," Pappas said.

"Keep quiet. If you don't want to hear this, just say so and I will stop wasting our time."

Pappas kept quiet.

"I moved around a lot after high school, and I managed to find trouble everywhere. I was lucky to avoid a criminal record. Laura and I had always stayed in touch. When I returned, I looked her up. We spoke on the phone every few weeks and we made it a habit to get together at least once a month. Then she married you, and the calls stopped coming. Until last night."

The man pulled something from his jacket pocket with his gloved hand and placed it on the table between them.

"Recognize this?"

It was a chrome-plated thirty-eight caliber six-shot revolver.

"Is that my gun?"

"It is, properly licensed and registered. I borrowed it from your mansion on the park, and it is going to convict you for Laura's murder."

"That's not the gun that killed my wife."

"No, Jimmy, it's not. But it *is* the weapon that killed Stanley Wilson and Charlie Sanders."

"You *are* insane."

"That's Stanley Wilson's blood on the grip, and they found a hair sample in the blood on his back that will come up positive for your DNA. I pulled it off a comb in your bathroom on Cheesman Park. They will find a gold cuff link in Charlie's place, with the initials JP, and will find a matching cuff link in your bedroom."

"If you think you can frame me for Wilson and Sanders, and somehow connect it to the murder of my wife, you're as stupid as they were. I'm sure I can come up with airtight alibis. So, go for it, fucking take me in. I will never be convicted. I was no-where near the house when Laura was killed."

"I'm not here to take you in."

"What then? Are you going to murder me in cold blood?" Jimmy Pappas said, grinning.

"In self-defense."

One bullet to the forehead from the Glock nine was all it took to wipe the grin off Jimmy's face forever.

The shooter holstered his weapon and pulled a second latex glove onto his bare hand.

He held the Smith and Wesson in the dead man's hand and fired a shot into the kitchen wall.

It was the last round. One in Wilson, two in the hall ceiling at Wilson's place, two in Sanders.

He removed the gloves and reached for his cell phone.

"Denver PD, Sergeant Maldonado speaking."

"Sergeant, this is Detective John Holden. There's been a shooting, one civilian dead."

Holden gave the dispatcher the address and then moved into the living room to sit and wait.

VOLUNTEERS

The expression *feast or famine* may well have been coined to describe the business of private investigation.

There have been times when I had waited days for an inquiring phone call—or a walk-in by a prospective client anxious to discover what he or she would be much better off not knowing.

Sitting idly at my desk, fighting to ignore the irresistible aromas drifting through the window from Molinari's Salumeria on Columbus Avenue below my office.

And other instances when there were more intrigues than I could handle without enlisting the aid of Darlene Roman or Vinnie Strings. Or, when in dire straits, the less than enthusiastic assistance of Lieutenant Laura Lopez or Detective Roxton Johnson of San Francisco's finest.

The case in question found me on my own. Darlene was in Miami Beach with her father who was catching up with his old friends from Cuba, Vinnie was down in the City of Angels visiting his mother, and I had absolutely no idea what I was getting myself into until I was neck deep in it and it was nearly too late to reach out for help.

It began innocently enough with a telephone call, at eleven on a Tuesday morning, from a man who called himself Daniel Rossi. He asked if I could find time, as soon as possible, to talk at my office. Over coffee. Rossi said he had a *proposition*—not a term I often hear when I'm being approached to conduct an investigation.

Nevertheless, I needed work and was willing to at least hear him out.

With Darlene gone, negotiating the coffeemaker was more than I cared to handle.

In fact, if Darlene were not running the office, we would likely have no electricity.

I suggested Rossi meet me at Caffè Trieste on Vallejo Street.

He said something like *that will be fine.*

I asked how I would know him.

Rossi said he would know me which he apparently did because, when I walked into the cafe twenty minutes later, I spotted him waving me over to a two-top near a window facing the street. Six-foot tall, full head of dark hair and an exceptionally good suit.

When I reached the table, he stood and offered a handshake.

"Call me Danny," he said.

"Jake," I said, as we sat.

A waitress appeared almost immediately with two lattés.

"I ordered for you," he said, unapologetically.

"Perfect," I said, if only to keep it simple.

Rossi got right to it.

"I would like to hire you to find my wife."

I have learned the hard way that a private investigator, or anyone for that matter, is wise to avoid any involvement in the domestic maneuverings of others at all costs. Wives or husbands that go missing from their spouses often do not wish to be found.

So, my initial impulse was to say, *I may not be able to find her. There are so many places she could hide.*

But decided it might sound insensitive.

"I'm sorry, I won't be able to help you," I said instead.

"It's not what you think," he said.

Danny Rossi, mind reader.

"Samantha would never leave voluntarily," he added, "not in a million years."

I had heard that one many times before.

Normally, at this juncture, I would recommend contacting the police. But, before I could articulate the suggestion, Rossi was again a step ahead.

"Jake, I am reaching out to you because I know how the police work. First, they will have me wait two or three days to file a missing person's report and then they'll waste more valuable time looking at me as a suspect instead of looking for Sam."

Good points.

"Here's my advice. Go see Detective Johnson at Vallejo Station and give him all you can. Mention my name. He may or may not owe me one, depending on his mood. If he feels he does, he may be able to grease the wheels. In the meantime, I'll see if we can get a leg up. Your wife is missing, and you are certain she didn't simply walk away. What *do* you think?"

"I try not to," Rossi said. "It scares me too much."

"I'll need more than that if there's any hope I can help you. Let's start from where and when you last saw your wife."

"Yesterday morning. We had coffee at our townhouse on Filbert Street, up on Telegraph Hill. I left for the airport around nine, an overnight business trip to San Diego. That was the last time I saw Sam."

Filbert Street was very high-priced, nestled below Coit Tower with a view of the Bay.

"Did she say anything about her plans for the day?"

"She said she planned to do some shopping and run a few errands before going to North Beach Citizens Center on Kearney Street, where she volunteers several days a week preparing free meals for seniors and needy families. She usually worked there from one in the afternoon until six. Then she planned to meet a close friend for dinner. I tried calling her last night when I was done with business, at home and on her cell, and got no answer. I tried again this morning before my early flight back here. Again, no answer. When I arrived at the townhouse, Samantha wasn't there and I could tell she had not returned home last night. I called North Beach Citizen's Center and was told the volunteers and volunteer coordinator, who would have worked with her yesterday, would not be arriving before noon."

"How could you tell she hadn't been home?"

"I could tell just by looking around the place. There was not the usual early morning disarray. You know. When you've lived with someone for a long time, you just know."

I wouldn't know.

"Have you talked with the friend she planned to meet for dinner?"

"*That* friend of hers dislikes me, for reasons I don't fully understand. I'm sure she would be more willing to talk to a stranger than to me. So, I called you."

"Why me, Mr. Rossi?" I asked.

As I had asked the heavens many times before.

"I heard you were very good at your job."

Flattering.

"From who?"

"I can't recall."

Okay.

I wrote down the information on how I could find his wife's *close friend,* Nicole Turner. Phone numbers, place of employment, and home address. We parted in front of the café.

Rossi headed in the direction of the Vallejo Street Police Station to see if Detective Johnson was willing to lend an ear.

I told him I would call him later in the day to report progress.

If any.

I decided to grab a quick bite before heading to the North Beach Citizens Center.

Capo's Italian Restaurant was only a hop, skip and a jump down Vallejo Street.

After a plate of Broccoli Rabe with house made hot Calabrese sausage, I was ready for action.

I arrived at the North Beach Citizens Center just past one.

VOLUNTEERS

They had just served lunch to nearly one-hundred people in their large dining hall.

I was directed to the kitchen, where a dozen volunteers were preparing meals that would be delivered free throughout the neighborhood.

Jack Scott, Head Chef and Volunteer Coordinator, was pointed out to me.

Scott continued prepping food the entire time we spoke, never missing a beat or chopping off a finger.

"Samantha Rossi?" I began.

"What's your interest?"

"I'm from Publisher's Clearing House."

"Cute."

"Her husband has been trying to reach her with no luck. He's worried."

"Are you a police detective?"

"Private."

"She's not here. Samantha was scheduled, but she never showed."

"Was she here yesterday?"

"From around one until six."

"Anything unusual? Anyone come to meet her? Did she leave with anyone?"

"Anthony."

"Anthony?"

"Another volunteer. They often left together. I believe they walked in the same direction, heading to their homes."

"Is Anthony here now?"

"Not scheduled until tomorrow."

"Could you tell me how to reach him."

"I can't."

"Do you know if he has work other than this?"

"I don't."

Anthony would have to wait.

"Thanks for your time," I said.

"Speaking of time," he said, having never looked up from his worktable, "if you ever have some extra time, we can always use help here."

Suggesting I could be any help in a kitchen was like suggesting pigs could fly. Once, while watching my mother do her magic, she asked me to pass her the paring knife, and I asked her which two knives she wanted. And when Darlene proudly showed me her new mandolin, I asked where the strings were.

I thought about saying, *I'll try to find the courage.*

"I'll see what I can do," I said instead.

Daniel Rossi had given me three phone numbers for Nicole Turner.

Business. Home. Cell.

As a general rule, I avoid interrupting people at their workplace.

Particularly someone who doesn't know me.

An ironic policy, perhaps, for one who has spent countless hours staring at my office phone hoping a stranger would call.

I called Turner's home number, expecting I could leave a message.

No dice. No answer. Voice mailbox full.

Plan C.

I texted her cell phone.

Ms. Turner. My name is Jake Diamond. I am a friend of Samantha Rossi. Could you please call me at your earliest convenience.

Okay, I was stretching the truth.

But, from what he had said about Turner's feelings for him, I felt mentioning Daniel Rossi's name could be counterproductive.

I called Rossi to provide a quick update.

"Your wife did work at the center yesterday, and seems to have left without incident. Do you know Anthony?"

"Anthony who?"

"I don't have a last name. Another volunteer."

"Why would I know him, and what has he got to do with Sam?"

"Probably nothing," I said, sorry I had mentioned it at all and hoping that a quick change of subject would keep him from pressing it. "I left a message for Nicole Turner, asked her to call me. I will let you know as soon as she calls, *if* she calls. Did you talk with Detective Johnson?"

"He wasn't in," Rossi said. "I'm extremely worried. Please let me know the minute you learn anything."

"I will," I said, and that was that.

I was about to call Johnson myself, when my cell rang.

Nicole Turner.

She neglected to ask me what I wanted, but said she could meet me at Charmaine's Rooftop Bar and Lounge on McAllister at six.

I decided calling Johnson could wait.

It was a beautiful Autumn afternoon, and I had several hours to kill.

Rather than going back to an empty office to stare at a mute phone, I headed to my house in the Presidio.

There, I could sit in the backyard, look out at the Golden Gate Bridge, sip a George Dickel sour mash, and pick up where I had left off in Thackeray's *Vanity Fair*.

When I walked into Charmaine's at six, I was immediately greeted by a young woman whose nametag identified her as Taylor.

I often wondered what happened to women's names like Anne, Susan and Mary.

"Good evening," she said, "one for dinner?"

"Actually, I'm meeting someone."

"Is your name Jake?"

"Lucky guess?" I asked, which elicited a smile.

"Please follow me."

I followed her.

She pointed to a cocktail table.

"I believe that is your party," Taylor said. "Can I bring you a drink?"

"George Dickel, rocks."

"George Dickel?"

"Make it Jameson's," I said, and I walked over to the table.

Looks aren't everything.

But in Nicole Turner's case, they were definitely something.

For lack of a better term, she was a knockout.

"Have a chair, Mr. Diamond."

It was actually a stool. I sat.

There was a glass in front of Turner, holding a liquid the color of very expensive single malt Scotch.

"I imagine you are wondering why I didn't ask what you wanted before inviting you to meet me."

I had thought about it.

"I thought about it," I said, as Taylor delivered my drink.

"You said you are Samantha's friend. I know Sam very well. I know who her friends are, and I have never heard her mention your name. I wanted to share that knowledge with you, face-to-face. What is this about?"

"I understand you had plans with Mrs. Rossi last evening."

"That is correct. But it doesn't answer *my* question."

"She didn't return home last night, and her husband is concerned."

"That concerns me also. How do you fit in?"

"He asked me to try to find out why his wife seems to be missing."

"Are you a cop?"

"Private investigator."

"Why not the police?"

"Mr. Rossi felt the police would not act with urgency."

"Why didn't he call *me* last night. He obviously knew Sam and I had plans."

"He didn't discover her absence until this morning. He was

in San Diego overnight."

"Then why didn't he call me *this morning*?"

"Mr. Rossi is under the impression you don't care for him."

"I don't. Daniel Rossi is a spoiled brat and Sam is too good for him. But I do care for *her*. A great deal. And Sam loves her husband, so I tolerate him."

"Can I ask you a few more questions?"

"Sure, unless you are only here for the ambience."

"You did have dinner with Mrs. Rossi last evening."

"If that is a question, then yes. And please refer to her as Samantha. If she may be in some kind of trouble, I can't bear your formality."

"Can I ask where you had dinner?"

"At my place, in the Mission."

"Did Samantha drive over there?"

"No, she wouldn't have driven. I assume she took a cab or the 12 Folsom/Pacific bus from the Citizens Center where she volunteers."

"And, following dinner?"

"We planned to watch a movie here. But, just after dinner, she received a text and said she had to leave. So, I invited a neighbor over for the movie."

"A text from who?"

"She wouldn't say, which was unusual now that I think about it. I'm her best friend. Sam and I shared everything."

"Around what time was that?"

"Eight, maybe quarter past."

"And you don't know where she was headed when she left you."

"I do not."

"Have you tried reaching her since?"

"I texted her earlier to ask about *you*, but never heard back. And Samantha is very good at returning messages. I'm becoming more and more worried and you are doing little to assuage my fears. I will keep trying to reach her. Please let me know as soon as you learn something."

"Absolutely," I said.

Any doubt that it was a dismissal was erased when she rose to leave.

"I'll take care of the tab," she said, and walked off.

She was *definitely* something.

In fact, she somehow reminded me of Becky Sharp in the Thackeray novel.

Then again, maybe it was too much drink and no food.

I was hungry, but a twenty-six-dollar hamburger at Charmaine's was not my idea of cost effectiveness, any more than was the nineteen-dollar Irish whiskey that Nicole Turner was good enough to cover.

I left a five-dollar tip for Taylor, regardless.

There was a food truck usually parked in front of the Vallejo Street Police Station that sold a decent pulled pork burrito, so I headed that way.

At the same time, I could try to see Detective Johnson—if he was back at his office.

I had a much better chance of catching him if I dropped in without warning.

If Johnson knew I was coming, he usually managed to avoid me.

Burrito devoured, I walked into the police station and tried to slip past Desk Sergeant Jefferson.

"Diamond."

Caught.

"I'm here to see Johnson," I said, trying to sound innocent.

"He's not in."

"Day off?"

"Not that it's any of your business, you just missed him. You're probably better off. He was in a foul mood. He was trapped at his desk all day with end-of-month reports. Lopez buried him under paperwork."

"All day?"

"Since nine this morning. Couldn't even get out for lunch."

"Anyone else come in asking for him?"

"Not since eleven. When I took over the desk. What's it about, Diamond?"

"Not important."

"In that case, I have a lot of funny things to do before I can get out of here and lipping with you ain't one of them."

If nothing else, I can take a hint.

I nearly crashed into Lieutenant Lopez at the door to the street.

"I'd ask what brings you here, Diamond," she said, "but I have a homicide to deal with."

I left her to it.

The following morning, I discovered the homicide victim was Samantha Rossi.

According to the *San Francisco Examiner*, Samantha Rossi, nee Rogers, was found strangled to death in a dense growth of flowers and shrubbery at the Fort Mason Community Garden. She was the only child of the late millionaire land developer Samuel Rogers, and heiress to his fortune following his death a year earlier.

I felt calling Daniel Rossi would be inappropriate. Instead, I left my place in the Presidio at nine.

Using public transportation, I arrived in front of Molinari's Salumeria fifty minutes later.

I grabbed coffee and a buttered hard roll and went up to my office.

I checked voicemail.

Darlene, reporting she was having a great time splashing around in the Atlantic and wolfing down vegetarian Cuban Picadillo.

My mother, reminding me to bring a bottle of wine for dinner at her place on Sunday afternoon.

Preferably a good Chianti.

And a message from Daniel Rossi.

Mr. Diamond, Daniel Rossi. As you may have heard, I will no longer have need of your services. Thank you for your time and for your attention. I hope one-thousand-dollars is fair compensation. I will send a check for that amount to your office.

End of message.

End of investigation.

Except something I couldn't put my finger on had me convinced it was closer to the beginning.

Too many unanswered questions.

Like why Rossi said he tried seeing Detective Johnson when it seemed as if he had not.

And who sent the text message to Samantha Rossi that interrupted her after-dinner movie plans with Nicole Turner.

It may have been a good idea to bring these ambiguities to the attention of Lopez or Johnson, but good ideas were not my forte.

Besides, I thought I might wait until I knew more about *their* findings.

I was particularly interested in the estimated time of Samantha Rossi's death.

All of this overthinking was giving me a headache.

Then I remembered the other volunteer, Anthony, who had left the Citizens Center with Samantha on Monday, and may have been the last person to see her before she met Nicole Turner for dinner.

It was just past noon, so I headed out to Kearney Street to see if Anthony had anything to offer.

One of the perks of volunteer work, on top of the feeling of *doing something good*, is you can take a break whenever you choose.

When I told Anthony DiMarco who I was, and that I wanted to talk about Samantha Rossi, he agreed without hesitation.

We sat together on a bench at Portsmouth Square, several blocks from the center.

"I truly liked Sam," DiMarco said. "She was a terrific person. I can't imagine anyone wanting to hurt her that way."

"You were friends."

"Yes, we were friends. And we had something in common. We both inherited lots of money from very wealthy fathers, and we both wanted to pay it forward somehow."

"Were you *more* than just friends?"

"No. Maybe I would have thought about it if I weren't married, but I love my wife and Sam really loved her husband."

"Have you ever met her husband?" I asked.

"Never."

"What can you tell me about Monday evening?"

"Nothing unusual. We left the center together, around six. We walked up Kearney Street to Green Street. Samantha continued north to Filbert Street where she lived and I turned east to Montgomery, where I live."

"She was heading home?"

"As far as I could tell."

"Did she say anything about meeting a friend for dinner?"

"She did not."

DiMarco was clearly upset.

I gave him a few moments.

"Did you ever meet any of her friends?" I asked.

"I've met her best friend."

"Nicole."

"Amy."

"Did she ever mention Nicole?"

"Not that I recall."

"What can you tell me about Amy?"

"Amy Vargas. She came to meet Sam here at the center several times. They had known each other since high school."

"Do you know how I can find her?"

"Sam's husband should know."

"Other than that."

"Sam mentioned Amy was a lawyer who worked for the city."

"A district attorney?" I suggested.

"I guess."

I thanked Anthony for his time and promised I'd let him know if I learned anything new.

I sat on the bench, plagued by more questions.

If Samantha Rossi was scheduled to have dinner with Nicole Turner in the Mission, and she did not plan to drive, why would she be heading toward her home on Telegraph Hill? Away from the Mission District.

And if Samantha's *best* friend was Amy Vargas, why did Nicole Turner claim the title?

I could have used Darlene's counsel, but she was three-thousand miles away at the beach.

I could have used Vinnie's assurance that I always knew the right thing to do, but he was down in Los Angeles.

So it was time to consult either Detective Johnson or Lieutenant Lopez.

I decided to flip a coin.

Heads, Johnson.

Tails, Lopez.

I used my two-headed coin.

I walked over to Vallejo Street Station.

"What's your interest, Diamond?" Johnson asked.

"The victim's husband hired me to find his missing wife."

"When was that?"

"Yesterday morning."

"And?"

I told Detective Johnson all I knew for certain and delineated everything I felt did not add up.

"What are you suggesting?"

"I don't know."

"Okay, Diamond. I will tell you what we *do* know. Mrs. Rossi's death, as determined by the coroner, occurred between nine and eleven Monday evening. Daniel Rossi has an iron-clad alibi. He was in San Diego. We spoke with six people he met with down there who can testify to his whereabouts from noon until five. We spoke with the hotel where he stayed. He ordered room service dinner at eight and checked out very early Tuesday morning. And there were calls made from the phone in his hotel room to his home phone and his wife's cell phone on Monday evening and early Tuesday. When Rossi was interviewed, he led us to Nicole Turner, and she repeated what you say she told you about the text message calling Mrs. Rossi away sometime around eight."

"I'm sure your people checked Samantha Rossi's cell for text and voice messages."

"No phone was found with the body. We asked Nicole Turner what *she* did after Mrs. Rossi left. Turner said she invited a neighbor over to her place to watch a movie. The neighbor confirmed she was with Turner from eight-thirty until nearly one in the morning. So, if you are suspecting either of them, I'd say you are barking up the wrong tree. You were made aware of their alibis *before* Samantha Rossi was found, which would make you a terrific witness for their defense. Don't make our jobs harder by trying to play Sherlock Holmes. If you know what's good for you, you'll steer clear."

If I knew what was good for me, I would have studied medicine.

"What's *your* theory?" I asked.

"I don't really have one. But it looks as if she was meeting someone. Someone who sent her the text message. And something went wrong."

"Okay," I said. "I simply thought I would fish for a second opinion, and I got one. I'll keep my nose out of it."

"Glad to hear that," Johnson said.

As I left his office, I found it hard to believe *he* believed I would.

On the other hand, knowing Johnson, it would not surprise me at all if it was a dare.

I decided I would try to track down Amy Vargas.

Vargas was not difficult to find. She was an Assistant District Attorney, working out of the DA's Office on Rhode Island Street.

I don't favor bending the truth, but I occasionally will for the sake of expediency.

The advent of caller identification necessitated deceptive measures.

I walked into the SPCA Adoption Center on Florida Street, trying my best to look like a guy in great need of a four-legged companion. I was invited by a young man named Bobby to check out the inventory.

"If you see a dog you are interested in, let me know," Bobby said, "then I can outline the adoption process."

Several minutes later, I returned from the kennel.

"I saw the perfect puppy," I said enthusiastically, "but I will need permission from my wife. Is there a telephone I can use? I left my cell at the office."

"Sure," he said, and he led me to a phone on a desk in the lobby.

I phoned the District Attorney's office and asked for Amy Vargas.

"Can I help you?"

"Ms. Vargas, I'm sorry to disturb you. My name is Simon. I'm calling from the SPCA Adoption Center."

"Yes?"

"Nicole Turner is applying to adopt a puppy, and she gave us your name as a reference."

"I don't know who that is," Vargas said.

"I see," I said. "I'm *very* sorry to have bothered you."

Well, Nicole, Simon says who's your best friend now?

"Well?" Bobby asked, "did you get the answer you wanted?"

"I'm not sure it was what I wanted," I said, "but I believe it was the answer I needed."

If Darlene had been around, she would have wanted the puppy. She would also have challenged me. Would have asked why I was continuing the investigation after the client had stopped paying for it.

Darlene was the pragmatist.

But Daniel Rossi said he would be sending a thousand dollars, which, with regard to time put in, I had not yet earned. There were too many things not right about both Rossi *and* Turner. And, after seeing Samantha Rossi's haunting eyes in a photograph in the *Examiner,* and hearing Anthony DiMarco speak about her, I felt she deserved more of my attention.

On top of that, I found I liked the idea of volunteering my time.

I returned to my place in the Presidio. I sat in the backyard and hoped George Dickel and the late Jimmy Pigeon could help me develop a plan.

I tried coming up with reasons for Daniel Rossi to want his wife dead.

I came up with what I imagined might be two good reasons.

Money and Nicole Turner.

Rossi's wife had lots of money, and Nicole Turner had looks to kill for.

I had a strong feeling that somehow they were in this together.

And what Johnson had said about me being a perfect witness for their alibis had me thinking that somehow I was being played.

It was not a happy feeling.

Nicole Turner seemed to be in the clear as the hands-on strangler, unless her neighbor lied about watching a movie with Nicole at Turner's apartment until midnight.

Rossi was in the clear if he was in San Diego but, even if he was actually down there, it didn't rule out a hired assassin.

If two or more conspirators were involved in a murder, it was a good bet one would eventually let the cat out of the bag.

Except, perhaps, in the case of the Kennedy Assassination.

Just about everything I knew about investigation I had learned from Jimmy Pigeon.

Jimmy taught me that when you suspect someone of a crime, you can proceed in one of two ways.

Pretend you don't have any suspicions and wait for a damning mistake.

Jimmy called that *patience*.

Or, reveal your suspicions to the suspect and suggest you have some sort of proof.

Jimmy called that *bluffing*.

I am not a particularly patient fellow.

But in order to bluff, you need an angle.

And though I was sure there was *something* right in front of my nose staring me in the face, I just couldn't see it.

I finally admitted to myself that I needed help.

I called Darlene.

"Miss me, Jake?"

"You have no idea."

"I have some idea. What's up? Forget to pay the electricity bill?"

"I'm sorry to bother you while you are frolicking down in the Magic City."

"Obviously, not sorry enough. What's the story?"

I spelled it all out.

"Okay," Darlene said. "Johnson told you not to try playing Sherlock Holmes, but that's exactly what you need to do. Look at all the possibilities and eliminate those you consider least likely. It's not foolproof, but it's a place to start. You suspect Rossi is guilty of murdering his wife or, if he was in San Diego, having her killed."

"Yes."

"Rossi said he tried reaching his wife on Monday evening and Tuesday morning, and the hotel records confirm the calls were made."

"Yes. And?"

"Who uses hotel phones anymore? And, what would be simpler and more practical? To locate a contract killer or find someone to order food and make calls from a hotel room phone? Rossi could have left San Diego as early as five-thirty Monday evening."

"Why didn't I see it?"

"You were too close to it. The forest for the trees and all that."

"Daniel Rossi would have had enough time to get back here and could have killed his wife himself."

"Could have."

"And how does Nicole Turner figure in?"

"What do you think, Jake?"

"Anthony DiMarco said Samantha was heading toward home. I don't believe she ever had dinner plans with Turner," I said.

"So, why stage all of that?"

"The text message calling Samantha away. The suggestion she was meeting someone. Someone who may have ended her life."

"You said you wanted to try *bluffing*. We need to convince Rossi we know it was *not* him making those calls from the hotel room, or that someone saw him back in San Francisco Monday night."

"Did you say we?"

"I did, Kemosabe. I'll grab the earliest flight I can find and I'll meet you at the office in the morning. Nine. Sharp."

"What about your father?"

"He's having so much fun with the Cubans, he won't even

know I left. Besides, I miss the Pacific."

I was exactly on time.

For a change.

Darlene had coffee made.

And two breakfast sandwiches from the deli below.

Egg, cheese, and bacon on hard roll.

Hers without the bacon.

And a prepaid cell phone in a sealed plastic package sitting on her desk.

"What's this?" I asked.

"We wouldn't want Rossi to suspect we're calling from our office," Darlene said.

Good thinking.

Breakfast in the books and cell phone unpacked, Darlene went to work.

"Hello."

"Is this Daniel Rossi?"

"Yes. Who is this?"

"I'm who delivered dinner to Room 1208, your room at the Wyndham Bayside in San Diego, and who knows it was not you in the room. As I understand it, being there is your alibi for when your wife was murdered."

"A business associate stopped by my room for a drink, I stepped out for ice and he accepted the dinner delivery for me."

Rossi was quick on his feet, but Darlene was quicker.

"That would not explain your *business associate* approaching me in the hotel bar and inviting me up to *his* room for a drink when I completed my shift. He said he would be *in* all night. Room 1208. If you're about to ask what I want, save your breath. I'll simply tell you. I want twenty-thousand-dollars. I will give you a few hours to think about it. If I don't hear back from you by one, I'll see how much I can score by starting a bidding war between the *Chronicle* and the *Examiner*."

And Darlene ended the call.

Rossi called back just after twelve-thirty and set up a meeting with Darlene for three, saying he would have cash in hand.

"How do I know you won't take the money and still talk?" he asked.

"That would make me guilty of extortion, and maybe an accessory after the fact to a felony. You can count on my discretion," Darlene answered.

We were sitting with Detective Johnson in his office on Vallejo.

The prepaid cell phone was on speaker.

"Well, there goes his San Diego alibi. But it doesn't prove he was here in San Francisco," Johnson said, after the location of the payoff was arranged and the call ended.

"Has anyone checked with the airlines?" I asked.

"I guess no one has," Johnson said, "the San Diego witnesses and hotel information looked solid."

"I'm pretty sure you could discover whether Rossi flew back here on Monday evening or Tuesday morning," Darlene said.

"Nicole Turner will collaborate. She didn't have dinner with Samantha Rossi that night. She wasn't a close friend. I doubt she even knew Samantha," I said, "and I'm sure she knows Rossi was back in town."

"How do we get her to spill the beans?" Johnson asked.

"Tell her you already know all of it, once you tell her you had Rossi picked up."

"That would be lying."

"Call it a bluff if it eases your conscience."

"We're looking at her as Rossi's lover, and future wife. And we're guessing Rossi spent the night at her place after he let his wife know he was returning from San Diego early, met her at home where she was headed after her volunteer work, offered to take her over to Fort Mason for a romantic walk in the garden, and strangled her," Darlene added.

"Okay," Johnson said. "Rossi is caught with a bag full of cash and his out-of-town alibi blown, and Turner is tricked into admitting she saw him here Monday night. Impressive work. But can you prove he actually killed his wife?"

"That will be the job of the prosecutors and *their* investigators," I said. "They get paid for it. We were just volunteers."

MEANS, METHOD
AND OPPORTUNITY

THE MYSTERIOUS NATURE
OF CRIME FICTION

During the course of an interview in 2016, coinciding with the publication of *Brooklyn Justice,* I was asked to share my thoughts on my writing choices, the genre known as *Noir,* and about the nature of *justice*—in Brooklyn or otherwise. Here is a good portion of that Q&A.

Q: Why do you write Crime Fiction?
JLA: Let me begin by saying that categorizing—giving a work of fiction a *genre* designation—is often vague. The label *crime fiction,* for example, could be used to describe some of the great classics of literature.

Crime fiction, film and television are extremely popular among readers and viewers worldwide. Fiction writers are often categorized, listed and known for their particular *genre*—be it crime, mystery, romance, horror, science fiction, and so on. Genre is defined by Merriam-Webster as *a category of artistic, musical, or literary composition characterized by a particular style, form, or content.* And as stated by Joyce Carol Oates in *The New York Review of Books,* "*In genre fiction there is an implied contract between writer and the reader that justice of a kind will be exacted. 'Good' may not always triumph over 'evil', but the distinction between the two must be honored.*"

I agree with the sentiment, but it is so broad it could just as easily portray *The Count of Monte Cristo, Moby Dick* and *The Bible* as *genre* fiction.

Categorizing is a double-edged sword. Calling something *crime fiction* can pigeonhole the work and serve to *discourage* readers with no taste for the genre or, on the other hand, *attract* diehard fans.

So, as to why I chose mystery and crime fiction as my literary *genre*, it might be more accurate to say the genre chose me—and to add that a particular genre is simply the *vehicle* in which the writer journeys through the landscape he or she is compelled to explore. In my experience as a reader, it is the *theme* and not the plot of a novel that carries universal and lasting impact—making the particular genre secondary to the thoughts and feelings which the writer is consciously or unconsciously driven to express. *Crime and Punishment, Les Misérables, A Tale of Two Cities* are, on the surface, crime novels—classic literary works that greatly influenced generations of readers and future writers not as a consequence of their genre, but for their examination of the trials and tribulations of the human experience. Similarly, the same holds for visual art and music. A timeless painting or a lasting musical composition is one that leaves a profound impression on the viewer or the listener—be it renaissance, religious, impressionist, avant-garde, symbolic, dada, classical, folk, country, blues, jazz or rock n' roll.

That being said, the selection of crime fiction as my vehicle of choice was a consequence of my exposure to literary works which examined crime and its ramifications and which greatly influenced me as a young man and adult. Dostoyevsky, Arthur Conan Doyle, Raymond Chandler, Dashiell Hammett, James M. Cain. And my exposure to films like *The Big Sleep, The Maltese Falcon, On The Waterfront, Anatomy of a Murder, Witness for the Prosecution, The French Connection, The Godfather,* and countless others. And I have always found it to be the genre I am most adept at and most comfortable in—something akin to the well-broken-in pair of shoes you prefer slipping into.

So, the question arises. Are we, practitioners of the written word and members of professional guilds like the Mystery Writers of America and the International Thriller Writers, novelists or *crime novelists*? And the simple answer is we are *writers*, willing to use any means of transport which will help us tell our tale and help attract the attention of potential followers.

Q: That being said, what's up with *noir*? Why do you think it still holds appeal as a genre? Why is it timeless? Or is it?
JLA: *Noir* takes the *crime fiction* classification a step further—to what some might call *sub-genre*. *Noir*'s appeal comes from generations of readers, writers and film goers who were inspired and thrilled by the 1940's novels of Chandler, Hammett and Cain and the French *film noir* work of Jules Dassin, Jean Luc Goddard, Henri-Georges Clouzot and others in the 50's and 60's. One of the characteristics of *classic noir* fiction and film was that it was invariably *black and white*—and as timeless as the eternal struggle between the darkness and light in humanity.

Q: Has the *noir* definition slipped? I've been to some *noir* readings where it seemed like a bunch of horror writers trying to out-gross each other. Do you know what I mean? Can *noir fiction* be defined?
JLA: *Noir fiction is about losers, not private eyes,* says Otto Penzler, *the noir story with a happy ending has never been written, nor can it be.* Dennis Lehane suggests that *noir represents working class tragedy—noir is a genre of men and women unable to roll with the changing times, so the changing times instead roll over them.*

I respect Lehane's observation—though it also brings to mind works such as *The Grapes of Wrath, Tess of the d'Urbervilles,* and *Of Human Bondage.*

Defining a category of writing—or of any art for that matter—too specifically, can create controversy. It is or it isn't what you call it, so be careful what you call it. Either we redefine what is considered *noir* to make the label more inclusive, or we use more general terms like crime fiction, detective fiction, or simply good old fiction and not risk calling what is not a spade a spade. Otherwise, labeling a sub-genre—or in some cases a sub-genre of a sub-genre—has little meaning.

I've never considered my work *noir*. The Jake Diamond series is certainly *not*. Jake is more over-easy than hard-boiled. *Gravesend* and *Coney Island Avenue* are about NYPD detectives who are, for the most part, righteous. The closest I've come to *noir* is *Brooklyn Justice*. Protagonist Nick Ventura has a shady past and a subjective morality. But Nick *is* a private eye, a borderline professional, and he sometimes accidentally stumbles upon a happy ending.

Recently, I was invited to contribute a short story to a *noir* anthology—and I had a decision to make. Pass—with the justification that *it's just not my thing*—or try to round off the square peg.

I had a general idea. More James M. Cain or Jim Thompson than Chandler or Hammett. More *After Dark, My Sweet* or *House of Games* than *Harper* or *The Rockford Files*. But how much more. How many straight bourbons. How many non-filter cigarettes. How many sexy double-crossing dames. How much more than simply a body count.

When James M. Cain wrote *The Postman Always Rings Twice,* did he set out to pen *noir fiction* or did he—when he was a journalist covering the Snyder-Gray murder trial in 1927, where Ruth Snyder and her lover Henry Gray were accused of killing Snyder's husband for the insurance money—simply get a good idea from a pair who had a terribly bad idea. When an interviewer for *The Paris Review* mentioned to Cain that he was so well-known for his *hard-boiled* manner of writing, Cain replied, "Let's talk about this so-called style. I don't know what they're talking about—*tough, hard-boiled.* I tried to write as people talk."

A widely subscribed to *rule* of *noir* fiction has long been *choose a dame with a past and a hero with no future.* Private investigators may or may not be present. Two of the most acclaimed *noir* novels, *The Postman Always Rings Twice* and *Double Indemnity,* both by James M. Cain, do not feature private eyes. And the protagonists in many classic *private eye* works, from Philip Marlowe to Sam Spade to Mike Hammer, had both flaws *and* redeeming characteristics.

And then Jim Thompson came along.

The early *bad guys,* from Conan Doyle's Moriarty to Cain's Walter Huff in *Double Indemnity,* ranged from simply criminal to diabolical—Holmes and Barton Keyes could relate to their adversaries, and therefore so could the reader. In *The Killer Inside Me,* Thompson created a psychopath. Lou Ford was more than simply evil—he was a monster. To be able to identify with Ford would be a scary proposition. The book was shocking in an unprecedented way. It was more *horror* fiction than noir. It changed the landscape—and opened the door to crime fiction featuring villains like Michael Slade's *Headhunter* and Thomas Harris' Hannibal Lector. There are a number of younger writers today who choose the Thompson model over the Cain model in their writing, which would account for the observation you noted in your question.

The question, for me, is can one write *noir for noir's sake?* Can the gloom and desperation suggested by Penzler, Lehane and others be manufactured—or does it need to be called up from something authentic inside the writer? And what is the risk, psychologically, of stirring up such darkness?

Q: You quoted Joyce Carol Oates suggesting *justice* is inherent in crime fiction—and your latest work is called *Brooklyn Justice.* How do you go about establishing a moral code for your characters? How do you decide when they need to take *matters,* so to speak, into their own hands?

JLA: Justice can be a very subjective concept, both in terms of the *law* and in the minds of individuals seeking personal retribution. From King Solomon threatening to cut a baby in half to address a dispute over its true mother to Vito Corleone's admonition to the undertaker who asks to have the men who assaulted his daughter killed—*That is not justice, your daughter is still alive.* The more personally a violent crime affects a person—the more intimate the survivor is or was to the victim—the less willing that person may be to *trust* the *legal system* to exact fitting justice. However, even in cases where a protagonist *takes matters into his or her own hands—commensurate justice* must be considered if we wish our readers to remain *sympathetic* to our *hero.*

A BRIEF HISTORY
OF DETECTIVE FICTION

In the play *Oedipus Rex* by Sophocles, the protagonist discovers the truth about his origins after questioning various witnesses. John Scaggs suggests in *Crime Fiction: The New Critical Idiom* (2005) that *although Oedipus's enquiry is based on supernatural, pre-rational methods that are evident in most narratives of crime up until the development of Enlightenment thought in the seventeenth and eighteenth centuries, this narrative has all of the central characteristics and formal elements of the detective story—including a mystery surrounding a murder, a closed circle of suspects, and the gradual uncovering of a hidden past.*

According to Mia Gerhardi, the *One Thousand and One Nights* contains several of the earliest detective stories—anticipating modern detective fiction. The oldest known example of a detective story was *The Three Apples*, one of the tales narrated by Scheherazade. In this story, a fisherman discovers a heavy, locked chest which he sells to the Caliph. In the chest is found the body of a young woman who has been cut into pieces. The Caliph orders his minister to solve the crime and find the murderer.

Gong'an fiction is the earliest known genre of Chinese detective fiction. Some of the well-known stories include the Yuan Dynasty story *Circle of Chalk*, the Ming Dynasty story collection *Bao Gong An* and the 18th century *Di Gong An* story collection. The hero/detective of these novels was typically a traditional judge or similar official.

One of the earliest examples of detective fiction in Western Literature is Voltaire's *Zadig* (1748), which features a main character who performs feats of analysis. The Danish detective story *The Rector of Veilbye* by Steen Steensen Blicher was written in 1829 and the Norwegian detective crime novel *Mordet paa Maskinbygger Roolfsen* by Maurits Hansen was published in December 1839.

Detective fiction in the English-speaking world is considered to have begun in 1841 with the publication of Poe's *The Murders in the Rue Morgue*, featuring the eccentric and brilliant C. Auguste Dupin.

Émile Gaboriau was a pioneer of the detective fiction genre in France. In *Monsieur Lecoq* (1868) the title character is adept at disguise, which is a key characteristic of detectives.

Another early example of a whodunit is a subplot in the novel *Bleak House* (1853) by Charles Dickens. A Dickens' contemporary, Wilkie Collins—sometimes referred to as the *grandfather of English detective fiction*—is credited with the first great mystery novel, *The Woman in White*, while T. S. Eliot called Collins's novel *The Moonstone* (1868) *the first, the longest, and the best of modern English detective novels.*

In 1887, Arthur Conan Doyle created Sherlock Holmes, arguably the most famous of all fictional detectives. Although Sherlock Holmes is not the *original* fiction detective—Conan Doyle was certainly influenced by Poe's Dupin and Gaboriau's Lecoq—Holmes' name has become a byword for the role.

Martin Hewitt, created by British author Arthur Morrison in 1894, is one of the first examples of the modern style of fictional private detective. This character—described as an *Everyman* detective—challenges the *Detective-as-Superman* that Holmes represented.

The period between World War I and World War II (the 1920s and 1930s) is generally referred to as the *Golden Age of Detective Fiction*. During this period, a number of very popular writers emerged including primarily British (perhaps most famously Agatha Christie)—but also a notable subset of American and New Zealand writers

In the 1930s, the private eye genre was adopted wholeheartedly by American writers. One of the primary contributors to this style was Dashiell Hammett with his famous private investigator, Sam Spade. His style of crime fiction came to be known as *hardboiled*, which is described as a genre that usually deals with criminal activity in a modern urban environment—a world of disconnected signs and anonymous strangers. Told in stark and sometimes elegant language through the unemotional eyes of new hero-detectives, these stories were a uniquely American phenomenon. In the late 1930s, Raymond Chandler updated the form with his private detective Philip Marlowe, who brought a more intimate voice to the detective than the more distanced *operative's report* style of Hammett's Continental Op stories. And by the late forties into the fifties *hardboiled* was redefined and made harder by private detectives in the mold of Mickey Spillane's Mike Hammer.

Along came Lew Archer, Travis McGee, C.W. Sughrue, Spenser, Matthew Scudder, Amos Walker, Kinsey Millhone, Elvis Cole, Dave Robicheaux, Easy Rawlins, Nick Stefanos, Moe Prager, Alex McKnight, Duncan Sloan, Jake Diamond—and here we are.

THE PRIVATE EYE
AS COLD WARRIOR
Hammer vs. The Hammer and Sickle

When Mickey Spillane's first novel—*I, the Jury*—was accepted by E.P. Dutton in 1947—the editor warned his superior, "It isn't in the best of taste, but it will sell." The formula was straight out of Pulp Fiction of the twenties and thirties—lots of action and, of course, violence—all the dialogue spoken in tough-guy vernacular and a good share of tantalizing sexual innuendo. Mike Hammer was a straight, honest private eye who had soured on a real world of corrupt cops, crooked DAs, and judges who had sold out. He was the avenger, the man who took justice into his own hands, a man who shot first and asked questions later. However, Hammer's focus seemed to shift drastically by the time *The Girl Hunters, The Snake,* and *Survival...Zero* came along.

America's obsession with the Cold War was so great that it convinced Hammer to stop chasing the garden variety of gangsters and concentrate instead on stopping domestic Communist subversion. Kenneth Davis went so far as to call Hammer a reflection of the McCarthyite soul of the country—"the ultimate cold warrior, a super-hero for frightened Americans who had heard tales of baby-eating Stalinists. Hammer's methods went beyond loyalty oaths, smears, and blacklisting. The evil of the

Communists was battled by the only weapons Hammer possessed—a blast from his 45, a bone-shattering kick, strangulation by Hammer's meaty hands."

In the words of Maysaa Husam Jaber, "Mickey Spillane represents the extremes that characterized the post-war period. A right-wing writer, Spillane raised the anxieties of the Cold War to a new level. Spillane's fiction crystallizes the failures of the system, the threats of conspiracies. He does not shy away from pointing out the Red Scare—his work is full of enemies whose threat extends beyond the confrontations between the detective and gangs to crimes that affect the United States at large. The enemy in Spillane takes the form of communists and foreigners."

As much as Ian Fleming had, Mickey Spillane brought attention to a new kind of adversary, whose evil was universal. And Spillane's protagonist was more recognizable to the American working-class reader than the suave, cultured, and world-wise James Bond.

There seems to be little argument that Spillane, a Jehovah's Witness, leaned right. And his contributions to the genre, and influence on a generation of hard-boiled detective novelists, is unquestionable. The degree, if any, to which his extremely popular fiction contributed to the paranoia that had school children ducking under desks cannot be measured. But, in my humble opinion, those of us who command a public audience would be careless to underestimate our influence or to neglect our moral responsibility.

LOCATION, LOCATION, LOCATION

Dennis Lehane's Journey From
Boston To Brooklyn And Back

Most of what I know about Boston, Massachusetts—and everything I know about Dorchester—I have learned from Dennis Lehane. Like Loren Estleman's Detroit, George Pelecanos' Washington D.C., James Ellroy's Los Angeles, and Charles Dickens' London—Lehane's setting, his home town, is as compelling a voice as that of any of his characters.

I first came across Lehane's work at Mercer Street Books in Manhattan in the late nineties—a well-worn paperback copy of *A Drink Before The War*. It was his first published novel, a Shamus Award winner, introduced Patrick Kenzie and Angela Gennaro, and shouted working class Boston from nearly every page.

The fourth book in the series, *Gone Baby Gone*, was made into a film directed by another Boston son, Ben Affleck. Again, in the novel and in the film, the setting was an integral part of the action. When asked in a New York Times interview which adaptation of his work he most favored, Lehane said: "It's a bit like choosing between your children, but I've got a real fondness for *Gone Baby Gone*. Ben Affleck understood the material in an organic way because he'd grown up here. He picked the majority of his locations not just from Dorchester, where I grew up, but from the very parish where I lived."

In Lehane's world, differences in background and experience could differ from parish to parish—the Catholic school you attended, who your parish priest happened to be, what your father did for work. And in his work, Lehane can be that specific when writing Boston, Dorchester and the local parish.

I, in much the same sense, grew up in a Brooklyn where you were defined by the neighborhood you came from—Gravesend, Bensonhurst, Bay Ridge, Dyker Park, Midwood.

Other films have been made based on Lehane's work—most notably *Mystic River* and *Shutter Island*. *Mystic River*, novel and film, again feature South Boston as a very worthy antagonist. *Shutter Island*, particularly the film, is a departure which I could talk about for hours—some other time. But it is the story of *The Drop*, the only film adaptation penned by Lehane himself, and the novel of the same name which followed it, that I find most intriguing with regard to the significance of setting in Lehane's work.

Boston Noir was an anthology edited by Lehane and published by Akashic Noir in 2009. Lehane suggests in his introduction that noir represents working class tragedy—that noir is a genre of men and women unable to roll with the changing times, so the changing times instead roll over them. *Animal Rescue*, Lehane's contribution to the anthology, is a perfect example—and once again the setting, Dorchester, is a key element in the narrative.

When I saw the film *The Drop*, I was unaware until the closing credits that it was based on the Lehane short story, *Animal Rescue*. The film was set in Brooklyn—a Brooklyn this Gravesend native could feel and taste. Lehane nailed it.

I had always seen a little of Brooklyn in Lehane's Boston—as I had seen a little of Brooklyn in a small film set in Philadelphia called *Rocky*. Working class Irish and Italian-Americans in large east coast cities have striking resemblances.

What intrigued me, however, was how a short story set in Dorchester became a film set in Brooklyn and later a novel set once again in Boston.

Lehane satisfied much of my curiosity in a 2014 interview in conjunction with the opening of *The Drop*.

Lehane said he had stayed away from adapting his own work—he likened it to a surgeon operating on his own child. However, he saw expanding a short story as a different exercise—so he agreed to adapt *Animal Rescue*.

Before it became a short story, *Animal Rescue* had been part of a full-length work that failed to come together. Lehane shelved it in 2002. So, he explains, some of the characters from that work were floating around waiting to pop in.

According to Lehane, the producers felt Boston was somewhat played out in recent crime films—*Mystic River*, *The Departed*, *The Town*. Lehane responded, "Okay, just give me another world that is similar where I can set it." Brooklyn was suggested. Lehane investigated various neighborhoods in Brooklyn and decided, "this will work, no problem".

The first word of the short story *Animal Rescue* is 'Dorchester'. The film, *The Drop*, is unmistakably set in Brooklyn. In the novel, *The Drop*, which followed on the heels of the film, the words Boston, Dorchester, and parish never appear—but we know, without question, that Lehane has brought his story back home. To the place that surely inspired him—if not forced him—to write.

RESURRECTING JIMMY PIGEON

"Mr. Diamond, I came here to talk about my husband."

"Of course you did, Evelyn," I said. I think my voice may have cracked. "Have you thought about going to the police?"

"Finding my husband is already of interest to the Los Angeles Police Department, Mr. Diamond. I was hoping you could help me locate him before they do."

"Why are the police interested in locating your husband?" I plowed on.

"They suspect he killed his business partner."

"And why would they think that?"

"My husband's gun was found beside the body."

"Did he do it?"

"I don't believe so."

"But the murder weapon was found at the scene, and it belonged to your husband. Any theories about that?"

"My husband kept the gun in his office. The victim was killed in the office adjacent to his. The police have little else to go on."

"And?"

"They seem unwilling to grant that almost anyone could have taken the weapon and killed my husband's associate."

There you go—it could have been anyone. That should convince a jury.

"If your husband is innocent, why is he dodging the authorities?"

"I don't know. Perhaps he feels no one will believe him—he's always lacked persuasive ability. That is why I need to find him. Before he gets himself hurt. Someone suggested you could help."

Why me.

"Why me?" I asked, "There are plenty of very competent investigators in Los Angeles. I could highly recommend a good friend of mine down there. Jimmy Pigeon."

"I came to see you, Mr. Diamond, because my husband's business partner *was* Jimmy Pigeon."

I managed to delay my reaction long enough to get the sketchy details from Evelyn Harding and then I quickly sent her on her way—assuring her I would stay in touch. She was barely through the door before the surprise and shock of Jimmy Pigeon's death hit me like a sucker punch. I opened the top desk drawer and pulled out the ashtray and the bottle. This time it was the bottle of bourbon.

So ends the first chapter of *Catching Water in a Net*, the first novel in the Jake Diamond mystery series—where Jake discovers, from a total stranger, that his friend and mentor, the man who brought him into the PI business, is dead. And the book, winner of the St. Martin's Press/Private Eye Writers of America Award for Best First Private Eye Novel, becomes Jake Diamond's quest to find Jimmy Pigeon's killer.

After writing three Jake Diamond novels, I decided to take a detour and write a stand-alone crime thriller set in the neighborhood where I grew up. The result was *Gravesend*.

That accomplished, it was time to start thinking about Jake again, a fourth in the series—but without warning Jimmy Pigeon took center stage. Throughout *Catching Water in a Net*, and again and again in the subsequent novels *Clutching at Straws* and *Counting to Infinity*, Jake refers to Jimmy—recalling lessons learned from Jimmy and often posing the question, when an investigation hits a dead end, *what would Jimmy do?*

At ThrillerFest in New York City, I sat on a panel entitled: *Why Did You Kill Off My Favorite Character?*

Speaking for myself, killing off a character who the writer—and hopefully the reader—has come to care about is never an easy decision. And for me, it is never *premeditated.* There comes a time in a story when something has to happen to raise the stakes, and sometimes a sacrifice is required. And I am as surprised as the reader when a good guy or good gal is killed. And I have often heard from readers of their disappointment—fortunately, I have never been confronted with a reader like Annie Wilkes in Stephen King's *Misery.* But what about a character who is killed off before you even begin, who you have never really met, who you only learn about through fond memories? A character so important to the main protagonist of your series.

As his name kept popping up, I wondered more and more often—*who was Jimmy Pigeon?*

And here is the fun part. I could find answers to my nagging questions about Jimmy Pigeon by simply turning back the clock. Suddenly I was writing a prequel to the Jake Diamond series, which finds Jimmy alive and at work as a Private Investigator in Santa Monica in 1994. In the midst of the O.J. Simpson murder case and the Major League Baseball strike. And the result was the novel *Chasing Charlie Chan.*

I have no illusions of grandeur, but being able as a writer to bring a character back from the grave is pretty nifty. It was a great exercise for me, and I believe it resonated with readers—with new readers as well as those Jake Diamond fans who have at times also wondered about Jimmy Pigeon. Jimmy who said—among other things—*When it comes to private investigation, nine times out of ten the client is your worst enemy.*

BROOKLYN EASE
You Can Go Home Again

Thomas Wolfe's short story, *Only The Dead Know Brooklyn,* appeared in 1935—just three years before his death at age thirty-seven. Wolfe, a native of the American South, wrote the story in dialect:

> You ain't neveh gonna get to know Brooklyn. Not in a hunderd yeahs. Dere's no guy livin' dat knows Brooklyn. It'd take a guy a lifetime to know Brooklyn t'roo an' t'roo. An' even den, yuh wouldn't know it all.

There is no guy living that knows Brooklyn—so, therefore, only the dead know Brooklyn.

I grew up in one of the largest, most diverse cities in the world. At the same time, I grew up in a place that could hardly have been more *small town* or more homogeneous. Where Nick, who owned the corner grocery store, knew every kid by name—as did Frank the barber and Audrey at the laundromat and old man Baker at the candy store and Vito who sold fruit on the street out of a horse drawn wagon. Gravesend was exclusively *working class,* Italian-American, and segregated from other Brooklyn neighborhoods—and it was our entire world until we were brave enough to cross its borders. A baseball park in Bensonhurst, a high school in Fort Greene, a discotheque in Sheepshead Bay, a girlfriend in Bay Ridge—exploration—and savvy about the borough increased exponentially as we grew older, as we took to subways, buses and eventually automobiles. But most other neighborhoods—Park Slope, Canarsie, Midwood, Brownsville, Bedford-Stuyvesant, East New York—remained mysterious, some considered *off-limits*. Brooklyn was a loose conglomerate of autonomous neighborhoods, much too vast to ever fully know in a lifetime. Thomas Wolfe from North Carolina was on to something.

I left the bosom of Gravesend and Brooklyn in my early twenties, on an adventure in Cincinnati, Ohio called graduate school—and from there my migration, for the most part, carried me further and further west.

By the time I wrote the first detective novel, *Catching Water in a Net,* I was replanted—and its protagonist, Jake Diamond, became a Brooklyn expatriate working out of San Francisco.

After three Jake Diamond mysteries, set primarily in San Francisco and Los Angeles, I felt compelled to write a Brooklyn story—to return to my origins—and the result was *Gravesend,* titled for that neighborhood where I was born and raised. It was a more personal journey, and the setting was a very important character in that novel. I felt very comfortable writing Brooklyn—at home, at ease. Brooklyn is unique simply because it *is* Brooklyn—it is not like any other place—and it is a perfect setting for crime fiction because, admirably or not, it has such a rich history of criminal activity. I grew up around many people involved in *organized crime*—it was everywhere at every level—and at times I depended on some of these people to protect me from collateral damage. There is no shortage of *mobsters* in my Brooklyn stories.

Times have changed in Brooklyn since my formative years, but there is still a heritage that survives through generations of storytelling and family ties. Even today, there is still something recognizable in the words of Betty Smith from her seminal novel, *A Tree Grows in Brooklyn:*

> "There's a tree that grows in Brooklyn. Some people call it the 'Tree of Heaven'. No matter where its seeds fall, it makes a tree which struggles to reach the sky. It grows in boarded-up lots and out of neglected rubbish heaps. It grows out of cellar gratings. It is the only tree that grows out of cement. It grows lushly—survives without sun, water, and seemingly without earth. It would be considered beautiful except that there are too many of it."

Brooklyn is where there are still Brooklyn Dodger fans more than sixty years after the team left for California.

Brooklyn is where the Brooklyn Bridge *starts.*

Brooklyn is where you can take your eight-year-old granddaughter on the same rollercoaster *you* first rode when you were eight-years-old.

Brooklyn is Junior's Cheesecake, Nathan's Hot Dogs, and L&B spumoni.

Brooklyn is Coney Island.

Brooklyn is where the Atlantic Ocean defines summer.

Brooklyn is stickball and slap ball and hopscotch and *Johnny-on-the-Pony.*

Brooklyn is evenings on the *stoop.*

Brooklyn is refuge.

Writing stories set in Brooklyn gave me the opportunity to remember and reflect—as in this excerpt from *Gravesend:*

> Murphy and his dog, Ralph, walk past John Paul Jones Park toward the Shore Road Promenade. A heavy fog engulfs the ancient cannon

and the stack of cannonballs left over from another revolution.

They walk down to the water's edge.

Murphy can hear the scurrying of small animals in the dense bushes.

Ralph is all ears.

Murphy stands at the railing, gazing out at the Verrazano Bridge while Ralph chases shadows.

The massive concrete piling is the tomb of a luckless construction worker who fell into a molten grave. Another immigrant who came to build a new world.

Murphy looks out across the Narrows to Staten Island, once only accessible by ferry. Beyond the island, New Jersey and California and all of those unknown places in between.

And beyond, the Pacific and all of those unknowable places Murphy has only dreamt about.

Murphy takes an unsung pride in the fact that people from nearly every foreign land beyond both seas have come here—have carried their children, their hopes and their dreams to Brooklyn.

And this, also from *Gravesend*:

Lieutenant Samson stares at Joe Campo's back and waits patiently.

Campo remains at the edge of the roof, silently.

"Mr. Campo," says Samson, just above a whisper.

"When we were his age," Campo says, referring to the boy on the roof, "we would sneak up here to fly a kite—my friends Eddie and Frankie and me. The kite set us back ten cents at old man Baker's Candy Store across the avenue. We would pick up a bag of penny candies while we were there, when penny candies actually cost a penny—or two for a penny. Tiny wax Coca-Cola bottles filled with brown-colored sugar water. Giant fireballs. Pink and white sugar dots stuck on strips of waxed-paper. Chocolate covered marshmallow twists. And then we'd pick up hero sandwiches at Nick's Salumeria, before it was Angelo's and then Vito's and then ours. Ham, capicola, Genoa salami, Swiss cheese and gobs of yellow mustard on half a loaf of seeded Italian bread still warm from Sabatino's Bakery on Avenue S. Twenty-five cents each."

Vota is about to interrupt—Samson stops him with a hand gesture.

Joe Campo looks out toward Coney Island, at the 250-foot-tall steel framed Parachute Jump ride that had been moved from the 1939 World's Fair to Steeplechase Park in the forties. The landmark attraction had not carried a passenger in more than thirty years.

"This apartment house was one of the tallest buildings in the neighborhood. Still is, at that," Campo goes on. "We thought if we started up here, we'd be closer to the sky. One of us would need to run down to Baker's every ten minutes or so for another ball of string, two-hundred-fifty more feet for a nickel. We would watch the paper kite sail toward the ocean, followed by a long tail we had made out of strips torn from one of my father's old handkerchiefs. We were sure we could fly the thing all the way to Europe, wherever we thought that was. When the long pieced-together strings inevitably snapped, we were positive that the kite would eventually come down to land somewhere in France or Germany."

And, from *Brooklyn Justice*:

At ten the next morning I sat in my office which in turn sat above Totonno's Pizzeria on Neptune Avenue two blocks from the beach and the Atlantic Ocean that separated me from a thousand places I had only read about.

My great grandfather and Antonio Pero had been childhood friends, since the days at the Little Red Schoolhouse in Greenwich Village when it had been the neighborhood grade school for children of immigrants in Little Italy before it was a cost prohibitive private school of the new upper class. Pero bought the property on Neptune in 1924, a three-story brick apartment building attached to a one-story storefront, and opened a pizzeria with a coal-fired brick oven that would become legendary. The product was considered by many aficionados as among the best pies in New York City, never sold by the slice and never traded for anything but cash. When my grandmother died, and my grandfather Giuseppe Ventura refused to be moved into the home of any of his children, Pero's son offered him two small rooms above a beauty salon in the apartment building adjacent to the pizza shop. Antonio's daughter, who had been like an aunt to me growing up, now ran the pizzeria and still burned coal. When Giuseppe met his maker, and I needed a place to set up my private investigation business,

'Aunt' Carmella let me have the rooms for the same monthly rent they had charged the old man. I knew she could get a lot more for the space and I told her so.

"Think of it like a Grandfather Clause," Carmella had said, smiling, and we shook hands on the deal.

An ancient window fan was noisily trying without success to battle the elements. The dog day temperature had already soared into the low nineties and the humidity was off the charts. I stripped down to what was what was referred to as a white ribbed tank top by youngsters and a wife-beater t-shirt by the old-timers.

I went through the mail on my desk. All bills, no payments. I leafed through the sports section of the New York Post, which took up nearly the entire back half of the rag, looking for any news that would offer hope for the Mets. No luck. As it approached noon, I was so hungry I was about to run the two blocks to Nathan's at the board-walk for a hot dog appetizer when there was a light rap on the office door. I threw on my white button down Van Heusen and tucked it into my black Haggar pleated slacks.

Standard advice for writers has long been: Write what you know.

I would add to that: *Remember where you came from.*

Writing *Gravesend* and *Brooklyn Justice* were edifying experiences.

Thomas Wolfe wrote, *you can't go home again.*

I'll disagree.

Rather, as T.S. Eliot said:

We shall not cease from exploration and at the end of all our exploring will be to arrive where we started and know the place for the first time.

SAN FRANCISCO BEAT

The sights, the sounds, the tastes and the aromas of San Francisco are as unmistakable as they are unforgettable and provide a perfect setting for the fictional exploits of Brooklyn born, Italian-Catholic, Ukrainian-Jewish, unsuccessful movie actor and marginally successful private investigator, Jake Diamond.

Jake is more over-easy than hard-boiled and he is more likely to be carrying a dog-eared paperback classic novel than a firearm. Jake's thirst quencher of choice is Tennessee sour mash bourbon, his favorite foods are those with the highest cholesterol, and the closest he comes to being a purist is non-filtered cigarettes.

> The scent of deep-fried calamari floated in through my office window like an invitation to triple-bypass surgery.

So begins the third novel in the Jake Diamond series, *Counting to Infinity*, following *Catching Water in a Net* and *Clutching at Straws*. Jake's office sits above Molinari's legendary Italian Market on Columbus Avenue; in the heart of the rich history and the eclectic street life of North Beach. From Molinari's Delicatessen to the Vallejo Street Police Station, to the Shrine of St. Francis of Assisi—the streets of North Beach are often the backdrop for Diamond's most tense and funniest moments.

. . .

During the break between my first and second year of graduate studies at the University of Cincinnati, I hopped into a ten-year-old Volkswagen bus and headed west—crossing the Mississippi for the first time.

Having grown up on the Atlantic Ocean, I was curious about the Pacific.

I made the mandatory stops—the Grand Canyon, Las Vegas, Hollywood, and then up the coast to the City by the Bay.

It was love at first sight.

It was 1971. Richard Milhouse Nixon was in the White House. Vietnam was aflame. The *Summer of Love* had come and gone, People's Park sadly abandoned. But Haight Street and Berkeley were still tie-dyed colors and long hair and civil disobedience. The Jefferson Airplane and Grateful Dead were still thought of as local bands, and the city was a jewel still sparkling upon the turbulent sea of social change. I was escorted to the top of Twin Peaks, as was Jake Diamond in *Clutching at Straws*—and the 360-degree view of the city, the Bay and the Pacific was indelible.

I left my heart there also, Mr. Bennett.

I lived in San Francisco during the closing years of the seventies—post-Vietnam, post-Watergate, pre-Reagan.

First, in the Fillmore, where Jake Diamond lived before inheriting the house in the Presidio. Later, on Frederick Street near Masonic. A short block from Haight Street, where the last Flower Children were fighting to hold the line—with their headshops and music stores and street performances—against the other thirty-something residents who were trying to turn the Upper Haight into a respectable neighborhood. I worked part time at the Green Apple Bookstore on Clement, where Jake Diamond purchased paperback copies of *A Tale of Two Cities* and *The Count of Monte Cristo*. *Catching Water in a Net* became a tale of San Francisco and Los Angeles. *Clutching at Straws* became a tale of retribution.

I explored the city. Seldom in a car. Automobiles were impractical in San Francisco—there was no place to put them. As Jake Diamond once noted, *the only way to get a parking space in San Francisco is to buy a parked car.*

I explored San Francisco on foot—walking up and down the city's hills, from neighborhood to neighborhood, each with their unique personality and their own climate. The Fillmore, Castro (the setting of *One Hit Wonder,* a Jake Diamond short story included in this collection), the Mission (where Vinnie Strings squanders his savings at the Finnish Line, a gambling hall run by two brothers from Helsinki), the Sunset (where Jake parks his cherished 1963 Chevy Impala convertible in Joey Russo's garage), the Presidio, the Panhandle, North Beach and the Haight.

I explored by bike, bus, streetcar, cable car, and even sailboat. I was taken in by the frenzied activity of small theatre, the renaissance created in the redevelopment of Fort Mason, and by a theatre rag found in every small venue lobby. I began to write about art.

I took the knowledge and the passion to Denver where I founded and edited a monthly theatre magazine and placed it in all of the local theatres. I began writing for some of the smaller independent newspapers. I had become a budding arts journalist. I was a professional writer—inspired by my time in San Francisco.

I began *Catching Water in a Net*, with the simple wish to try my hand at first person narrative. The natural, unpremeditated form was the private eye narration, and the setting, in my mind, could be nowhere but San Francisco.

Jake Diamond was born.

I thank the city of San Francisco for the inspiration and, as often as possible I visit—preferably in the fall.

Autumn in San Francisco, as Jake Diamond muses in *Clutching at Straws.*

Late September, early October is my favorite

time of the year in San Francisco. In terms of weather, September is the mildest month. Most of the tourists are gone and that is a great blessing. In July and August they're as thick as Buddy Holly's eyeglasses. The kids are back where they belong; the nine-week challenge of trying to find a single square inch of ground not infested by swarms of loud and reckless adolescents is finally over. Unless you're insane enough to venture anywhere near a school. I can hardly imagine a better place to be in early fall.

Though I'll admit, I'll take Paris in the springtime.

I visit, I walk the streets, I duck into alleys, check out storefronts, and look for more magical places for Jake Diamond to discover while searching for a clue or two.

FOOD FOR THOUGHT
Even Fictional Characters Need To Eat

In mystery and crime fiction, as in life, characters exhibit degrees of good and evil, failure and success, they live and die and—unless they are androids—they need to eat.

Food had always been present and often telling in my stories. Whether a question of what they eat, where they eat, when they eat, if they have a chance to eat—food can reveal much about characters and their relationships. And meetings in cafés and restaurants can make for delicious encounters.

Jake Diamond, the protagonist in five novels, works out of a private investigation office above an Italian salumeria in San Francisco's North Beach. Food is always nearby. *Counting to Infinity* begins:

> The scent of deep-fried calamari floated in
> through my office window like an invitation to
> triple bypass surgery.

The delicatessen also serves to highlight the difference in the eating habits of Diamond and his associate Darlene Roman. Darlene does not eat meat, while Jake—as all good Ukrainian-Italian-Americans—cannot do without it. In *Circling the Runway*, when Jake voices strong dislike for Darlene's decision to act as bait for a sexual predator, Darlene reminds him:

> You don't like tofu either, but that never stopped me.

Describing food can add color and taste, and the presence of food can play into the action. In *Counting to Infinity,* Jake describes a meeting with his antagonist in a Chicago airport:

> Between the chairs stood a glass-topped table holding a silver tray covered with tiny sandwiches, crackers, and a mound of foie gras that cost some poor fowl a lot more than an arm and a leg. The bread was ink-jet black, the crusts had been cut off, and the beef spilling from the corners was so rare it made tartare look over-done. The crackers were multi-grain, ten or eleven at least. They had the appearance of untanned shoe leather. The chopped liver looked as appetizing as corned beef hash. Granted, I wasn't very hungry—and I'd had my fill of goose for the day. The cinnamon roll that I inhaled while dashing to make take-off was like eating a down comforter.

Later, the same food tray adds flavor to a physical confrontation:

> I began to turn toward the door when a can-nonball, which had to be Ralph Battle's fist, struck me in the back between the shoulder blades and knocked me straight to the floor. My right elbow hit the food tray, flipping it end over end into the air. The pâté did a terrific job of turning a Norman Rockwell on the wall behind Lansdale into a Jackson Pollock.

. . .

Food can help set the occasion. In *Circling the Runway,* as Jake prepares to celebrate St. Joseph's Day with friends, he considers inviting Darlene to join them:

> Darlene would not eat meat, and my dining habits and the variety of cooked animals I regularly brought into the office made it difficult for her to be in the same room. Angela's dinner table would be a meat lover's dream, but her salads and vegetable side dishes were legendary and meatless. Joey would surely have the very best Chianti on hand. And the Zeppole di San Giuseppe, fist-sized golden pastry prepared traditionally for St. Joseph's Day, was a cannoli cream-filled miracle even Darlene found tough to resist.

Later, the allusion serves to help Diamond describe a reluctant meeting with a killer:

> I would be discreetly followed to the rendez-vous, I would be well protected from any possible harm, and then the bad guy would be apprehended and brought to justice. A piece of cake. One far less appealing than Zeppole di San Giuseppe.

Food can also serve to add a bit of history to the proceedings. In *Chasing Charlie Chan,* Jimmy Pigeon and Ray Boyle meet at a landmark restaurant:

> "It is generally accepted as a historical fact that the French dip was originally created at

Philippe's in downtown Los Angeles in 1918.

"According to legend, Philippe Mathieu, the French born proprietor, accidentally dropped a sliced French roll into the pan of hot juices while preparing a sandwich.

"The patron, a Los Angeles policeman named French, told Philippe to use the bread as it was. The next day, Officer French returned with a group of fellow lawmen—each asking for their bread to be juice-dipped."

"So," Jimmy asked, "was the sandwich named after the Frenchman, the bread or the cop?"

"Who cares?" said Ray Boyle.

In *Counting to Infinity*, food is also employed to suggest regional cultural differences:

I suppose I expected Chicago-style pizza to be very thick, that a leftover slice could be used for a step exerciser. In fact, the deep-dish concoction looked more like the pan it was baked in. The crust was a thin circle with high sides, creating a large crusty bowl into which the ingredients were poured. First in was the cheese, followed by the Italian sausage, which Eddie claimed was a must, red bell peppers and Portobello mushrooms. Finally, tomato sauce covered the works. We sat at a pizza parlor not far from Eddie's place and the ballpark. Eddie assured me the pie was as good as any you could find in the city, that it was shipped in dry ice to customers all over the country.

"So, I could have one delivered to me in San Francisco."

"Sure, if you don't mind paying sixty bucks."
"For sixty dollars, the thing had better do my laundry when it gets there."

In the thriller, *Gravesend*, a scene in a diner introduces pivotal characters and sets up dramatic future events:

"Good morning, gents," says Bill Meyers, bouncing into Mitch's Coffee Shop and taking a seat at the counter, "long time, no see, Gabriel."

"Been very busy, Bill," says Gabriel Caine, working on a plate of eggs and home fries at the adjacent stool.

"I'll have the special, Mitch," says Bill, "scrambled well and with a little less hair."

"I add the hair for the extra protein," says Mitch, breaking two eggs onto the griddle.

"Drop a few fingernail clippings into my coffee cup," says Meyers. "That should take care of my minimum daily requirement. Been working, Gabriel?"

"Yes. And you?"

"I just began a major renovation over on Ovington," says Meyers, "remodeling the kitchen and bathroom and finishing a basement. Should keep me in groceries for the rest of the month."

"How well done do you want these eggs, Bill?"

"Burn them. Are you taking a vacation this winter, Mitch?"

"You bet. A week from today. Thirteen days in sunny San Juan," says Mitch Dunne. "Which reminds me, I'd better get a sign up on the door saying that we'll be closed."

"Closed?" says Harry Johannsen, walking into the shop.

"Vacation," says Mitch, plating the eggs.

"Where am I going to get stale rye toast while you're gone?" asks Harry, grabbing a seat next to Gabriel.

"I'll fix you a few orders to go before I leave," says Mitch, placing the plate on the counter.

"Where's the hair?" asks Harry, checking Bill's food.

"Mitch used it all up in my omelet," says Gabriel.

In *Brooklyn Justice*, Nick Ventura is treated to homemade delicacies while recuperating in a hospital from a gunshot wound:

Angela popped in at nine, moved the hospital table into place, and set down a plate wrapped in aluminum foil. I uncovered a perfect frittata—eggs, potatoes, garlic, onion, sweet red pepper and grated pecorino Romano. It was a beautiful sight.

"What, no Thomas' English muffin?"

"I couldn't resist, I devoured it on my way over."

"Did you whip this up?"

"All by myself."

"It's a work of art."

"I can have it framed for you."

"It looks too good to eat."

"Well, decide, either eat it while it's still warm or ask it to marry you. How did it go with Lawrence?"

And later, a touch of Italian culture:

> Angela returned at half past six with a large bowl of Ziti Siciliana. The bowl matched the breakfast plate.
> "Whip this up also?"
> "I could have, but it was a busy day. I pulled it out of the freezer. My mother never lets me go home from a Sunday dinner visit without taking leftovers. Eat while it's still piping hot from the microwave in the nurses' break room. I need to make arrangements for your release. I expect to see an empty bowl when I get back."
> "Or else?"
> "Or else I'll tell my mother."

And in *Coney Island Avenue*, Detective Murphy indulges in his favorite dishes at Joe's Bar and Grill in Gravesend, Brooklyn:

> Thomas Murphy took possession of a stool at the bar.
> Augie Sena, from the opposite side of the bar, set a bottle of Samuel Adams Boston Lager within Murphy's reach a moment later.
> "I haven't seen you move that fast since the last visit from the Health Department," Murphy said. "How did you know I wanted a beer?"
> "Wild guess. It's on me."
> "My birthday is not for another five months."
> "I might not live that long," Augie said. "The beer, my friend, is meant in way of congratulations."
> "You heard I won two bucks on a ten-dollar

lottery ticket?"

"I heard you're up for lieutenant."

"Bad news travels fast," said Murphy. "Thanks for the beer anyway."

"I'll bet you the two bucks you would love the fried calamari over linguini for dinner."

"Wild guess?"

"Just call me Sena the Psychic, but the calamari is not on the house."

"That, my clairvoyant friend, even I could have guessed. I'll take it with the hot sauce."

"There's a kid in a hurry," Augie Sena said, seeing a young man with a green gym bag race past the front window of Joe's Bar and Grill. "Maybe you should go after the kid. He may have knocked off the Jerusalem Pizzeria."

"He'd deserve a medal. The pizza there tastes like soaked cardboard."

"How is the linguini?"

"Not bad," Murphy said. "How did you get it delivered here so fast?"

"Anyone ever tell you you're a laugh a minute, Tommy?"

"I hear it every sixty seconds," Murphy said, slipping a forkful of calamari past his smile.

"My sister's boy is popping the question."

"What question is that? Why is the eggplant always greasy?"

"He bought a ring for his girlfriend."

"Jesus, Augie, what kind of uncle are you?" Murphy asked. "Couldn't you talk him out of it?"

"You're a hopeless cynic, Tommy. I haven't met her, but my sister says she seems like a very nice girl."

"They all seem like nice girls, Augie. And then they grow into their mothers. Which sister?"

"Rosie."

"The sister who married Cicero? I'm not too sure about her judgment."

Murphy shook his head and let out a deep sigh.

"What?" asked Augie Sena.

"The cynic and the psychic," Murphy said. "What a pair."

The setting of a story—San Francisco, Los Angeles, Chicago, Brooklyn—can be as an important a character as any other.

Similarly, the cultural backgrounds of protagonists and antagonists can add color and authenticity.

Food serves well in contributing to a stronger sense of the flavor of a place and the character of a person.

Good appetite.

FIFTY ANSWERS

I have been told that readers like to know something about the authors they read.

Since I am not stalked by paparazzi, I decided to tackle a questionnaire that came my way—aimed at revealing a little about the responder.

If nothing else, it was something to do while eating Cherry Vanilla Ice Cream.

1. One of your scars, how did you get it?

I was hit on the head with a big rock. I was told it was an accident.

2. Do you snore, grind your teeth, or talk in your sleep?

You tell me.

3. What type of music do you listen to?

Music with words.

4. What do you want more than anything right now?

To know what question 50 will be.

313

5. What do you miss?

The Brooklyn Dodgers and holding hands.

6. What are your most prized possessions?

All of the teeth I have left.

7. Do you get claustrophobic?

Only in very tight spaces.

8. Do you get scared in the dark?

No. It's what I can see that scares me sometimes.

9. What is your worst fear?

That I won't get it all done.

10. How would you describe your ideal match?

Happy.

11. Coffee or energy drink?

Coffee.

12. Favorite pizza topping?

Italian sausage from Faicco's on Bleecker Street.

13. If you could eat anything right now, what would it be?

Cherry Vanilla Ice Cream—and I *am* eating it right now.

14. Have you ever eaten a goldfish?

I hope not.

15. What was the first meaningful gift you ever received?

A sense of humor.

16. Are you double-jointed?

No, but I can bat from both sides of the plate.

17. If you could go anywhere on earth, right now, where would it be?

The Mediterranean.

18. What time did you go to bed last night?

Too late.

19. What's one thing you have done that you never told your parents?

I spent three days in jail, once.

20. What is the best subject to learn about?

Trust.

21. Blondes or brunettes?

Okay.

22. Favorite quote?

You're going to need a bigger boat.

23. Favorite place?

Atlantic Coast.

24. Your weaknesses?

Caffeine and nicotine.

25. Ever made a prank phone call?

Not yet. What's your phone number?

26. What were you doing before you began filling out this questionnaire?

Putting Cherry Vanilla Ice Cream into a bowl.

27. What do you get complimented most about?

My writing. My wit. My witty writing.

28. Have you ever had braces?

Yes. So what?

29. What do you want for your birthday?

Another year.

30. Were you named after anyone?

My paternal grandfather, Giuseppe.

31. What is the biggest turn off of the opposite sex?

Trying too hard to be opposite.

32. What did you like most about high school?

Weekends and summers.

33. What kind of shampoo do you use?

Who cares?

34. Any bad habits?

Some, but only potentially harmful to myself.

35. Jealous person?

Have been—a bad habit I have managed to break.

36. If you were another person, would you be friends with you?

I'd give it my best shot.

37. Do looks matter?

Unfortunately.

38. How do you release anger?

If you make me angry, I'll show you.

39. Snow?

No.

40. What was your favorite toy as a child?

A ball.

41. What do you look for in a guy?

I am a guy, so I look for a brother.

42. Favorite ice cream flavor?

Guess.

43. Plans for tonight?

Try to get through the rest of these questions.

44. Have you ever really and truly had a best friend?

I have really good friends—I don't rank them.

45. Favorite restaurant?

It closed.

46. Hair color?

The color formerly known as brown.

47. Republican or democrat?

Ukrainian-Italian-American.

48. Do you have all of your fingers and toes?

Last time I checked.

49. What book are you reading now?

The book I am writing.

50. Have you been a writer your entire life?

Not yet.

CLOSING WITH OPENINGS

In 1987, I had the honor of meeting Kurt Vonnegut Jr.

I had recently produced and directed his play, *Happy Birthday, Wanda June*, in Denver and had corresponded with him several times before the show opened.

Vonnegut was unable to come out for the production, but he offered to buy me a cup of coffee the next time I was in New York City, and I gladly accepted the invitation. We spent most of our time together talking about our children, we both had five-year-old daughters in 1987.

I had been writing quite a lot by that time, but I was an arts journalist not a fiction writer. However, since I was thinking about trying to pen a novel, I asked Vonnegut what he considered the most important consideration.

"Simple," he said, "most critical are the opening lines. Your first and possibly last shot at capturing the reader's attention."

The present collection is an opportunity to feature a healthy sample of more than twenty years of my shorter works. But I would be foolish not to introduce the reader to a little taste of my full-length fiction while I have the chance—and I can think of no better way than to present opening lines from my novels.

None as legendary as *Call me Ishmael* or *It was the best of times, it was the worst of times*, and not necessarily simple, but I have tried my best to follow Kurt Vonnegut's counsel.

. . .

The phone on my desk rang so unexpectedly, I nearly spilled the Mylanta onto my only unstained necktie.

It was my trusty assistant calling from her sentry post out front.

Darlene Roman was unlike most office receptionists in that the words *do you have an appointment* were not in her vocabulary.

Darlene greeted anyone who walked through our door as if it were our very first client, or might be our last.

"Yes, Darlene." I tried not to slur the words, in case Darlene was using the speakerphone.

"There's a woman here to see you."

I'd figured we had a guest. The place was small. Usually when Darlene wanted me, she just hollered.

"Count to twenty Darlene, and send her in,"

"Is that one, two, or one Mississippi, two Mississippi?"

I quickly assessed the condition of the desk. "Make it one Montgomery, Alabama, two Montgomery, Alabama."

—*Catching Water in a Net,* 2001

Lefty Wright slipped the rusty blade of his trusty paint scraper between the frame and sill of the kitchen window and finessed the latch open. He slowly raised the window, squeezed through, and shimmied like an alligator across the sink. When his palms reached the linoleum, he went into a perfect handstand—which he would have held longer if not for the sore rib. He gracefully and silently tumbled into an upright position. Once inside the house he stood motionless for a full minute, infinitely patient, listening.

Known as a top-notch second-story man by his peers, and a two-time loser by the courts, Lefty had been relegated to ground-floor entries since falling from a dry-rotted cedar balcony a few weeks earlier.

—*Clutching at Straws,* 2003

. . .

The scent of deep-fried calamari floated in through my office window like an invitation to triple-bypass surgery. I could almost have tasted the squid if not for the Camel Non-Filter dangling from my lip. I was working the Sunday Examiner crossword, grasping for a four-letter word for Egyptian goddess. I was sure Darlene would know it, but I was being stubborn. It was well after noon on a Sunday and not a single telephone call. I had vowed that I would hold off ordering lunch until my desk telephone rang at least once. The last time I'd tried that, I hadn't eaten for two days. When Darlene called out my name from the front room my heart sank.

"Use the telephone," I called back, "while we have one."

The phone rang. The blinking button indicated that it was Darlene. I wanted to call in my food order to Angelo at Molinari's Salumeria two floors below before picking up the interoffice line. I got a grip on myself.

"Yes, Darlene," I said.

"Get out here, Jake, before this gorilla trips over his shoelaces and blows my head off."

—*Counting to Infinity*, 2004

It is a cold and cloudy afternoon, the first Friday in February.

The wind chill factor races across the rooftop.

Joe Campo turns away from Detectives Vota and Samson and the small body lying on the tar surface behind them. Campo gazes down at the street corner, directly across the avenue, where his wife stands at the door of their family-owned and operated food market. A pair of teenage boys take turns slapping a rubber ball against the west brick wall of the grocery.

Campo's Food Market is the only grocery, delicatessen, newsstand and produce shop remaining in the neighborhood that is not owned and operated twenty-four hours a day by Korean immigrants or owned by Boston or Canadian entrepreneurs and operated by Indian or Pakistani clerks. Not necessarily a bad thing. Just not the way things used to be.

Little was as it used to be in Gravesend.

Lieutenant Samson stares at Joe Campo's back and waits patiently.

Only Detective Vota looks down at the body, and then only for a moment before looking away again. He nervously works at the buttons of his coat.

"I could use my jacket," Vota says, "to cover the body. He looks so cold laying there."

—Gravesend, 2012

When Lenny Archer managed to open his eyes, the first thing he saw was a small black circle with a white spot at its center. As he began to focus the circle became deep red and he recognized the white object. A tooth. Lenny probed the inside of his mouth with his tongue and found the space where the molar and a few of its neighbors had once been. And he could taste blood.

Lenny realized he was face down on the floor and made an effort to move. The pain in his lower abdomen was unbearable. He shifted his gaze to the significantly larger red pool that spread from the floor up into his shirt below his waist.

Archer let out a ghastly sound, part animal moan and part angry prayer.

"This mope is still breathing," said Tully.

"Put him out of his fucking misery."

"Maybe he'll tell us where he stashed it."

"If he was going to spill, he would have talked before you knocked his fucking teeth out," said Raft, "the guy is a fucking mess. Kill him. You'd be doing him a favor."

Lenny Archer tried to remember where he was, remember what he'd been doing before taking a bullet in the stomach and a kick in the face.

He wondered if it really mattered.

—Chasing Charlie Chan, 2013

James Bingham stood at the curb in front of the high-rise residence, talking with the taxi driver who had dropped off the occupant of 3501 a few minutes earlier. Bingham was inquiring into the availability of deeply discounted cartons of cigarettes. The cab driver assured Bingham he would hook him up that weekend.

Bingham walked back into the lobby as the cab pulled away.

As James Bingham approached the security desk, he heard footsteps from behind. Before he could turn to the sound, his head was clamped between two large hands and with the twist of two powerful wrists Bingham was dead.

—Circling the Runway, 2015

Bill Heller could not shake the feeling he was being followed.

Heller was driving up 18th Avenue toward Ocean Parkway to pick up the Prospect Expressway.

When he stopped at a red traffic light on 77th Street, he noticed the OPEN sign in the window of Il Colosseo.

He decided to go in and have something to eat and try at the same time to determine if he was being tailed.

The restaurant was nearly empty by nine-forty. They had stopped seating at eight-thirty.

The sign on the front door had been flipped over to the side that read CLOSED.

A young couple rose from their chairs at the back of the dining room. The young man placed a tip on the table and escorted his girl to the front door. Three twenty-something females were putting money together to cover their bill.

Heller sat alone at a table near the front window. The bus

boy had already started clearing vacant tables. A waitress was refilling salt and pepper shakers. The restaurant manager stood at the cash register.

Heller spotted a big man in a jogging suit out on the street, straining to look inside.

He had paid cash. His waitress brought his change and his receipt—a carbon duplicate of the three-by-five-inch guest check. He asked her for a pen and a rubber band.

The large man in the jogging suit made his way back to a car parked on the opposite side of 18th Avenue. A second man was seated behind the wheel.

"Well?"

"He's still there. He's sitting alone in front."

They watched the young couple leave the restaurant.

"How many others inside?"

"Looks like three more customers. There are at least three others working the floor, and maybe one or two in the kitchen. They're shutting the place down."

"Let's wait," the man in the vehicle said.

—Coney Island Avenue, 2017

They were born less than one year apart, in a poor village full of boys so like one another they could all have been brothers.

It was the 1890s. The Gay Nineties for much of the Western World and, in the New World across the Atlantic, a time for casting off the restraints of the Victorian Age.

In the rocky hills surrounding Naro, on the ancient island of Sicily, time seemed to stand still. For Vincenzo Leone and Giuseppe Agnello, the approach of the twentieth century had little consequence—and offered less promise.

In another time and place, these two boys could have been friends.

Amici. Compagni. Fratelli.

The two young boys often crossed paths, and there was a

mutual attraction—although part of their curiosity to know one another was likely encouraged by the taboo. Both had been educated from birth to mistrust and forswear the other and as they grew to adolescence they succumbed to the prejudices of their fathers—blindly accepting the ageless dissension between the two families if not totally adopting the fierce hatred.

Vincenzo Leone and Giuseppe Agnello might have spent their lives in the hills of Agrigento, working the miserly earth and perpetuating the blood feud that had existed for so long no one could remember when it began.

Or why.

And, as both approached adulthood, this looked to be their fate.

But each young man, independently from one another, had a common dream.

To escape.

To escape the barren land.

To escape the senseless and violent antagonism.

To escape the archaic island prison.

All that was needed was a catalyst, an inspiration, a reason to break away from family and home, a motivation too strong to resist.

And the incentive came for each of them in the form it had taken for all ages—for as long as restless sons struggled to gain a foothold on manhood.

Romance.

—American History, 2018

"Vinnie. Vinnie. Vinnie."

Vinnie would have rather been sitting on a bed of hot coals than sitting face-to-face with William Conway across Big Bill's oak desk in the back office of the Blarney Stone Saloon.

"I know," Vinnie said.

"You knowing isn't doing you much good, and it does me no

good at all. And don't insult me by telling me you are working on it. You have witnessed how I make examples of those who fail to pay what they owe. You know I will have no choice but to make an example of you. I didn't twist your arm to put down bets with me, but both your arms will be twisted until they snap if you can't cover your losses. I have a reputation to uphold. You may want to ask your guardian angel to bail you out again. I heard he squared your debt to Sandoval, and I heard Manny's two gorillas are still on crutches."

"I didn't ask him to do that."

"Whatever you say. In any case, do Jake Diamond a favor and explain to him that I am not Manny Sandoval and I don't employ morons."

"Can you give me more time?"

"Of course, Vinnie, that's why you're sitting here and not in traction at Saint Francis Memorial Hospital. One week. Go."

—Crossing the Chicken, 2019

ACKNOWLEDGMENTS

I would like to thank all of the short story anthology editors who have accepted my contributions over the years. *Mystery Readers Journal*, for publishing my musings about the art. Bloggers and interviewers who have taken the time to grill me. And Down & Out Books for entertaining my whims.

J.L. ABRAMO was born and raised in the seaside paradise of Brooklyn, New York on Raymond Chandler's fifty-ninth birthday.

A long-time journalist, educator and theatre artist—Abramo earned a Bachelor of Arts degree in Sociology and Education from The City College of New York and a Master of Arts Degree in Social Psychology from The University of Cincinnati.

Abramo is the author of *Catching Water in a Net*, winner of the St. Martin's Press/Private Eye Writers of America Award for Best First Private Eye Novel; the subsequent Jake Diamond novels *Clutching at Straws, Counting to Infinity, Circling the Runway* (Shamus Award Winner) and *Crossing the Chicken*; *Chasing Charlie Chan*, a prequel to the Jake Diamond series; the 61st Precinct novels *Gravesend* and *Coney Island Avenue*; *Brooklyn Justice*; the generational novel *American History*; and the full-length non-fiction work, *Homeland Insecurity*.

For more about the author please visit:

JLAbramo.com

On the following pages are a few
more great titles from the
Down & Out Books publishing family.

For a complete list of books and to
sign up for our newsletter,
go to DownAndOutBooks.com.

Killin' Time in San Diego
Bouchercon Anthology 2023
Holly West, Editor

Down & Out Books
August 2023
978-1-64396-328-0

Welcome to San Diego, where the perpetual sunshine blurs the line between good and evil, and sin and redemption are two sides of the same golden coin.

Killin' Time in San Diego is a gripping anthology featuring twenty of today's best crime and mystery writers and published in conjunction with Bouchercon 2023.

From the haunted hallways of the Hotel del Coronado to the tranquil gardens of Balboa Park, from the opulent estates of La Jolla to the bustling Gaslamp Quarter, *Killin' Time in San Diego* is your ticket to the hidden side of "America's Finest City."

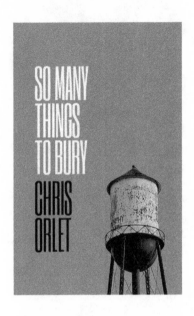

So Many Things To Bury
Chris Orlet

Down & Out Books
September 2023
978-1-64396-335-8

Al Heidorn is a working stiff, a Korean War vet and recently divorced father of three whose life is unraveling from decades of drinking and neglect. Now Al is determined to start over and put things right.

But that's easier said than done. Rather than get his life on track Al makes a tragic decision that seems likely to haunt him for the rest of his days.

Will he find redemption or will he squander the only thing that he has yet to lose—his young daughter's love and life?

The Duplication House
Nathan Singer

Down & Out Books
September 2023
978-1-64396-336-5

Emily Conlin, missing for twenty years in rural West Virginia, has recently been found alive in the forest, bloody and bedraggled. Now, with the "help" of a down and out novelist, she is finally ready to tell the story...but whose story is it?

The Duplication House is a twisted tale of the constructed self, identity in confined spaces, and all the dark things deep down. Just to let you know, should you decide to stay, there will be screaming.

Prohibition Peepers
Private Eyes During the Noble Experiment
Michael Bracken, Editor

Down & Out Books
September 2023
978-1-64396-337-2

The 18th Amendment created prohibition, which banned manufacture, transportation, and sale of intoxicating liquors and gave rise to bootlegging and gang violence. During the 1920s and early 1930s, private investigators were there working both sides of the law.

The hardboiled and fast-paced tales in *Prohibition Peepers*—written by today's hottest crime fiction writers—will have you reaching for your own highball glass of bathtub gin.

Printed in the USA
CPSIA information can be obtained
at www.ICGtesting.com
LVHW011733131023
760943LV00045BA/817